Waiting

For

A Promise

Chrissy Garwood/Chrisolite Books
email: chrissy@chrissygarwood.com

Sorell, Tasmania, Australia, 7172
www.chrissygarwood.com

Direct quotations from Scripture are taken from the World Wide Bible (WEB) and are available in the public domain. Other verses are written from memory and are not direct quotes.

Book Layout ©2017 BookDesignTemplates.com

Cover Design: Belinda Pollard

Waiting For A Promise/ Chrissy Garwood —1st ed.

ISBN: 978-0-6489651-8-3 paperback

ISBN: 978-0-6489651-9-0 eBook

Waiting

For

A Promise

A River Wild Romantic Suspense Novel

Chrissy Garwood

Chrisolite Books
Sorell, Tasmania, Australia

I dedicate this book to
my newest niece, Michelle Rainbow.
It is an honour to welcome such a passionate,
independent young woman to the family.

ℬ☼ℭ

Contents

A Trying
Introduction

ᘓ ☼ ᘖ

Proverbs 16:9 CG - Your heart makes plans,
but the Lord directs your steps.

ᘓ ☼ ᘖ

The barroom fell silent for a moment, then conversations resumed in a more subdued manner. Sigrid drained her bottle and raised her hand to order a replacement from Harry McHenry, stationed behind the bar.

Heavy footsteps announced the uniformed police officer who appeared at Sigrid's elbow.

"Good evening, Kurt," the barman said.

"Evening, Harry. A nice crowd for a Sunday. Everyone behaving themselves?"

"No worries," Harry said, but glanced towards an eight-ball table in the furthest corner.

The corners of Sigrid's mouth twitched. A drunken brawl might still be on the evening's menu.

The policeman leaned his back against the counter, addressing her without taking his eyes from the room. "You're Sigrid Ericson. I saw you at yesterday's wedding. What are you doing here?"

"I didn't know I had to report to you," she replied. "I'm waiting for my counter meal."

"I'll check if it's ready," Harry said and disappeared through the door to the kitchen.

"You make him nervous," Sigrid said.

"I'm about to go off duty," Kurt said. "And I don't want any trouble."

"You've come to the right place then. There's no trouble here."

Finally, he faced her. "Your reputation precedes you, Miss Ericson. Why didn't you go to Newcastle with the other bodyguards? I know you're always eager for a fight."

"Who's been talking about me? My money's on Butch Kidman. Don't believe anything that kid says."

His brown eyes studied her.

Sigrid analysed her intense response without looking away. "Did you do a background check on everyone, or did I do something to annoy you?"

"You weren't named in the report I read, but there's no hiding your red hair or fiery temper. I saw you arguing with that woman in charge of security yesterday." Kurt leaned closer and lowered his voice. "Then there was the unsolved murder in your Melbourne apartment building – a woman in Witness Protection. I've also accessed the sanitised version of your military service record. So I'm asking again, why are you here? You're like dynamite searching for someone to light the fuse."

Pushing aside the barstool, Sigrid rose to her full height. "Thanks for the psych analysis, Senior Sergeant Jensen."

Kurt grimaced.

Sigrid was taller than the policeman by several centimetres, thanks to the heels on her dressy shoes. Kurt straightened his shoulders and took a step back. All conversation ceased. The only voice in the room came from the Wurlitzer jukebox – Billy Ray Cyrus, singing the final refrain from his hit, *Achy Breaky Heart*. The song ended, and a few seconds later, Billy Ray was replaced by Shania Twain, singing *Man! I Feel Like a Woman!*

Harry reappeared behind the counter. "One chicken parmi, chips and salad." He pushed the generous plate of food towards Sigrid, and she rewarded him with a genuine smile. "Here's your cutlery," Harry added. "Is there anything else I can get you?"

Sigrid accepted the bundled knife, fork and spoon, wrapped in a paper serviette. After picking up the plate, she said, "Thanks, Harry. I'll have another beer."

Without waiting for a response, Sigrid sashayed across the room, aware that every eye marked her progress. She smiled, pleased that she had chosen a dress instead of her usual jeans and loose-fitting shirt. After selecting a table near the rear, the redhead set down her plate before moving a chair to put her back to the wall. From here, she had a good view of the room.

Conversations resumed.

Kurt was still at the bar. Harry placed a fresh beer on the counter. The pair talked, Harry shrugged, and Kurt took the bottle. Kurt crossed the space towards Sigrid, checking where other patrons were situated as he moved.

She smiled. Her boss Piper Maxwell had briefed her about key locals before the wedding. Kurt carried his forty-five years well, especially since he devoted his life to managing other people's problems. He walked with confidence, his uniform straining at the shoulders and looser around his trim waist. She wasn't the only one to spend too much time in the gym.

She stabbed a golden fried potato wedge and shoved it into her mouth. It was hard to hold onto her annoyance. The policeman wasn't her type – too intelligent, too cautious, too concerned about keeping the peace. But something about his intensity was breaking through her defences.

When he arrived, Kurt placed her beer on the table but kept his fingers around the bottle. "Harry says this is your fourth drink since you ordered your meal."

"There's no law against a girl having a few drinks."

"You need to be careful. There's more than one man here who would try to take advantage of you."

"Don't worry about me. I can take care of myself." She reached for the bottle, and he released it.

"Harry says you've booked a room for the week. Ours is a close-knit community, and most of these men have wives or girlfriends waiting for them at home. I've already told you I don't want any trouble."

The next song began to play on the Wurlitzer – another old familiar tune – *Girls Just Want to Have Fun*, sung by Cyndi Lauper.

"Hey, Sarge," someone shouted, "give the new girl some breathing space."

"He's making sure she's safe from the likes of you," a voice yelled from the opposite corner.

Laughter and taunts ricocheted across the room.

Sigrid drank from the bottle and grinned at Kurt. "If you're going to stay for the fun, you'd make a smaller target if you sat down."

Trying
to Solve a Mystery

ഓ ✪ ☾

*2 Timothy 2:15a CG - Try to present yourself
as a worker who doesn't need to be
ashamed of the truth.*

ഓ ✪ ☾

Kurt muttered to himself as he combed his hair, still damp after his brief shower. He was wearing faded blue jeans and his second-best shirt – he had worn his best one to Freddie's wedding. Rubbing the stubble on his chin, he glanced at his watch. How much trouble could Sigrid Ericson have caused since he left her?

Going out for a pub meal had never been on his schedule. That woman had disrupted his plans for a quiet evening reading the new novel that had arrived in the mail. He lived alone, in the flat attached to the Meredith Crossing Police Station.

As Kurt closed his door, he glanced down the street to the Meredith Crossing Motel, known to locals as Top Pub. He acknowledged the constable on night duty as he hurried past the front window of the station. He had already asked for the roving patrol to visit the pub before closing time at eleven.

Kurt paused in the foyer outside the bar. The refurbished motel reception area was brighter and more spacious than the one arsonists had destroyed last year. The family dining room had also benefited from the renovations, but not the main bar. Venturing through the glass panelled doors was like stepping back a hundred years. Generations of farmhands, stockmen, and locals who supported the rural industries had made this bar their favourite refuge.

Straightening his shoulders, Kurt pushed into the room. This time, silence did not immediately descend as he headed to the bar. Removing his uniform had rendered him temporarily invisible.

"Good timing," Harry said, appearing through the door from the kitchen. He placed a large bowl of fettuccine carbonara on the counter. "Can I get you a beer to go with that, or something stronger?"

"Thanks, but I'll be sticking to soft drink tonight. Cola, no ice," Kurt said.

"On the house." Harry selected a tall glass and filled it from the soda gun. "It's not often that you favour us with more than a quick visit, and this is the least I can do to show you my appreciation."

"I'd rather pay," Kurt said, placing coins on the counter. "We both know that your takings are going to be down because I'm here."

Harry laughed awkwardly. "Take your meal to a table, and I'll bring your drink over."

After crossing to the table Sigrid had used earlier, Kurt settled on the chair she'd left propped against the wall. This vantage point removed the risk that anyone could approach him from behind. *Interesting.*

Sigrid stood beside an eight-ball table, surrounded by a group of local men. She had a bottle of beer in one hand and a wooden cue in the other. When it was her turn, she moved with graceful confidence. The targeted ball flew into the corner pocket. As she repositioned herself to take the next shot, her eyes rose from the table and met his gaze. For a moment, time stopped, and then she smiled.

Kurt dropped his eyes to his pasta, his heart racing. He was still puzzling over his reaction when Harry arrived with the soft drink and dropped onto an empty chair.

The barman kept his voice low. "If Sigrid keeps up her patronage for the week, what she and her followers spend in the bar will more than compensate for whatever you think I'll be losing tonight."

Kurt nodded and continued eating. Harry took this as encouragement. "Is there any truth to the rumour that she's related to Samson? Or is she connected through his military past?"

"You know better than to ask me."

"But you know something, or you wouldn't be here." Without waiting for a response, Harry returned to the bar to serve another patron.

Kurt emptied the pasta bowl and sipped his drink as he contemplated Harry's remarks. He leaned back in his chair to watch the room watching Sigrid.

The attractive redhead would be taller than most of the men even if she dispensed with those heels. The short dress she was wearing did nothing to hide her muscular physique, yet there was no mistaking her feminine curves. When she sent the final ball into the pocket, a cheer rang out to celebrate her victory. The loser demanded a rematch, while others in the crowd tried to challenge her to a game.

Sigrid laughed. "I'm going to buy another drink. No, I don't want anyone else to pay..."

Emptying his glass, Kurt crossed to the counter and perched on a stool, waiting for Harry who was at the other end of the bar. As the barman stopped before him, Sigrid appeared on the adjacent barstool.

"I thought you'd be back," she said to Kurt, placing her empty bottle on the counter and smiling at Harry. "I'll have another of these, and whatever the sergeant is drinking."

"How many have you had?" Kurt asked.

"Not enough for you to worry about." She accepted the fresh bottle. "We both know Harry wouldn't risk his licence by serving me if I was drunk." She frowned as the barman reached for the soda gun and filled a glass to the brim with cola. "Is that what you're drinking?" she asked. "I knew the Kidman brothers abstained, but I didn't expect you to belong to the same camp."

"Thanks for the drink," Kurt said. "How much of Samson and Freddie's story do you know?"

Sigrid sipped her beer. "Their nephew Butch told me plenty, but that kid can be liberal with the truth."

"The whole district learned more about their home life after Ol' Jack's confession yesterday," Harry said, leaning on his side of the counter. Sigrid welcomed the barman into the conversation with an encouraging smile. Harry spoke softly. "Last night, the bar was full of speculation about whether the old coot was genuine or if he'd had too much to drink. Nobody expected him to admit to being an abusive alcoholic. It's been years since he's come into town to drink."

"What do you think?" Sigrid asked Harry. "Did he get baptised in the river to impress the visitors? Will he revert to his old ways when they've gone back to Melbourne?"

"I know Ol' Jack Kidman better than most." The barman chuckled as he began to move away. "But I'd be in trouble with Ma if she caught me gossiping about her cousin."

Kurt glanced in the direction Harry was heading. Waiting near the swinging doors were three well-respected older ladies. Harry rounded the counter, and one of the women wrapped her arms around him.

"Mrs Mac is his Ma?" Sigrid asked.

"Don't be fooled by her old-lady disguise," Kurt said. He pointed to a framed certificate on the wall. "After her husband died, Muriel McHenry managed this place alone for thirteen years.

"Harry's been in charge for twenty years now, but that doesn't mean she's given him free rein. She's lived in Meredith Crossing all her life, and she knows everything about everyone. She doesn't hesitate to interfere if she deems it's necessary."

Sigrid gracefully swivelled on her stool to survey the room. She crossed her legs, drawing his attention to her black lace stockings. He recalled the Melbourne crime scene photos. The medical report said she'd been lucky to survive, and had pushed herself through rehab for an early release. There must be scars...

Kurt tore his eyes away. The comments from her admirers were growing louder. She waved towards the rowdy group near the eight-ball table.

"We were talking about Ol' Jack," Sigrid said. "Was he drunk, or did he mean what he said?"

"Ol' Jack values his privacy," Kurt said. "He wouldn't have been baptised in front of the whole community if he didn't mean it."

"I wasn't expecting such a large crowd. From Freddie's comments, I didn't think religion was a priority here."

"There have been believers here since first settlement," Kurt said. "But yesterday, Samson's wife was the drawcard. Everyone wanted to see her transformation for themselves."

"Do you think it will last, her 'transformation'?"

"Do you?" Kurt countered.

Sigrid slipped off her stool.

After taking a step away, she spun towards Kurt. "Piper refuses to call her Ruth. He's certain she'll revert to Jezebel at the first opportunity, but Evie insists that he's wrong. I'm not ready to declare which side I'm on."

Trivial

Annoyance

ᏸ ✿ Ꮳ

*Proverbs 13:20 CG - One who walks with the wise,
grows wise, but a companion
of fools suffers harm.*

ᏸ ✿ Ꮳ

Sigrid sipped the warm beer in her bottle. It had been too long since she'd ordered this drink, and the crowd had dwindled. Less than a dozen patrons remained in the bar. She was the only audience for the quartet of men vying for her attention.

The pub would close in an hour, and she was still sober. She craved something more potent, but that off-duty policeman still guarded the bar. Whenever she glanced towards him, his disapproving frown remained.

She swallowed the tepid liquid. Meredith Crossing had lived up to its reputation as a community where everyone took an interest in their neighbour's affairs. The locals weren't afraid to call their neighbour to account for an exaggeration or a lie.

A noise from the second eight-ball table drew Sigrid's attention.

"Did you see that great shot?" shouted a skinny teenager. He waved his cue in the air.

His companion congratulated him before shoving him. "The game's not over yet."

The two teenagers were less proficient with the cue, but their enthusiasm was refreshing. Earlier in the evening, the youths had introduced themselves to Sigrid. They hadn't lingered among those trying to impress her. The skinny boy was Roo, which was short for Rupert. What was the other one's name? Something obscure – she reviewed what she remembered of that conversation.

The two friends worked at the hardware store.

When they had entered the bar, they carried motorbike helmets under their arms, and Kurt called them over. After that interaction, they only ordered soft drinks. The older patrons teased them about a recent escapade involving complaints about excessive noise, and the threat of losing their provisional drivers licences—

Brum! That was his nickname: Abraham "Brum" Callahan and his friend, Rupert "Roo" Armitage.

The older men's voices at the first eight-ball table grew louder, reminding her of her prospects for a suitable companion. She offered her potential suitors a smile before retrieving her phone from her pocket.

The flashing icon on her screen confirmed that the micro-camera was working. The concealed device was in the silver ornament on a chain around her neck. She jiggled the oval locket. It was not the technology that bothered her – activating the camera was a simple process. It switched on and off with a firm squeeze between her fingers.

When it was on, every interaction was recorded, analysed and processed by an anonymous work colleague in Melbourne. She had the option of turning it off, but Sigrid knew she had to be judicious with that privilege if she was to prove she was ready for active duty.

Opening the digital notes on her phone, she added a quick reminder about the boys' names. When this "holiday" was over, her employer, Piper Maxwell, would expect a comprehensive report. He wouldn't question her expenses if she delivered enough intelligence about everyone she encountered.

A shadow appeared beside her. "You're asking for trouble."

Before looking at her visitor, Sigrid slipped her phone into her pocket. She wasn't surprised to see the publican's relative standing there.

"You're Harry's mother?" Sigrid said. She remained seated so that her shorter visitor didn't have to crane her neck.

"That's correct. I'm Muriel McHenry, but most people call me Mrs Mac."

Mrs Mac was of average height and stocky build. Her face was lined, with the steel-grey hair cropped short—she'd foregone the traditional perm. The shapeless floral dress and hand-knitted cardigan all screamed "country gran".

But Sigrid wasn't fooled. Those thick glasses could not disguise this septuagenarian's keen interest. Muriel McHenry was a shrewd, self-sufficient businesswoman.

"There's no need to introduce yourself," Mrs Mac said. "You're Sigrid Ericson, one of the Melbourne bodyguards at Freddie's wedding."

"Would you like to sit down?" Sigrid asked, indicating a chair.

"I won't be staying that long," Mrs Mac replied. "I only came to introduce myself and to give you some advice."

Sigrid had a flashback to a long-ago conversation with her own grandmother, which had led to the disclosure of too many secrets. Sigrid's hand flew to the locket, but she pulled her fingers away without deactivating the camera. There was no way this stranger could loosen her tongue or unlock her heart.

"This is not the city," Mrs Mac said bluntly. "It would be unwise to pit friends against each other to keep yourself entertained."

Those words took Sigrid's breath away, but she kept her face neutral. "That was never my intention."

Mrs Mac stared into Sigrid's face before nodding. "Then I'll bid you good evening. I'll be praying that your stay brings you the peace you need and returns you to the right path."

Sigrid swallowed the last of her tepid beer as she watched Mrs Mac cross the room and leave with her friends. Pushing aside unwelcome memories from her last conversation with her own grandmother, Sigrid surveyed the room. She was shocked to find she was now the only female present. The four men at the nearest eight-ball table had concluded their game and were bickering.

Sigrid headed towards the bar.

She had taken only a few steps when one of the men appeared beside her.

"Lemme buy the next drink," Cowboy Joe said, reaching for her empty bottle. His other arm appeared around her shoulder.

At the start of the evening, Cowboy Joe had seemed the most promising of her new acquaintances. In his mid-thirties, he was tall enough to be a good match for her height, and she liked his cheeky grin and quirky sense of humour. But since then, she'd learned that he wasn't a cowboy, despite his Akubra hat, denim jeans and scuffed RM Williams boots. Tomorrow morning, he would swap his cowboy gear for a suit and tie. The bank manager's name wasn't Joe, either, but that wasn't what had ruined Jeremiah Friedman's chances: he hadn't denied the wife and three children waiting at home.

Sigrid shook off his embrace. "I've already told you I'll get my own drinks."

"Now, don't be stand-offish, Siggy. How's a bloke supposed to show his appreciation if ya won't let 'im—"

"It's time you went home, Joe," his mate Hank Binshaw said, pushing himself between Joe and Sigrid. "Your wife's going to forget what you look like—"

"Take your own advice, Hank," a stockman called Connor Portman said as he joined the huddle. "You married men clear off."

"I'm getting a divorce!" Hank protested.

Cowboy Joe was undeterred. "I'm not going anywhere. At closing time, Siggy's going to need a *real* man to escort her to her room. Not some no-hoper who can't—"

"Can't what?" Connor asked, his face darkening. Drew Radcliffe, the fourth member of their group, gave Joe a shove.

"Enough!" Sigrid snapped, and they fell silent. Her fingers tightened around the glass bottle. A surge of adrenaline washed through her system. She took a calming breath. This was neither the time nor the place to lose control of her temper. With a false smile plastered on her face, she lowered her voice. "Have you *boys* forgotten there's a policeman present? You don't want him to ban me from this pub on my first night."

She didn't wait for their response, approaching the counter with long strides. Behind her, the four men argued among themselves about how to regain her favour.

"Another beer?" Harry asked, placing an open bottle before her.

"Thanks," she said, "and I'll have a whiskey too."

Harry raised an eyebrow before he reached for the whiskey bottle. After he placed the shot glass on the counter,

Sigrid downed the contents in one gulp. The liquid fire did nothing to appease her thirst.

"Another," she said, refusing to look towards Kurt. There were three empty barstools between them.

Harry paused with the whiskey bottle above her glass. "What did my mother say? I should have come to rescue you."

Sigrid shrugged her shoulders and gestured for her drink.

He measured her drink and stepped back. "Whatever Ma said, she was only concerned for your welfare."

The second whiskey followed the first. "Having someone concerned about my 'welfare' is not what I'm used to. This is a good whiskey. I'd like a bottle to take back to my room."

CHAPTER 4
(Sunday 27th May)

Try
My Patience

ဆလ ✿ ငခ

John 14:27b WEB - Don't let your heart be troubled,
neither let it be fearful.

ဆလ ✿ ငခ

Kurt glanced from the bickering men in the centre of the room to the fuming redhead beside him. When she ordered a third shot of whiskey, his concern ratcheted up.

"Don't you think you've had enough?" Kurt asked, moving closer. He reached out to stop her offering the glass for another refill.

Her eyes dropped to his hand, and then she lifted her chin. "Make it a double," she told Harry, and then she skewered Kurt with a glare. "Who appointed *you* my keeper?"

His first instinct was to step back, but something kept him in place; for a second, he glimpsed pain in her eyes. Then she blinked, and the vulnerability was gone. Now those green eyes gleamed with a warrior's defiance. He'd encountered that kind of fire recently when he'd tried making his friend Samson see reason. Was Sigrid a kindred spirit forged in the same battlefield cauldron? If that were true, this woman would make a dangerous enemy—

Or a faithful friend to stand by your side to the end.

Time stopped.

This was not the first occasion when he had heard *that* voice. He pondered the significance. Perhaps the audible hallucination had been triggered because he was thinking about his childhood friend? Earlier today, Samson had warned him that God always found a way to make Himself heard.

A dangerous smile appeared on her face. "You can let go now."

Kurt looked down as her fingers wriggled under his hand.

"Is this how a policeman asks for a date?" she murmured. "Why else would you be holding my hand?"

Before Kurt could unscramble his thoughts, someone grabbed him from behind. He let go of Sigrid's hand as he flew through the air and smashed into a table.

"Keep ya hands to yourself, Sarge!" Cowboy Joe shouted, launching himself after Kurt.

Taking evasive action, Kurt scrambled out of the intoxicated man's reach. He backed into another obstacle.

"Are you alright, Sarge?"

Kurt glared at Constables Gavin Mallory and Clifford Briggs, the roving patrol he had ordered. The two uniformed police officers reached down and pulled him to his feet.

"We almost missed the floor show," Mallory said. "You should have sold tickets."

Kurt shook his head as he surveyed the room. What had become of his attacker?

All the people in the room had gathered near the broken furniture, frozen in place as if someone had pressed the pause button on a cosmic remote control. The closest spectators shuffled out of his way when Kurt approached. He glanced at their faces, recognising Joe's friends. They would not meet his eye, staring instead at a familiar figure sprawled on the floor.

Kurt leapt forward. "What happened to Joe?" He checked that Cowboy Joe was breathing before he rolled the unconscious man into the recovery position. A quick inspection revealed no visible injuries.

Nobody answered his question.

"Has someone phoned for the doctor?"

"There's no need." Sigrid became the centre of attention now, perched on the barstool, drinking beer as if nothing had happened. "He'll come round in a few minutes, a little sore for his troubles, but with no permanent damage."

"What did you do?"

Sigrid sipped from her bottle.

"Someone tell me what happened!" Kurt said.

He spotted Harry edging away, with a baseball bat concealed behind his back. The barman had been too far from the casualty to be able to claim responsibility. "Harry."

"I didn't see anything," Harry said, retreating behind the bar. "One moment, Joe was charging at you – I thought you needed help, so I reached down to get my trusty enforcer. When I looked again, he was flying through the air. I reckon he was unconscious before he hit the floor."

There was a murmur of agreement. Scanning the group again, Kurt spotted his nephew trying to hide. Here was someone who wouldn't be able to hold his silence.

"Brum!" Kurt said. "Tell me what you saw."

The others stepped away from the teenager.

"She's a ninja!" Brum said. "She leapt off the stool, like this, high into the air." He waved his arms wildly. "Then she went flying over Cowboy Joe, and I thought she'd missed him. But she flicked out a hand as she went past." The teenager darted his hand forward. Some in the crowd flinched. "He went down like a sack of spuds."

Brum's performance enthralled the spectators. "He wasn't going nowhere, but she – um, she—" He took a deep breath, and his face lit up. "*She* placed one hand on the floor and rebounded into the air like an Olympic gymnast going for gold. A spin and a flip, and she was back on that stool, reaching for her drink as if nothing happened."

A few others nodded in agreement.

"If you don't believe me, Harry can show you the recording." Everyone knew the insurance company had demanded a camera be installed over the bar after the trouble last year.

"Don't forget our body cameras," Constable Briggs reminded Kurt with a grin. "We'll be able to slow down the action and confirm how this female ninja saved you."

Cowboy Joe began to stir. Hank, Connor and Drew rushed to his aid. They spoke quietly together as they helped him to his feet.

"Nobody leaves until they give their names to my officers," Kurt said. He kept his distance from Sigrid, choosing a stool closer to the door.

Harry appeared beside him without an invitation.

"Harry, a word of warning – take care of that camera footage," Kurt said. "Miss Ericson works for a powerful organisation, and they don't welcome publicity. There's the possibility the evidence will *disappear*. Email me a copy as soon as you've locked up tonight."

Harry straightened, his eyes narrowing as he considered this request. He moved to the wall-mounted brass bell.

Clang! Clang! Clang!

"Closing time! Off you go."

Protests rang out as men rushed to order a final drink. "It's not time yet."

Harry ignored them, moving along the bar and removing empty glasses from their hands. "There's been enough excitement, and I can't stand looking at your ugly mugs any longer. Go home and get some beauty sleep. Don't forget to give your names to the officers at the door."

୫୦ ✧ ୧୫

Sigrid finished her drink while Harry progressed along the counter towards her, flicking nervous glances in her direction. When he arrived, she offered him her empty bottle. He checked to see who was listening before he spoke. "Now you know I wasn't referring to you when I used the word ugly. These regulars won't show me any respect unless I insult them."

"I've been called worse," she laughed. "I'll be wanting that bottle of whiskey before I go." He didn't budge. "I'd say I'm sorry," she said, "but we both know I'm not. I'll come to Reception in the morning and put extra on my account to cover tonight's damage."

"There's no need—" Harry began, but she put up her hand.

"I don't know what Senior Sergeant Jensen said, but I can see that he's spooked you. I'm on holiday, but I have an expense account. My employer would be disappointed if I didn't take *full* advantage of his generosity."

Harry nodded, reaching to the top shelf and bringing down an unopened bottle of whiskey. He showed her the label. "Is there anything else I can help you with?"

The bottle rested on the counter between them, and she resisted the urge to grab it and leave. She hesitated for a moment before she spoke. "I've checked out your gym, and I'm going to need more than an exercise bike and a treadmill. Is there anywhere in town where I can access some heavier weights or a punching bag?"

"There's not much call for that in Meredith Crossing," Harry said, rubbing his chin. "Most of the men here do more than enough heavy lifting while they're working on the homesteads. I know there's a gym over in Brumby's Run— But you don't have any transport? Hmm – the only other option is Kurt's set-up at the police station." The barman raised his voice. "Hey, Kurt! Sigrid needs a proper gym. Is there any reason she can't train with your officers?"

Kurt paused in his conversation with his nephew. One of the other police officers was closer to her.

This officer addressed Sigrid: "He runs a session at six am that you're welcome to join. Sarge is big on fitness, and he's got certificates to prove it. He can even design a workout to help you improve any weakness. But from what we've seen tonight, you're already in great shape."

"You're premature with that offer, Constable Mallory," Kurt said, his eyes lingering on the unopened bottle on the counter. "Miss Ericson is on *holiday*. She won't be wanting an early morning workout."

Denying herself the urge to smack the disapproval from his face, she forced a smile. "Stop calling me Miss Ericson. You already know my name. Six am would be perfect."

She gathered the bottle to her chest and took a step towards the door.

"Before you go, Cowboy Joe has something he wants to say," the second patrol officer said.

All eyes turned towards the bank manager. He seemed a shadow of himself. "Siggy, I want to – um – apologise for – ah—"

"Apology accepted," she snapped. "But if you call me 'Siggy' again, I'll not be responsible for my actions. I'm *Sigrid* to my friends, and that is how we'll part company."

Without waiting for a reply, she pushed through the doors into the foyer. Footsteps followed close behind, yet she kept going until she was outside. Without turning to acknowledge his presence, Sigrid spoke. "There's something you wanted to say to me, Sergeant?"

"You're not really on holiday, are you?" Kurt asked. "I told you I didn't want any trouble."

"And here I was, thinking you followed me into this dark car park to thank me for stopping the fight. My room is here." She unlocked the door, lowering her voice. "I was minding my own business when the action kicked off." She pushed the door open, and it thumped against the cupboard in the narrow passage between the kitchenette and the bathroom. She carefully set the whiskey bottle on the counter. "You're the one who couldn't keep his hands to himself."

The corners of her mouth twitched as she waited for a reply. The policeman blinked as he stared at her, and she lost her temper. Sigrid grabbed Kurt and pressed his back against the door frame. Holding him prisoner with her upper body, she invested all her frustration into one kiss. His hands squeezed her arms making it clear that her attack was unwelcome. He pushed her away, and shame washed over her.

Then someone else spoke.

"Ah-hum. Sorry to interrupt, Sarge." The two uniformed officers from the roving patrol were standing outside her room.

Sigrid stepped into the car park. She risked a peek. Kurt's eyes gleamed with fury, and his face was red.

"We're finished here," Officer Mallory said, "and came to tell you that we're continuing our rounds."

"Why are you still here?" Kurt said.

The officers took a step back, glancing at each other and then at Sigrid.

"We didn't mean to interrupt—" Mallory said.

The other one scuffed the ground with his foot. "Are you alright, Sarge? It looked as if she was using her ninja magic—"

"Of course I'm alright. *Miss* Ericson's just discovered that I'm immune to her 'ninja magic'."

He pushed past them and marched off towards the police station. The officers watched his departure, and then Mallory spoke again.

"There's a lot of respect for our Sarge in this community."

"I'm sure there is," Sigrid replied. "He seems like an honourable man."

"Don't mess with him unless you're prepared to stick around and deal with the consequences."

The two officers moved away, talking quietly to each other. Sigrid waited, playing with the locket at her throat. On, off, on, off... Let fate decide whether the final conversation for the evening would be recorded. On...

One of the officers retraced his steps. It was Constable Mallory. "You're asking yourself, if he's such a great catch, why is he single?"

"I wasn't, but since you mentioned it, I'd appreciate your explanation."

"Everyone knows Kim Kidman broke his heart when she involved herself in the death of his younger brother. She keeps turning up, trying to con him into making allowances for her petty crimes. He's not going to let anyone else get that kind of hold over him."

"Thanks for the information," Sigrid said, stepping into her room and closing the door. She switched off the camera and reached for the whiskey.

Trial
by Ordeal

ଞ ☼ ଛ

*1 Chronicles 16:11 CG - Seek the Lord
and His strength.
Seek His face forever.*

ଞ ☼ ଛ

With an annoying click, the plastic number on the old-fashioned clock flipped over to the next minute. Thirty clicks more, and this day would be over.

Then only six more days before she could say goodbye to this town.

Half a glass of whiskey sat on the table, calling her name. Sigrid paced the compact room. The first half of the drink had disappeared in a few gulps.

To stop herself from downing the rest in a rush, she had hidden in the shower, remaining under the hot blast until the water ran cold.

Sigrid swapped her dress for an oversized tee-shirt.

She had already rubbed moisturiser into her exposed skin, her fingers massaging each limb to unlock the tension in her muscles.

The surgery scars on both forearms and her left leg, below the knee, were a constant reminder that staying alive had come at a price.

She paused in her pacing to examine the tattoo on her left ankle: crossed swords over a round shield. Freddie's new wife, Alixanda, had created the design.

It represented a shared vow to honour their dead friend by making their lives count.

The clock clicked again. Twenty-nine minutes to go...

Sigrid dropped onto an armchair and frowned at the drink on the table. She would empty the glass the next time that annoying clock clicked again. She raised her eyes to the ceiling and uttered a challenge.

"Okay, God. If you're listening, do something to stop me."

Click.

The glass was in her hand when her phone began to chirp.

She hesitated, waiting until the noise stopped and the display went dark. With the glass halfway to her lips, she checked the notification:

Oliver Johnston reached your Messenger Service and did not leave a message.

The phone began to chirp again, and she answered it. "Oliver, did you forget that I'm on holiday?"

"We both know nobody working for Piper is ever *on holiday.*"

Her fellow agent sounded like he was in the room, instead of hundreds of kilometres away in Melbourne.

Sigrid visualised his crooked smile. They were regular sparring partners in the *Maximum Security* gym – one day, she would defeat him.

Her respect for Oliver was more than loyalty towards a superior officer. He was like the brother she had never had.

"Are you free to talk?" he asked. "Or do you have someone with you?"

Sigrid grimaced. "Just a bottle of whiskey keeping me company."

"The evening didn't go to plan?"

She took a sip and let the silence speak for itself.

Oliver didn't wait for a response. "I've had a call from the duty officer."

"What did he say?" Sigrid gulped another mouthful.

"He thought the new camera might have malfunctioned. Did you intentionally turn the device on and off repeatedly and then go off-line without the correct procedure?"

Her answer required more liquid courage. "Guilty as charged."

"Don't do it again," Oliver said.

Sigrid sat up at his tone and offered him an unseen salute with her glass. "Yes sir!"

"I know you don't like being the guinea pig for Piper's new technology, but if it improves safety for Evie and *the others*, it will be worth the intrusion into your privacy."

Her supervisor knew which buttons to press. Sigrid examined the empty glass. Could she cross the room and retrieve the bottle without alerting him?

While wrestling with temptation, she redirected the conversation. "Did the duty officer say anything about the quality of the signal?"

"He tested an audio sample and obtained an accurate transcript – I have it on the screen in front of me. He said the final image you transmitted was crisp – clear enough for him to read the fine print on the whiskey bottle you carried to your room."

"Ha! I knew it. You phoned to find out if I was drunk," she said. "There's still two-thirds of the bottle left. I'll send you a photo to prove it."

"You don't have to prove anything to me."

Sigrid wasn't listening. "I wish everyone would stop meddling in my life..."

There was no stopping her now. The words of frustration and anger poured from her poisoned heart until the atmosphere was heavy with recrimination.

He waited until she ran out of complaints.

"Feeling better now you've got that out in the open? That's the alcohol talking. If you don't stop drinking yourself into oblivion, the misery you're trying to escape will overpower you."

"Tell me something I don't already know."

"I thought you'd never ask," Oliver said. His laughter broke something in the air. "I've wanted to tell you, but you've been busy with the wedding security."

"You sound excited," Sigrid said, hoping for a distraction from the call of that bottle. "Is this something personal, or has there been a breakthrough with Piper's family project?"

"Both. Are you telling me Piper and Jenny haven't said anything?"

"Jenny's been organising the wedding, and Piper has big plans for creating a mountain sanctuary there. He's been busy with purchase negotiations."

"Sara's been liberated," Oliver said.

Sigrid pumped the air with her fist and leapt to her feet. At last! Oliver had fallen in love with Sara Messinger before her disastrous marriage to Nero Mariani.

The young lawyer had not been seen outside the husband's apartment without a chaperone since the death of Nero's uncle, Valentino.

But Valentino had predicted this and secretly recruited Piper and Oliver to give Sara back her freedom. "How did it happen?"

"On Friday afternoon there was a violent argument with Nero. Sara's injuries gave us an excuse to get her out. I recruited my mother to smuggle Sara from her hospital room – my father's a patient again."

Sigrid murmured her sympathy. Oliver's mother and father were the kind of parents she had dreamed of as a child. Loving and generous. Willing to do anything to see their child prosper. Never burdening him with shame and reproach.

His father's cancer diagnosis was one more injustice on Sigrid's list.

Oliver continued speaking. "Nero's furious – the listening devices we snuck in are still providing valuable intelligence. He doesn't suspect that his wife is hiding at the *Maximum Security* Compound."

"Is Piper going to tell him?"

"The family asked Piper to find the runaway wife. Piper's waiting until she's safely evacuated from Melbourne before he tells them what he knows. Friday's revelations have ruined any chance he'll cooperate with them."

"What revelations?" Sigrid asked. Had they finally found the missing information that would confirm the conspiracy theory?

"That cousin you befriended – Gina Gregorio – has been having an affair with Nero. Her long-term plan is to seize control of the family empire."

"The family won't let that happen," Sigrid muttered. "She's a party girl—"

"She confessed to organising Valentino's assassination."

"What! No way!" Sigrid dropped back into the chair. Eighteen months ago, she had gone undercover and spent time getting to know Gina.

There had been nothing to suggest the twenty-one-year-old had anything significant to contribute to the case. "Gina's responsible for Valentino's death? I can't believe all this happened while I'm away."

Mentally, Sigrid was already packing. "I can be back in Melbourne tomorrow afternoon." There was an awkward silence. "What?"

"Piper was supposed to tell you. You're not coming back. I've sent someone to your flat to pack. You're staying there to protect Sara."

"I'm WHAT?" Sigrid grabbed a pillow from the bed and launched it across the room.

"I'm flying Sara to New South Wales on Friday. She'll be hiding with Samson at *Mountain Rise* until the new base is operational. Piper's using this situation to test Samson's security."

Sigrid joined the dots and snarled, "*That's* why I was ordered to *holiday* here?"

"I'm sorry you had to find out like this." Oliver had too much integrity to say something he didn't mean. Even before he "found God", the truth had been important to him.

"You were supposed to spend a week there," Oliver said, "and then come back to Melbourne to be fully briefed."

"Briefed? What else do I need to know?"

"Gina's on the run. She went to Sydney with Quin and Matteus, but we've lost her."

Oliver paused, which suggested what he said next was going to hurt. "The evidence suggests she's in partnership with their father, Ricardo Barononi."

Sigrid forgot how to breathe. She was back in the past, broken and bleeding – watching helplessly as that evil man murdered her friend. Xanda had not been the intended target. She had sacrificed her life...

Tears fell freely, and Sigrid did nothing to stop them. Oliver wouldn't tell.

Piper had refused to permit public mourning for Xanda. He argued that his agent's death would be wasted if the assassin discovered his mistake.

The fugitive had to survive, and Xanda no longer needed her identity...

Alixanda was a living reminder of the price that had been paid.

When Sigrid returned from the flashback, her phone was lying on the floor.

Oliver's voice was the only sound in the room.

"...and give Sigrid the strength to overcome the darkness. Shine Your light into her heart, and show her the way forward. Give her the wisdom to wait for You to lead her. She wants justice. If it is in her future to face her enemies again, provide her with what she needs. Keep her safe and protect her heart—"

"I'm okay," she said. "You can stop praying now."

"I'll never stop praying," Oliver said. "That's a promise you can count on. I can sense God's hand in this. Piper's preparing for a confrontation, and he's put you right in the middle of the battleground. That's the only explanation for committing valuable resources to Samson's mountain."

"I hope you're right. Otherwise, I'll die of boredom."

Try a Little Harder

ଥି ☼ ଓଃ

*2 Corinthians 5:7 WEB -
For we walk by faith,
not by sight.*

ଥି ☼ ଓଃ

Fifty minutes before sunrise, Kurt turned on the lights in the small gym. Thankful that he had set everything up yesterday, he rechecked the equipment before opening the sliding patio doors.

In passing, he threw a solid punch towards a bag suspended from an overhead beam. The punching bag rebounded, catching Kurt a glancing blow.

His responses were slow, and his head ached. A red-haired ninja warrior had pursued him in his dreams. In the final manifestation, his dream-self turned to face her. The memory of her alcohol-flavoured kiss tormented him now.

Hoping to banish the distraction, Kurt walked to a wall-mounted whiteboard. He reviewed the training goals for each of his officers. The individualised weight programs needed adjusting.

He was more severe with himself than the others, and commenced his warm-up routine.

As Kurt neared completion, fragments of conversation reached him from the street. Constables Gavin Mallory and Clifford Briggs, from last evening's roving patrol, were not expected this morning.

So why were they here?

The remaining voices belonged to Constables Des Wilmot and Ben King. Ben was the eldest member of his team.

The group fell silent when they entered through the side gate.

"Good morning, Sarge," Mallory said. "We weren't sure you'd be here."

"Where else would I be?" Kurt asked, preceding them into the gym to prepare for the group warm-up exercises.

"You might have waited until we left and returned to the pub," said Briggs. "Or that woman could have come after you."

"Miss Ericson had no further interest in me," Kurt said.

"Then you're not expecting her this morning?" Mallory asked. "I can hear Helena talking to someone, and we're all here."

"I'll go and tell them to hurry up," Wilmot said, rushing away before Kurt could stop him.

He returned a few moments later with Constable Helena Avery. The troublemaking redhead was with them.

"Good morning, Sarge," Avery said. "Sorry I'm late. I got stuck behind the morning delivery truck. I found Sigrid outside on the footpath. She said you invited her."

"Morning, *Sarge*," Sigrid said. "Do you want me to follow my usual program or fit in with your class?"

"Go over to the board and add your name. You asked to use the weights, so start at the power rack while the others go through their warm-up. If you add your personal best achievements to the other sections, I'll have a better idea of what improvements you're working towards."

Sigrid dropped her bag and crossed to the whiteboard. After studying the information, she selected a marker. She was wearing a long-sleeved lycra top and matching black leggings. The tight fabric emphasised her muscles while enhancing her feminine curves.

Kurt swallowed. It had been a long time since any woman had made it this difficult for him to maintain his focus.

With great effort, he turned his back on Sigrid to begin the preliminary exercises. It took longer to gain his team's attention, and it proved even trickier to keep it. Sigrid loading the bar with weights had become a captivating spectator sport.

Today's class was set up in a circuit, using both the indoor and outdoor space. Kurt cut the warm-up short, hoping that spreading out would help keep them on task.

Moving among the group, he corrected posture and offered advice. The effort to keep his back to Sigrid was exhausting, especially as each of his officers said the newcomer was staring at him.

Only when his team had completed a circuit, and he could find no fault with them, did he turn. Kurt watched Sigrid work through five repetitions before he approached the power rack. He delivered his assessment. "You're favouring your left shoulder. What exercises did your regular trainer give you to address that?"

"There's nothing wrong with my shoulder," Sigrid said, loading yet more weight.

"I disagree. Turn around, and I'll prove it."

For a moment, he thought she was going to argue with him, but then she shrugged her lycra-covered shoulders. He stepped closer and probed her back muscles with his fingers.

When he found the tightness he was expecting, he increased the pressure. "Tell me this isn't sore—"

Sigrid swore. Before Kurt could take evasive action, she spun towards him. After grabbing him with both hands, she sent him crashing to the floor. He landed hard and lay still, waiting for the pain to subside. He half expected her to put one foot on his chest to confirm his defeat.

The other officers reacted, but it was Sigrid who hoisted him to his feet.

"Sorry," she said, studying his face. "I wasn't expecting that level of pain. That's the second time I've assaulted you – it's time I went."

"No!" Kurt wasn't sure which of them was more surprised when he caught hold of her arm. Did he think he was strong enough to prevent her from leaving? "I should have given you some warning, and it's not your fault that my reflexes are too slow."

೮☼ಐ

Shaking herself free, Sigrid stared at Kurt. Adrenaline was surging through her system. Her fingers throbbed with the temptation to deactivate the secret locket camera. She should escape—

"You said you're here for the week?" Kurt asked.

He glanced towards the other officers. "Come back tomorrow, and I'll drag out the mats. I'd like you to show me how to improve my landing."

Kurt continued, "My team could also benefit from your expertise — if you're interested in taking them on as a challenge."

"You want me to come back?"

"That's what I said."

"Are you feeling alright, Sarge?" Wilmot asked. "Are you sure you didn't bang your head?"

"There's nothing wrong with me," Kurt said. "Except my wounded pride — and a few bruises — to remind me that I'm getting old. Your concern is admirable, but I'd be happier if you returned to your exercises."

Kurt waited until they moved away before he faced Sigrid again.

"If you promise not to throw me, I'm going to take another look at your shoulder."

Heat started in the middle of her chest and moved skyward. "There's no need."

"I'm going to phone your boss when this class is over. I'd rather not tell him you're concealing an injury and refusing advice to remedy it."

Sigrid ground her teeth. "I'm not concealing anything." *And I'll prove it.*

She reached for the hem of her top and pulled it over her head. Now she stood before him in her sports bra. Before the violent assault that ruined her career, she had taken pleasure in showing off her body.

She adjusted her posture to emphasise the surgical scars on her arms.

He blinked.

Sigrid smiled, confident he would retreat.

Instead, he reached for one of her hands and studied the raised pink scar near her elbow.

She shoved the other arm in his face. "A dodgy shoulder is the least of my concerns."

"I can't undo these injuries," Kurt said. "But I'm confident I can strengthen your shoulder."

Without saying anything further, Sigrid faced the wall and closed her eyes. She held her breath, her senses alert to his proximity. A shiver ran through her upper body as Kurt's hands brushed the skin on her back.

She could hear his measured breathing and familiarised herself with his aftershave. It was not strong enough to mask his perspiration.

His fingers traced the line of muscles where the pain had flared, and she tensed in anticipation.

"Hold your left arm straight out to the side."

She obeyed, and he took hold of her wrist.

"I'm going to raise and rotate your arm. I want you to describe the level of pain," Kurt said. "Use a scale where zero is no pain at all, and five is painful enough to restrict your movement."

"Is ten when I'm tempted to kill you?" Sigrid asked. "I'm already at three. The nerves are still sending out danger signals. Sometimes it takes half an hour before the pain returns to a comfortable level."

"Thanks for the warning." He let go of her arm and edged away. "I'll let you control your shoulder movement. Show me how high you can raise your arm before you get to five."

"I can raise it to here and still ignore the pain," Sigrid said, calculating the angle at thirty degrees above horizontal. "I can push up to here if I must."

Her straightened arm raised a further twenty degrees. "Any higher, and I'm in danger of losing control."

Kurt held her arm at the easier level. He lightly tapped the painful area with his other hand.

Sigrid didn't make a sound.

"You can lower your arm now."

With relief, she obeyed, shaking off the pain as she faced him. His familiar frown was in place.

Walking to the sliding patio door, Kurt reached for a liquid chalk marker. "I'm going to show you some exercises to strengthen this muscle group."

In swift strokes, he illustrated his instructions on the glass surface, asking her to demonstrate her understanding as he went. When he seemed satisfied, he sent Sigrid back to her training schedule. She watched him show the same level of dedication to each member of his team.

When the circuit session was over, Sigrid joined the others for the cool-down routine. Afterwards, Kurt walked with her to the footpath. He waited until the others were too far away to hear him. Was he about to deliver another lecture?

She decided to get in first. "Will you be joining me at the Top Pub for dinner this evening?"

"I'm on patrol," Kurt said. "So you'll have to stay out of trouble without my supervision. What's on your schedule today? I can't visualise you sitting around idle. You could catch the morning bus to the city."

"I'm not going anywhere. I thought you knew that I didn't choose to stay here. My 'holiday' here is a test."

"What happens if you fail this test?"

"I go back to desk duty in Melbourne."

"And if you pass?"

Sigrid leaned closer, wrapping an arm around his shoulder. She didn't hide her grin when he flinched. "If I pass, I'm going to be your problem for a *long* time."

Tricky
Question
∞ ☼ ∞

∞ ☼ ∞

The afterglow from Sigrid's small victory was fleeting. It
lingered during her leisurely shower but had disappeared by
the time she went in search of a cooked breakfast. When
Harry glanced up from the motel reception desk, his
customary smile was missing. He pointed to a cardboard box
in the corner. "There's been a delivery for you. You went out
early and weren't answering your phone, so I signed for it."

"Thanks, Harry. I'll take it to my room later. Have I missed
breakfast?"

"It's only eight-thirty," Harry said. "I'm in charge of
cooking breakfast, and I'm always here until eleven, so it's
never too late. Take yourself through to the family dining
room." He directed her towards a glass-panelled door. "I'll
come and take your order in a few minutes. But before you go,
your Melbourne office phoned. You should have told me your
room was too small."

"Is that what they told you?"

"They requested an upgrade, and they also extended your stay."

Sigrid frowned towards the box. "Did they offer any other information?"

"Perhaps you should open the box before you order breakfast?"

Sigrid dismissed his suggestion. "Let's maintain the illusion that I'm on holiday for as long as possible. Breakfast first, and then you can show me my new room—"

"It's an apartment: five bedrooms, three bathrooms and a study."

"What?"

Harry continued as if she hadn't interrupted him. "There's a fully-equipped kitchen and a private outdoor entertaining area. You could cook your own meals."

Sigrid laughed. "My culinary skills extend to using a can opener and pressing buttons on the microwave." She hesitated with her hand on the dining room door. "Did Melbourne say how long I'd be staying?"

"They didn't specify an end date, but they've sent a payment for the next month. I'm to provide them with a weekly invoice for your meals and other expenses. Which reminds me, I need you to sign for last night's damages."

ഇ ✿ ൽ

When she finished the second cup of coffee, Sigrid returned to the motel reception. "Breakfast was great, Harry. You've missed your calling. There are cafés in Melbourne that charge twice as much and leave me dissatisfied."

"I'm pleased to hear your compliments, but I'm happy here. Do you want me to get a trolley for that box?"

"That won't be necessary," Sigrid said, making a preliminary inspection. It looked like a standard removalist box, one of the smaller variety. It didn't have any company identification markings. "There's no heavy-lifting warning on the outside."

Sigrid raised the box from the floor and discovered her error. Gritting her teeth, she held it close to her body. "Lead the way, Harry. My delivery is heavier than I thought, but I'm too stubborn to put it back down." Using Kurt's pain scale, the agony in her weakened shoulder spiked at nine.

As she followed Harry outside, Sigrid worried about the contents. The box had come from Sydney, so it would not contain the promised possessions from her Melbourne flat. Had Piper Maxwell, the *Maximum Security* commander, made the arrangements? Or had Jennifer Prescott, his second-in-command, organised this delivery?

Neither of her superiors had briefed her about the new mission. Was this one of Jenny's weird – and potentially dangerous – tests? Sigrid owed her shoulder injury to an earlier one of those. Or was this the kind of mission she would never volunteer to undertake? Her stomach churned. Perhaps the large breakfast had been a mistake?

Instead of heading towards her current room, Harry turned left. He led Sigrid towards the detached wing, situated at right angles to the main complex. This wing was constructed from brown brick to match the other buildings, but it had an upper storey. Harry approached the fourth door, the one closest to the street. It bore the legend "Forest Retreat".

Sigrid assessed the security of her new accommodation. From the front windows, she would be able to observe more of the neighbourhood. There was also a clearer view of the road that delivered traffic into Meredith Crossing.

She hesitated as a familiar figure exited the police station. Kurt climbed into the driver's seat of a patrol car and drove away with the lights flashing. The wailing siren drifted across the quiet town long after he had disappeared from view. Sigrid loitered until his distant vehicle appeared on the winding road leading into the hills. Where was he going in such a hurry? In Melbourne, that information would be at her fingertips, but here—

The pain in her shoulder flared, bringing Sigrid back to her present situation. Harry watched her from the concrete pathway outside the door. She stepped across the threshold and dumped the box onto a convenient dresser on the right-hand side.

The inward-opening door and the wooden dresser created an illusion of a separate foyer. There were tiles beneath her feet. A few steps into the room and the tiles gave way to a luxurious carpet. The mottled brown pattern reminded Sigrid of fallen leaves. The painted walls were a shade of misty green, and the left wall featured a forest mural.

A pair of archways punctuated the opposite wall, with a huge wall-mounted television between them. The television rivalled in size the digital screens in her Melbourne headquarters. In a smaller room, it would have dominated the space.

Sigrid walked forward, spinning to survey the room. She swallowed her immediate response, a string of expletives that seemed inappropriate here. "Harry! My whole city apartment is smaller than this room! What kind of crazy inspired you to create this?"

Harry walked towards an arrangement of seating near the window. He rested his hands on an upholstered armchair, gazing out at the car park and the motel beyond. "Ma had a grand vision for writers' retreats, family reunions, and small

44

conferences." He faced back into the room. The weight of the investment seemed heavy upon his shoulders, but then he smiled. "You're the first guest to stay here since we upgraded. Satellite TV and internet, automated lighting and heating. There's seating for twenty in here..." She followed him through the righthand archway. "And this dining table extends to twenty-four."

Sigrid dropped onto one of the bentwood chairs. "Twenty-four! Why do I need a dining table for twenty-four?"

"I was hoping you could answer that question for me."

"How many people can sleep here?"

"The Melbourne office asked the same question. I told them there's an additional charge for each guest, but they said there were no immediate plans for anyone else to stay," Harry said. "We advertise this apartment as sleeping fifteen. Upstairs there's a double, a twin double and the master suite. There's a twin-single downstairs and another bedroom with two sets of bunks, plus there's a sofa bed in the study."

Sigrid frowned, unable to keep track of Harry's description.

He finished his monologue. "You will let me know if you find out when anyone else is coming?"

"The 'Melbourne office' hasn't told me anything," she said, moving through another archway into the tiled kitchen. There was a smaller table here, plus a breakfast bar that accommodated half a dozen chairs. Sigrid crossed the kitchen towards the rear door, which opened onto the enclosed courtyard.

She ignored the brick barbecue and the tables sheltering under a green shade-sail. A high wooden fence surrounded the courtyard, concealed behind native trees and shrubs. Closest to the street was an artificial waterfall that trickled into a rock-lined pool. Orange fish swam up to the surface and blew bubbles at her through the wire mesh.

"There's a family of kookaburras living nearby," Harry said. "My kitchen staff leave out meat scraps to encourage them to stay. Don't be surprised if you find them perched in the trees or on your fence. They see these fish as an easy meal. But I don't discourage their visits – the water's deeper than it looks, and these fish are survivors."

Harry opened a cupboard, bringing out a canister of fish pellets. After watching the fish feeding for a few minutes, he returned the food to the shelf. "The kookaburras catch any snakes that come down from the scrub."

Sigrid shuffled her feet, resisting the urge to scan the undergrowth. Harry grinned. "My priority is to ensure the comfort of my guests. The birds take care of the snakes, and I take care of the fish. Don't thank me; it's all included in the room charge."

Returning inside, Sigrid dismissed Harry's offer to show her the upstairs bedrooms. "I've taken up enough of your time. I'll retrieve my things from the other room and bring you the key when I'm done." She escorted the hotel proprietor to the door. He hesitated beside the unopened box on the dresser.

"You're worried about these changes," Sigrid said, "and my inability to give you any answers. Go and talk with Senior Sergeant Jensen. He's in contact with my boss, and he should be able to allay your fears. I promise to let you know if I learn anything relevant, and I hope you'll repay the favour."

Trinkets
and Gadgets
ॐ ✿ ॐ

*Isaiah 54:4a WEB - Don't be afraid, for you will not be ashamed.
Don't be confounded,
for you will not be disappointed.*

ॐ ✿ ॐ

Sigrid set aside the empty cardboard box. Half an hour had elapsed since Harry's departure. Frustrated by a fruitless search for written instructions, she sank to the floor. With her back to the television, she sat cross-legged with the delivery items on the coffee table before her.

Four cartons, similar in size, formed a small tower. Each one held an electronic gadget. All the printed information for the plastic-and-polystyrene-wrapped enigmas was in Chinese.

She broke the seal on each one, sliding out the contents to check for anything written in English. Finding nothing except the model number and manufacturer's logo, she reclosed each carton and set these items aside.

The next object was a laptop computer. The seal on this box was already broken. Inside was a note from Macy Mancini, a Sydney-based operative:

"Preloaded with everything you need."

Sigrid dismissed the urge to turn on the laptop immediately.

The next bundle of items filled her with unexpected dread. Two sets of military uniforms, still wearing plastic shrouds. Camouflage pants and shirts – jungle pattern, not desert.

Why would she need a combat uniform in rural New South Wales? The shirts were embroidered with an unfamiliar emblem: the letters O and P surrounded by flames arranged in a sunflower design.

Sigrid tried on the shirt. The crisp, heavy fabric against her bare skin triggered a heightened awareness. There was a time, best forgotten, when she had only felt complete when dressed in a military uniform.

She heard her father's voice: "A good soldier wears his uniform with pride."

He had wanted a son to carry on his name, and she bore his disappointment like a wound that never healed. If only he had lived to see his sole child become a decorated Special Forces officer.

Her fingers fumbled with the buttons. Sigrid closed her eyes, waiting for the memories to lose their potency. Her father had left her life when she was nine, forever a fallen hero on a distant battlefield.

Other ghosts from her more recent past pushed his memory aside. Names and faces from other conflicts. The daughter who had brought him only disappointment had trained hard.

She had grown strong, winning service medals and commendations worthy of his praise. But all this meaningless when balanced against her greatest failure.

No!

Opening her eyes, she banished the living nightmare to the corners of her mind. When she regained control, Sigrid considered the garment which had triggered the mental storm.

The shirt was broad at the shoulders and long, but not too wide at the waist. She stretched to appreciate the ease of movement before unfastening the buttons.

To familiarise herself with the weight, she did not take it off. The long pants remained in their plastic. Sigrid needed no further confirmation that this uniform was custom made.

How long had Piper and Jenny been planning her involvement in this unknown mission? Oliver had told her that she was staying here to protect Sara, but this uniform said more. She rammed the broad-brimmed hat on her head. The crown bore a matching OP metal badge.

The final item to explore was an oversized shoebox containing a pair of heavy leather boots stuffed with scrunched paper. Sigrid discovered a hidden object in the toe of the right boot.

She examined the blue hinged box with trembling fingers. The camera locket had come in a similar box with an identical gold logo. The lid opened with a snap to reveal a pair of silvery oval disks.

She recognised them – "dog tags" – the disks worn to identify a soldier found on the battlefield. The top one had an embossed image, identical to the badges on the military uniform. She frowned, and then slid that disk aside to read the engraving on the second one. She recognised her name, date of birth, and her *Maximum Security* personnel number. It took a few seconds for the rank to register: MAJ Sigrid Ericson. *Major!*

When she had resigned her commission five years ago, she had only been a Captain. An overwhelming desire for a strong drink burned within her. She remained still, haunted by the death of the Major in charge of her company. Memories from a distant battle transported her away. If Sigrid had challenged that Major's last order, the unit would not have driven into an ambush.

Enough!

Sigrid leapt to her feet, and the forgotten boots thumped onto the floor. Swearing at her lack of self-control, she returned them to the coffee table. She looked at the metal disks in her hand. The tags were held together by a solid metal ring, but they did not have an accompanying chain.

Sigrid fumbled with the clasp on the chain around her neck. Careful not to drop the locket, she slipped the new tags onto the chain. They nestled behind the silver pendant as if the tags and hidden camera were a matching set.

€☼cs

Back in her previous room, the whiskey bottle disappeared into her suitcase. Having abandoned her holiday expectations, Sigrid denied herself even the smallest sip as she focused on her tasks. She surveyed the room. With a sense of purpose, she seized her luggage. A few minutes later, she stood at the reception desk, waiting for the proprietor to respond to the bell.

Harry appeared in the doorway. His smile wavered. Sigrid had forgotten she was wearing the unbuttoned camouflage shirt.

"I've brought you my old room key," she said. "As you can see, my uniform was in the box. Don't be surprised if you see me stomping around in my new size twelve boots. I'll be trying to break them in before my holiday officially ends."

As she talked with the man behind the counter, an idea came to her. Perhaps the uniform was part of a public relations stunt? Piper's plans for the area included a sanctuary for ex-military personnel, especially those who found civilian life challenging. He recruited agents from among the damaged, the disillusioned and the lost. Sigrid was among their number.

Confident that she had chanced upon the right idea, she straightened her shoulders. Starting with a lone uniform made sense. A subtle preparation for a greater paramilitary presence.

Harry stepped closer. "I don't recognise the insignia."

"I'd be surprised if you did," Sigrid said, holding a finger to her lips. "I'd stay and talk, but I've got to finish unpacking. I won't be here for lunch. I've got errands to run – you said there was a laundrette in town? The washing machine in my apartment is too small."

"Yes, the laundrette is next to the chemist. Go towards the police station and turn left. You said you have new boots? Then you'll be wanting leather conditioner. Continue past the chemist towards the next corner. There you'll find the hardware store. The entrance is down the side street."

"Thanks for your help," Sigrid said.

With a confident stride, she marched to her new apartment. Once she was inside, she carried her case towards the second archway. Choosing the downstairs twin-single, she put the suitcase on the first bed and unpacked.

She ignored the whiskey bottle until it was the only item left. After placing the bottle in an empty kitchen cupboard, she paused to allow her Melbourne observer to mark the occasion. Then she firmly closed the door, determined to prove that she was worthy of this commission.

CHAPTER 9
(Monday 28th May)

Trifling
Discomfort
ೞ ✿ ೞ

*Galatians 1:10 CG - Am I seeking God's approval?
Or am I striving to please others?
If I were still pleasing people, I wouldn't be a servant of Christ.*

ೞ ✿ ೞ

The laundrette's heavy-duty washing machine was large enough to accommodate both starched uniforms. Sigrid selected the longest cycle and inserted the coins in the slot. Retrieving her phone from her pocket, she activated the timer to schedule her return. She smiled at the flashing red symbol on the screen, confirmation that the locket camera was on.

Alone in the building, she described the town to the Melbourne observer. "I don't know what I expected, but it wasn't this. Old weatherboard cottages with overgrown front gardens and open verandas, red brick monstrosities that look as if they have been transplanted here from the seventies. And the occasional grey brick box with the glass frontage that passes for a modern shop..."

Walking from the laundrette, she passed the chemist and turned onto a rose-lined path. The cream weatherboard building ahead looked as if it had been there for a century. When she came to the front door, she hesitated. "You will

53

have to keep yourself company," she said to the locket. "This is the Medical Centre. I don't want people to think I'm crazy."

The woman behind the reception counter looked up when Sigrid entered. "Good morning. How may I be of assistance?"

"I'm Sigrid Ericson. I'd like an appointment to see the doctor."

The receptionist's expression lost some of its warmth. Sigrid kept her smile in place.

"You're staying at the motel?" The receptionist didn't wait for a reply. She ran her finger down the old-fashioned appointment book and then flipped a page.

Sigrid studied the woman's nametag: Lizette Friedman. The surname seemed familiar. There must be some connection with someone she had met the previous evening.

"I'm sorry," Lizette said, "but Doctor Chappell has no free appointments for the next few days." Her eyes challenged Sigrid to disagree. The receptionist turned another page. "The earliest I can give you is three-fifteen on Thursday afternoon. Perhaps you should try the larger medical practice in Brumby's Run. I can phone them—"

"Thursday afternoon will be fine." Sigrid pretended not to notice the empty lines in the book. "I only want to introduce myself to the doctor, as I'm going to be working in the area. I'll need your contact information to have my medical records forwarded from Melbourne."

"Are you sure you don't want me to phone Brumby's Run—" Lizette looked past Sigrid as the front door opened again.

A slim young man with shoulder-length sun-bleached hair entered the waiting room. He carried an old-fashioned medical bag. Sigrid had seen Doctor Tim Chappell at Freddie and Alixanda's wedding. Why would someone like him exile himself to the bush?

Lizette's cheeks reddened. "You're back early, Doctor."

Doctor Chappell looked at the clock on the wall. "I told you I'd be back before eleven." He offered Sigrid his hand. "I'm Tim Chappell. I saw you at the wedding, but we weren't introduced."

She shook his hand, unimpressed by his light grip. "Sigrid Ericson."

"You've already made an appointment?"

"Unfortunately, there's nothing available until Thursday afternoon."

"Thursday?" Doctor Chappell reached across the desk and spun the appointment book towards him. "How fortunate that I've come back *early*. There are twenty minutes before my next patient is due. Plenty of time for Ms Ericson to see me, Lizette." He held out his hand, and the receptionist surrendered her pencil. He wrote Sigrid's name and the initials O.P. against the 10:45 appointment.

"But Doctor," Lizette said. "Ms Ericson hasn't registered yet."

"The new patient file is waiting on my desk, and I've written the billing code in the book. Ms Ericson's employer has been in contact, and her records are already in the database." Doctor Chappell stepped back from the counter and gestured towards a hallway. "This way, Ms Ericson."

There were four closed doors in the hallway. Doctor Chappell's name was on a brass plate on the first one on the left. When Sigrid was inside the office, he closed the door. After dropping his medical bag beneath his desk, the doctor settled on his chair in front of a computer. "Please sit there." He indicated an adjacent padded chair. "I hope you're not offended by Lizette's unfriendly welcome – the whole town is talking about how her husband made a fool of himself last night."

Sigrid sat before she responded. "Her husband?"

"Jeremiah Friedman, the bank manager," Doctor Chappell said. "He likes to call himself 'Cowboy Joe'."

"Ah. She has nothing to worry about. As soon as I found out he was married, I crossed Cowboy Joe off my list. I'm only interested in *single* men."

It was the doctor's turn to hesitate. Sigrid smiled. To cover his reaction, he tapped the keyboard. The computer screen burst into life. "Let's check your records."

"I'll put my phone on silent," Sigrid said, entering the code required to turn off the locket camera. She placed the phone on the floor at her feet, discreetly glancing at the screen while her hand played with the locket. Once the red light on the phone screen had extinguished, she relaxed in her chair and studied the doctor.

He tapped more buttons and frowned at the new windows that opened on his screen. After a few minutes, he turned from the computer. "I now understand why your employer wanted you to introduce yourself. Can I see the surgical scars on your arms?"

With a swift movement, Sigrid removed her long-sleeved top, and Doctor Chappell examined both arms.

He entered information into the file. "The surgeons did an excellent job. I'll take your blood pressure and listen to your heart while you're undressed."

She endured the procedures, and he signalled that she should replace her clothing.

"Do you want to see my leg?"

"Not today. I will conduct a more comprehensive examination during your next visit. You had a top surgical team, and their report is comprehensive. I'm more concerned about what's missing from your medical records. Are you seeing a psychologist?"

"Why would I be seeing a psychologist?" Sigrid asked.

"There's a single line about the violent physical assault that led to your surgery. But no mention of a referral for trauma counselling. Nor any reference to follow-up appointments to monitor your mental health."

"I went through the hospital's rehabilitation program," Sigrid said. "That information should be there. The doctors signed the release forms."

"So you're not taking any medication?"

"No."

"Not even non-prescription drugs."

"Only alcohol and the occasional painkiller. You can take a blood test if you don't believe me."

Doctor Chappell stared at her for a moment. "That won't be necessary today. Why do you think Piper Maxwell wants you to see me once a week?"

"Who knows, with Piper?" Sigrid shrugged. The doctor raised an eyebrow and waited for her to continue. "I came to make an appointment because the local police sergeant thinks there's a problem with my shoulder. He told me to get it checked before he reported it to Piper."

Doctor Chappell switched from one digital document on his screen to another. "Piper has medical power of attorney?"

"That's the same for all his employees. It makes it easier for him to organise treatment if, um—" Sigrid shifted in her chair. "If something... goes... um, wrong."

"The kind of *something* that happened to your arms?"

Keeping her eyes fixed on the doctor's face, Sigrid answered. "I survived. My teammate didn't. Piper paid the doctors to fix me. Don't think I'm ungrateful. He made good decisions, and I'll be better prepared next time."

"Is that why you take risks?"

Leaning forward in her chair, Sigrid asked, "Who told you I take risks?"

He gestured towards the screen. "What about this reference to obsessive behaviours? Do you know your triggers?"

She held her breath and loosened her fingers from the arms of the chair.

His smile tightened, no longer matching the concern in his eyes. "Can you tell me what signs and symptoms I need to watch for?" He lowered his voice and pushed his chair away from the desk to put a little more space between them. The silence lengthened. "Have you ever been treated for an addiction?"

"No to the last question," Sigrid said, keeping her tone even. "I'll concede that I'm a 'risk-taker' because that's how my supervisor described me in my last review. I'd prefer to say that I'm an adrenaline junkie. I enjoy the thrill of living on the edge. He believes I drink too much, go looking for physical disputes too often. And I don't exercise any caution when seeking sexual satisfaction. But you already know that."

"What makes you think I already know?"

The phone on his desk rang, and he frowned towards it.

"You'd better answer that," Sigrid said, leaning back in her chair. "Your receptionist's worried about you."

Doctor Chappell picked up the receiver and listened. He glanced at Sigrid. "Lizette, you know better than to interrupt when I'm with a patient. I don't need you to tell me that my next patient has arrived."

Sigrid waited until he ended the call. "She has good cause to be concerned. I've only been in town for less than twenty-four hours, and I've already lived up to my reputation."

The doctor frowned. "Is there anything else you think I should know?"

Sigrid thought for a moment. "The contact information for my real relatives is missing. Freddie and Samson are listed as my next-of-kin, but that's a convenient cover story. If anything happens to me, let Oliver Johnston know."

"What about your family?"

"I've taken enough of your time," Sigrid said, reaching for her phone, which lay under the chair. She frowned; the red recording indicator was flashing. Rising to her feet, she shook the doctor's hand again, keeping his fingers captive while she looked him in the eye. "Thank you for taking the time to see me, Doctor Chappell."

"Don't hesitate to contact me anytime, Ms Ericson—"

"My friends call me Sigrid."

He took a step back, and then he smiled. "Of course, Sigrid. And you must call me Tim." Then he rushed to open the door and escaped towards reception.

Sigrid smiled and followed him. She arrived at the desk as the receptionist presented him with a slim file.

"The next patient—"

Tim Chappell nodded. "Lizette, Ms Ericson will not be requiring that Thursday appointment." The receptionist brightened. "But she will require an appointment for next Monday, preferably at this time. Please set aside half an hour for that consultation. There will be weekly appointments for the duration of her stay."

Lizette mumbled a reply and turned the pages in her book. The doctor was already ushering his next patient towards his office.

Sigrid entered the appointment into the planner on her phone. Occasionally, she glanced over to confirm that the receptionist was following his instructions.

"How long will you be in Meredith Crossing?" Lizette asked, her pencil hovering over the pages.

"I'm booked into the Top Pub for a month."

The pencil scribbled the required entries. Lizette sniffed. "Would you like me to write the details on a card?" Without waiting for a response, the receptionist scrawled the information onto a business card. "The practice number is here," Lizette said, tapping the card with her manicured nail. "In case you need to cancel."

"Thank you."

Sigrid was halfway to the door when Lizette spoke again.

"Is it true that you hooked up with Kurt Jensen last night?"

Sigrid kept walking, only pausing at the door to look over her shoulder. She grinned. "I wouldn't believe everything you hear."

Trial

by Rumour

ଅଠ ☼ ଓଷ

*Proverbs 3:25 WEB - Don't be afraid of sudden fear,
neither of the desolation
of the wicked when it comes.*

ଅଠ ☼ ଓଷ

The hardware store was Sigrid's next destination. As she neared the entrance, a battered LandCruiser pulled into the car park. Samson Davidson climbed out. The bearded mountain man nodded towards her, before turning to his passenger.

One of the city guests unfolded his giant frame from the LandCruiser. Sigrid smiled as Sebastian Romano rose to full height. The Melbourne businessman always made everything seem miniscule in comparison to himself.

"Good morning, Sigrid," Romano said, striding towards her. "Enjoying your holiday?"

She remembered the watchful camera as she continued towards the hardware store entrance. "I've survived so far. I didn't expect to see you in town."

Romano adjusted his steps to walk beside her. "Business at the bank, and a few maintenance projects to organise before I return to Melbourne."

A dozen questions went unasked. Romano wouldn't know why Piper had dumped her here, and she didn't want to hear about his "projects". Sigrid excused herself, disappearing into the shadowy depths of the store.

A teenager wearing a royal-blue protective coat appeared from nowhere. He grinned as he stood in her way. "Sigrid! You're the prettiest customer I've seen all morning. I know where everything is, so tell me what you're looking for, and I'll take you straight to it."

Recognising him as one of the boys from last evening, she glanced at his nametag: Brum Callahan. Was this Kurt's relative?

"Hello, Brum. I need some leather conditio—"

He spun around and disappeared between two shelves. "This way!"

She trailed behind him.

"The leather conditioner is here." Brum selected several items and passed them to her.

Handing the smaller tubes back to him, Sigrid examined the label on a larger tub. "I'll need several of these. I'm breaking in a new pair of boots."

Brum glanced down at her running shoes and then back to her face. "What kind of boots? Dressy ones with heels or classy riding boots?"

"Sorry to disappoint you," Sigrid said. "You seem to think I live a glamorous life. My boots are the standard military issue."

A frown appeared on Brum's face, and he snatched the tub from her hands. He reached down to a lower shelf and presented her with a much larger container. "All the locals swear by this brand for their workboots."

"That sounds perfect."

Brum retrieved the product and headed towards the front counter. He checked that she was keeping up with him as the words flowed from him like water from a fountain. "Make sure you stop off at the chemist and get yourself some protective tape. New boots always rub, but I suppose you already know that." He didn't pause for her to respond, dumping the container on the counter, and continuing to talk as he waited for his turn to use the cash register. Romano and Samson were concluding a transaction with an older man.

"I should have guessed you were military," Brum said. "What's your rank?"

"That's a good question," Romano said. "We're all waiting for your answer, Sigrid. Samson needs to know if he has to salute you next time he sees you."

"Nobody's saluting anyone here," Sigrid muttered. "If you've finished, I'd like to pay—"

"Put it on the *Operation Phoenix* account," Romano told the manager behind the counter, and then he faced Sigrid again. "That's what it's for. Piper said you're on active duty."

"I'm supposed to be on holiday!"

"Call it a holiday if you like," Romano said. "But you wouldn't be buying a bucket-sized tub of leather conditioner if you were planning a leisurely stroll."

"Thank you," Sigrid said to Brum as he handed her the shopping bag containing her purchase.

The teenager rushed to open the door for her.

"You still didn't tell me your rank. Is it a problem that Uncle Kurt's only a sergeant?"

"Why would Kurt's rank be an issue with Sigrid?" Samson asked. Brum opened his mouth to explain, and Sigrid escaped. The ringing bell promised to drown out Brum's voice. But she still heard him mention a "ninja warrior".

಄ ✿ ಇ

Sigrid took an extended detour. She arrived at the laundrette, bundling the wet uniforms into the dryer. After activating the machine, she stepped onto the footpath.

Her plan for a quick visit to the chemist went awry while she was standing at the counter. The shop assistant gasped. The other customers craned their necks. Seconds later, Romano loomed over Sigrid.

"I need your help with Evie's list," he said.

A handwritten document appeared in her hand. Sigrid withdrew from the counter, frowning at the crumpled paper. After surveying the shop, she found a shopping basket and shoved it towards Romano. He followed as she wove between the shelves. Evie had given birth to twin boys five weeks earlier. Nursing pads, nappies and an assortment of creams and lotions went into the basket.

On her way to the counter, Sigrid paused at the perfume display. "This is Evie's favourite." She selected the largest gift set and added it to his basket. Renowned for his generosity towards his wife, Romano wouldn't quibble about the price. The successful businessman was a multi-millionaire.

"Let me pay for your purchases," Romano said, picking up the box of tape she had abandoned on the counter. "You don't need anything else?" He gestured towards a contraceptive display on the countertop.

"Why would I need advice from you?" Sigrid asked through gritted teeth.

He matched her stare, and her face began to glow. Only then did she realise that the shop assistant was watching her with interest. Sigrid straightened her shoulders and held her head higher, turning to face the woman.

"I'm not sure why your friend is worried. You look like you can take care of yourself. We haven't been introduced. I'm Eliza Callahan. My son Brum met you last night. From his colourful account, I believe you already *know* my brother Kurt."

Sigrid snatched up her purchase and headed towards the door. "Nothing happened last night."

"It's not what *didn't* happen last night that your friend is concerned about," Eliza called after her. "It's what might happen *tonight*..."

The door slammed behind her and Sigrid blindly walked into Samson. She had forgotten he would be waiting for Romano. She took a step back and glared at him. He straightened but did not retreat. Sigrid compared him to Kurt. They were childhood friends: the same age, the same height, the same disapproving expression.

"You met Kurt's sister?" Samson asked. "You should be careful who you kiss."

Her fingernails dug into her clenched fists. "It's – none – of your – business!"

Romano emerged from the shop and placed a massive hand on her shoulder. "Sigrid," he growled.

For a moment, Sigrid saw red, but then sanity returned. Romano was Piper's closest friend. Not even Jenny Prescott showed him any disrespect. Besides, he had the strength of two men. Losing control of her temper would end with a humiliating – and very public – defeat. It would also destroy any chance that Piper would ever trust her with a *real* mission.

"You're wrong about this not being *our* business," Romano said. "You work for Piper, and that makes you family. Evie prays for you every day. And Kurt is Samson's friend. So be careful."

Sigrid shook off his hand and stomped away, realising too late her mistake. The police station was ahead of her, not the laundrette. She stubbornly refused to change direction.

Try and Find Me

ஐ ✪ ☾

*Psalm 90:12 WEB - So teach us to count our days,
that we may gain
a heart of wisdom.*

ஐ ✪ ☾

Although he preferred to be in the driver's seat, Kurt insisted Constable Helena Avery take the wheel for this evening's patrol. He was determined not to criticise her slow progress until he had fully considered the implications. The journey from their earlier call out – a longstanding neighbour dispute – to their current location had taken half an hour longer than it should have.

There had been no traffic to justify her caution, yet the vehicle crawled forward through the darkness. The scrubby trees on both sides of the winding country road emerged from the shadows and then faded from view like characters in a flickering, slow-motion black and white movie. The occasional kangaroo or possum that wandered into the beam of the headlights was never in any danger.

Their involvement at the scene of this minor traffic accident was coming to an end. A learner driver had swerved to avoid a possum on the road and crashed into a sign which warned drivers to watch out for nocturnal animals. It was debatable who was more embarrassed, the teenager or her father, an animal welfare officer employed by the local council. He'd gone to a lot of trouble getting the road crew to crash-proof the signpost which contributed to the damage to his daughter's car.

The occupants of the car had already been collected by a relative. Kurt watched the lights of the departing tow truck disappear into the distance as he finished inspecting the accident site. He gestured for Avery to get back into the police vehicle. "We'll head back to Meredith Crossing."

Ten minutes later, the tow truck's red lights appeared ahead of them. It was travelling at a snail's pace, and Avery reduced her speed. Kurt made a quick decision.

"We need to get to the next major crossroad ahead of that truck," Kurt said. "Take the side road coming up."

"Yes, Sarge."

The unmarked intersection appeared on the left. Replacing the signpost had been on the local council's maintenance list for six months. It was time to send them another reminder.

"Are you sure this is the road you want?" Avery asked, making the turn onto the gravel road and coming to a stop.

"I grew up in the area," Kurt assured her. "This road is a well-known shortcut. Even the local school buses use it."

He watched her shift into gear, and the vehicle crawled forward. Why was she so hesitant? The young woman may be the newest addition to his team, but nine months in the district should have familiarised her with the road conditions. In that time, she had worked her share of evenings. Even if she had never driven on this particular road, there were many others like it.

Perhaps it wasn't the road that was making her anxious? Had she picked up on his concerns about her work performance? He had recently discovered that some of his team were making unnecessary concessions to cover her shortcomings.

He continued to dwell on his concerns, including the unequal division of tasks. He doubted any of the team would show the same leniency for a male rookie. Kurt was convinced someone else had taken over writing her reports. And why were experienced officers claiming responsibility for what were beginner's mistakes? If this practice continued, Helena Avery might develop a false sense of privilege. That attitude would be detrimental to her career.

Kurt frowned into the darkness. The only benefit from the tension between them was Avery sparing him her regular update about the latest gossip. Tonight, he was thankful for her silence. He'd already fielded more than enough enquiries relating to last night's incident. The rumour that he was romantically involved with an exotic outsider had inspired his mother to phone...

Pushing aside that distraction, Kurt considered the other topic that he had expected Avery to raise. It was puzzling that she hadn't asked about her potential transfer to an "elite city squad". That had been all the young constable had talked about since returning from last month's five-day Sydney getaway, where she had partied with the rich and famous. Somebody there had suggested that her family connections would fast-track her career. They also told her about a position for which she should apply. Perhaps Helena Avery would soon become somebody else's problem...

As Avery navigated the sharp bends that brought them down to a single-lane bridge, the digital screen on the dashboard lit up. An incoming call from the Meredith Crossing Station. Ben King was the night duty officer this week. Kurt tapped his earpiece to send the incoming call to the dashboard speaker. "Ben, we're crossing the one-lane on seven-twenty-nine."

"Right, Sarge. Good thing you don't need to turn around. Is the city girl driving?"

"Yes."

"Then you won't get to Meredith for another hour," Ben chuckled. "She's as slow as a wet week in July."

Kurt glanced at his companion as the vehicle lurched forward with a sudden burst of speed. Avery accelerated into a tight bend, recognised her error immediately and now fought to make the necessary correction. The wheels locked as the vehicle slid on the gravel surface. He resisted the urge to grab the steering wheel. Instead, he braced one hand against the dashboard. "Slow down!" The rear end of the police vehicle narrowly avoided a guidepost.

"Sorry, Sarge," Avery said, bringing the vehicle to an abrupt stop. Visibly shaken, she fumbled with her seatbelt. "You'd better take over."

"No. Learn from your mistakes and drive to the conditions."

The female constable nodded, and the vehicle rolled forward again. Only the engine noise broke the silence as they laboured around the next corner and began the climb into the hills.

Kurt made a mental note to book Avery into an off-road defensive driving course. Returning his attention to the duty officer's call, he allowed his frustration to moderate his tone. "Constable King."

"Like that, is it?" Ben said. "It's not like you to pull rank on an old mate. I can't wait to see the dash-cam recording—"

"Stop wasting time. Why did you call?"

"Oh-kay, Sarge." The mocking tone had vanished from Ben's voice. "Harry wants you to call at the Top Pub at your 'earliest convenience'."

"Trouble?"

"He wasn't sure," Ben replied. "Seems your *girlfriend* didn't show for dinner, and she's not answering her phone."

Kurt took a calming breath. "The visitor probably went to the Bottom Pub."

Ben laughed. "Half the Top Pub's been down there to check, and nobody's seen her."

"Why is this a police matter?" Kurt asked.

"I wouldn't have bothered you, but when I put her name into the database, the system blocked me."

"I see. Anything else?"

"Within five minutes," Ben said, "someone from Sydney rang, wanting to know why I tried to access her file."

"What did you say?"

"A standard background check into a potential witness. They requested the incident number, and I gave them the one from last night. I didn't recognise the department code that showed on the call log, but I checked with someone I know. He told me to be careful. That's why I haven't entered the intel Harry gave me into the system – I thought you'd want to check out the situation first. Didn't think you'd appreciate the anti-terrorism squad breaking down doors without your knowledge."

"What intel?" Kurt's heart was pounding, and he straightened in his seat.

"She received a suspicious consignment this morning. Harry said she's been upset, angry even."

Kurt stared out the window, considering his options. If he had been alone, he could have contacted Piper Maxwell, the mysterious *Operation Phoenix* commander, and demanded an explanation. Kurt wasn't prone to letting his imagination influence his decisions, yet there was no ignoring his churning stomach.

"Let Harry know we're on our way."

"Will do, Sarge. Over and out." The digital dashboard indicated that the call had terminated.

"Will I activate the siren?" Avery asked. Kurt glanced towards her. She was leaning forward as if that would get them to their destination faster. He hadn't seen this much enthusiasm from the young constable for a while.

"No. Harry's probably worried about nothing."

He turned towards the passing landscape. The shadowy trees flashed past, temporarily lit by the headlamps before fading back into the night. Avery had finally increased her speed.

When they arrived at the intersection with the sealed road that led to Meredith Crossing, the vehicle's speed leapt up to the permitted limit. There was little traffic, and Avery drove down the centre of the road.

Trio

of Intruders

ဆဝ ✿ ൦ദ

Isaiah 63:19 WEB - We have become like those,
over whom you never ruled,
like those who were never called by your name.

ဆဝ ✿ ൦ദ

Checking the time, Kurt acknowledged that Avery had beaten Ben King's disparaging deadline by twenty minutes. She screeched to a halt outside the Top Pub.

There were ten cars in the motel's well-lit car park. Kurt paused on the steps leading to the main entrance, recording the registration plates in his notebook, and identifying the owners. There were no unknown cars among them, a reminder that Sigrid had arrived without transport.

He glanced in the direction Sigrid had led him last night. The curtains were open, and the motel room was in darkness. It was not the first time he had asked himself whether the whole evening had been a deliberate ploy.

Was Sigrid a honey trap? And if she was, what did Piper Maxwell want with a middle-aged country policeman?

"Sarge? Are you coming to talk to Harry?" Avery asked. She stood with the reception door open. "Or will I interview him on my own while you go straight to her room?"

Kurt moved past Avery. "We stay together."

Harry came bustling through the swinging doors before Kurt had taken more than three steps into the foyer. The barman wiped his hands on his black apron.

"Thanks for coming," Harry said. "Follow me."

The two officers accompanied Harry as he hurried towards the separate double-storey wing.

"She changed rooms this morning," Harry said with a wave of his hand. "It's the last apartment, closest to the road."

"What makes you think there's a problem?" Kurt asked.

"The lights are on, but she didn't answer when I knocked. I tried phoning her while I was outside the door, and I could hear her phone ringing. I used my master key, but she's hooked up the chain, so she has to be in there."

When Harry stopped outside the green door, Kurt made a note of the number and name: "Forest Retreat". He stepped to the door and pounded the wooden surface with his fist. "This is the police, Ms Ericson. Please open the door!"

After waiting with his ear pressed against the wood, Kurt repeated the action. Satisfied that there was no sound from within, he stepped back. "Constable Avery, go around to the rear and see if you can gain access through the courtyard."

Avery rushed away. She phoned him a few minutes later. "The gate's locked, but I climbed over. There's nobody in the courtyard. The back door is locked, but the kitchen light is on. There's an open curtain at the window, but I can't see anyone inside. The curtains for the other windows are closed."

"Go back to the car and bring me what I need to deal with the security chain," Kurt told her. After banging on the door a final time, Kurt turned to Harry. "Use your master key and then step away. I'll give you an incident number for the insurance company."

Footsteps announced Avery's return. She passed Kurt the tool he needed and took up her position a few steps behind him. Before taking further action, he contacted the duty officer. "Ben, enter the time in the log. The motel room is secure, and the registered guest has made no response. I'm authorising a forced entry."

When the severed security chain dangled from the frame, Kurt pushed the door open. "Police!" He paused in the doorway. He had visited this room during the official opening. The furniture arrangement was exactly as he remembered it.

Every light in the main room was on. The flickering image on the widescreen television drew his attention – a music video channel, with the volume muted.

A cluttered coffee table sat in front of the television. A stack of unopened cardboard cartons and what appeared to be an empty shoebox. He moved back onto the path, allowing Avery to take his place while he talked to Harry.

"Do you have anyone covering the bar? Don't follow us into the room, but I want you to stay here. I might need you to answer some questions."

"I phoned Ma before I rang the station," Harry said. "She's in town visiting a friend, and she came straight over. There's no getting rid of her until I have some answers."

"Sergeant Jensen," Avery said. "Something is hanging on the corner of the television. I'm going in to take a closer look. I'm sure it's the silver locket Sigrid – Ms Ericson – was wearing this morning."

Avery rounded the coffee table, pulling on her blue disposable gloves. "There's a couple of credit cards on the floor here, a mobile phone, and what looks like the room keycard."

She bent down, picked them up, and then yelped when the phone began to chirp in her hand. "Someone named Oliver is calling. It looks as if he's made multiple calls during the past few hours."

Avery pressed on the screen. "Hello." She frowned and held out the phone. "He wants to talk to you."

Kurt entered the room and accepted the phone. "This is Senior Sergeant Jensen."

He gestured for Avery to put the cards on the coffee table.

"Tell your constable not to touch Sigrid's locket," the male voice said. Kurt looked up. Avery's fingers were reaching towards the object.

"Avery, leave it there," Kurt snapped, and she froze. He signalled for the officer to stand still.

"Send Helena Avery to search the kitchen cupboards," the voice said. "If there's half a bottle of good whiskey there, the only emergency you'll be dealing with tonight is Sigrid's reaction when she sees what you did to her door."

Kurt waved his officer towards the kitchen. He mimed opening the cupboards. When she left the room, he peered at the locket. "Tell me this isn't a camera," he said into the phone.

"Why would I lie to a policeman?" the voice asked. "It's a relief to see a familiar face. Although I'm not happy that you've upset Sigrid."

"I haven't upset Sig—" The words were out before he could stop them. Annoyed, he asked, "Who is this?"

"Oliver Johnston. I'm disappointed you don't remember me. You've been in my helicopter. Piper included me in the dossier when he recruited you."

"He didn't recru—"

"Shh! Keep your voice down. I'm not finished with Helena's background check. Even if she turns out to be squeaky clean, the fewer people who know of your alliance with Piper, the better."

Taking a deep breath, Kurt turned from the locket to investigate the boxes on the coffee table. "You said this isn't an emergency. How can you be sure?"

"Sigrid hung the locket where you found it. She phoned the duty officer here in Melbourne and asked for confirmation that it was transmitting a clear view of the room. Then she put her credit cards, her room key card and her phone on the floor where he could see them before she went offline."

"When was this?"

"Four hours ago."

Kurt walked from the television, which was silently playing a music video he recognised, towards the archway leading to the rest of the apartment.

There was light coming from an open doorway. He took a single step into that room. Sigrid was seated at the desk, with a laptop open in front of her.

She was wearing a pair of headphones, nodding her head as if listening to the unheard music. She was also playing a computer game.

"I've found Sigrid," Kurt told Oliver, watching for a reaction from the seated woman.

The last thing he wanted was to startle her. His body still complained about how the dangerous woman had sent him crashing to the floor this morning. She might kill him for intruding tonight.

"Hey, Sarge," Avery called out, appearing in the hallway behind him. "There was nothing in the cupboards but this bott—"

"Shh!" Kurt said, backing from the room. "Avery, find the remote and turn the television off. I've found Sigrid, but she's wearing headphones."

He spoke into the phone. "Did you catch that, Oliver? I'm placing this phone on the floor where she can see it, and I'm leaving you to deal with her." Without waiting for a reply, he beat a hasty retreat.

"I've found the remote, Sarge," Avery said as he moved past her. "The television's off now."

He continued until he stood behind one of the sofas that faced the big screen.

Kurt signalled for Avery to leave the apartment. Harry was standing at the open door, and Kurt waved him away before turning back to face the archway.

Despite the room full of furniture between him and that aperture, he felt vulnerable and exposed.

ᗮ ☼ ᘓ

What happened to the music? Sigrid rose from the desk and went towards the television. There on the floor, under the archway, lay her phone. She picked it up. Oliver was on the line, but she ignored the illuminated screen. Stepping into the archway, she noted two things. The front door was open, and there were two intruders. One of them was Kurt Jensen, wearing a bulletproof vest over his uniform.

"What are you doing in my apartment?" Sigrid demanded, crossing the distance in a few long strides. Kurt stood behind a sofa.

78

"Harry called us. You missed your dinner reservation, and you weren't answering your phone. Harry said you were upset."

"So you thought I'd harmed myself? Do I look like a girl who would do that over some trivial incident?"

"No," Kurt said. "It was more likely that you were planning to take out someone else. Be grateful that it's only Avery and me. The anti-terrorism squad would shoot first and ask questions later."

A string of words worthy of her grandmother's strongest reprimand poured from Sigrid's mouth.

She flopped into an armchair and put her head in her hands. "You THINK – I'm a – I'm a – TERRORIST!"

Her plan to send Piper a message had backfired. Now that she had triggered a security alert against herself, her commander would never allow her back on active duty!

This incident would give credibility to a medical assessment from five-years ago that had labelled her a damaged war veteran in need of psychological help. The kind of "help" that would see her committed to a *special* facility. She took a deep breath as the reality hit her. Piper had played her like a cheap violin.

"I need a drink," she said, rising to her feet. "Harry, is that you hiding outside the door? If I promise not to blow anything up, can I come to the bar?"

"Of course, Sigrid," Harry said. "You're more than welcome. It wasn't *me* who thought you were a dangerous terrorist. *I* was more concerned about your safety."

"You're not leaving this room dressed like that," Kurt said.

Helena Avery snickered. Sigrid looked down. She was wearing her combat shirt, with the buttons undone, over a plain white tee-shirt.

The latter garment barely covered her upper thighs, leaving her long legs exposed. In contrast, her feet were clad in heavy socks and stuffed into her new military boots.

"You're right," Sigrid said. "I've forgotten my hat."

Tricky Thoughts

ℰ ☼ ℭ

Proverbs 27:5 WEB -
Better is open rebuke,
than hidden love.

ℰ ☼ ℭ

It was a quarter past eleven when Harry escorted Sigrid back to her room. After closing the door, she leaned against it, reflecting on her evening. She had not been left alone during her time in the bar. If Harry hadn't been hovering at her side, then his mother insisted on keeping her company. Her first drink had to wait until she had eaten a "proper" meal. Mrs Mac laughed at Sigrid's suggestion that an apple pie from the supermarket was an adequate dinner for a "growing girl".

The first task for what remained of this day was to make herself more comfortable. Sigrid kicked off her running shoes and carried them to her bedroom, where she placed them on the lower shelf of the cupboard. It was a relief to peel off the faded blue jeans. She applied lotion to her leg and massaged the taut surgical scar.

Kurt had been right. Appearing in the bar without trousers would have delivered the wrong message. In the city, she could act out her fantasies – the worst she might expect was a little morning-after regret. But in Meredith Crossing, her promiscuous lifestyle had already proved a recipe for trouble.

Her thoughtless actions had brought repercussions everywhere she went.

Determined to show everyone that she had learned from her mistake, she hadn't consumed as much alcohol this evening and hadn't flirted with anyone.

But now, in the solitude of her room, pretending to be the perfect agent was futile. Sigrid picked up her phone, which had remained in the apartment while she was out. Oliver had sent her multiple messages. She banished the notifications without reading them. From the call register, she saw that her supervisor had remained on the line for fifteen minutes after she left for the bar. Kurt must have spoken with Oliver before going to the station to file his report.

Glancing at her phone again, Sigrid noticed the flashing red symbol. She went to the television and stared at the locket, hanging where she had left it. She waved to the unseen observer. Her induction to the *Maximum Security* Melbourne facility had included time watching the digital monitors. All the recordings were analysed and catalogued, cross-referenced to different investigations and stored for future reference. What this locket recorded of her comings and goings would be available to anyone with the right access.

At the time of her induction, she had not understood the value of an unguarded moment to an investigation. Working under Oliver's supervision, she now knew better. Yet, she had never expected to be under surveillance herself. The locket still hung on the corner of the television. She reversed it so that the camera faced the inactive screen.

Sigrid went to the kitchen, selected a coffee pod from the tray on the counter and followed the printed instructions beside the machine. When the coffee aroma filled the room, Sigrid's appetite reawakened. Another apple pie lurked in the freezer. After liberating it from the packaging, she tapped her fingers on the counter while the dessert went around and around in the microwave.

An unfamiliar nostalgia washed over Sigrid. The supermarket product was a poor substitute for the apple pie Oliver's mother could make. His parents welcomed Sigrid into their home, no matter the hour, and they were always happy to feed her. The Johnstons were kind, generous people who showered her with undeserved love. Their attitude hadn't changed, not even when it became clear that her relationship with Oliver would never be more than friendship.

A heavy sensation in her chest brought her thoughts back to Oliver. Despite her rudeness, her refusal to answer his calls or respond to his messages, he continued to try. She went to the main room, intending to find her phone and send him an earnest apology. While she deliberated how to begin, someone thumped on the apartment door.

Bang! Bang! Bang!

"Open up, Sigrid. We need to talk."

Recognising Kurt's voice, Sigrid hurried to the door. She swung it open, and he stepped inside. He was still wearing his full uniform.

"No Helena, this time?" Sigrid asked, looking past him to the car park. No patrol car? She pushed the door closed. Without trousers again, she slipped past him to the kitchen. "Coffee?"

"That would be great. Black with two sugars."

"There's apple pie," she said as the microwave pinged.

She divided the pie into equal portions and set the plates on the breakfast bar. Kurt settled on one of the stools, and they ate side by side. When his plate was empty, he wrapped both hands around his coffee mug, and his head fell forward.

A tingling sensation ran through Sigrid from the top of her head to her toes. She came fully alert and stared at him. "Are you praying?"

His head jerked. "What? N-no! Why would you think I was praying?"

"You reminded me of Oliver. He bows his head over his coffee just before he goes into big-brother mode." She moved around the breakfast bar until she was opposite him, resting her elbows on the counter. "He says talking to me without prayer is not worth the risk."

Kurt stared at her. "What kind of prayer?"

"Oliver asks for wisdom in how he delivers the message," Sigrid said, being careful to smile. "And protection, in case I forget that his only motivation is love." She lowered her voice and leaned forward. "He reminds God that if I kill the messenger, then someone else will have to deal with me."

One of Kurt's eyebrows edged upwards. He drank from his coffee mug, gazing into her eyes.

Sigrid's patience ran out. "What did Oliver want you to tell me?"

Kurt nodded. Instead of delivering the message, he asked another question. "You and Oliver are close?"

She shrugged. "We work together." The apple pie turned sour in her stomach, and she tried again. "Oliver's a loyal friend. He understands me."

Kurt's eyes demanded a better answer.

Sigrid groaned. "I don't have any secrets from Oliver. He doesn't care that I'm impatient and irrational. Or that I make too many mistakes and get myself into trouble. Oliver lets me scream and shout abuse at him, and when it feels like I'm ready to kill someone, he drags me to the gym. He's the best fighter I've ever faced, and even though he never lets me win, he doesn't try to crush my spirit either. He's patient and loyal, continually bailing me out and giving me another chance. Oliver even stands up for me when Piper's on the warpath. I don't know where I'd be without him in my life."

Sigrid's heart pounded in her chest. How would Kurt respond?

He drank what remained of his coffee and pushed aside the cup. With a sigh, he spoke. "You remind me of my kid brother."

Whoa! Sigrid flinched. His "kid brother" had been killed in a police shoot-out sixteen years ago. "He's dead."

Kurt frowned, and her imagination took over. It felt as if waves of pain flowed out from him, smashing against her cold, cruel heart. What madness was this?

Kurt rose to his feet. "If he'd had someone like Oliver in his life, he might still be alive."

Sigrid's mind screamed: *Don't say anything!* But her tongue was out of control. "But he had you."

"I wasn't here. I wanted to become a hot-shot lawyer, and I went away to university. I left my brother when he needed me most—"

"You can't take responsibility for someone else's mistakes. You weren't here. You don't know how many people tried to help him." Sigrid took a deep breath. "This is a close community – everyone has an opinion, and they don't hold back in sharing their advice, whether you want it or not." What else could she say? "And I'm sure your parents loved him. Your brother had more support than a lot of kids. He was a fool to throw it all away."

Something flashed in Kurt's eyes, and he straightened his shoulders. "The locket – put it back on."

"What?"

"Oliver says he hopes you've learned an important lesson."

Sigrid rose to her full height. "He *what?*"

"The next time you throw a childish tantrum, you'll be on your own." Kurt retreated towards the exit. "And if you get yourself arrested as a psychopath, you'll only have yourself to blame."

Sigrid rounded the kitchen counter with long, angry steps. "Anything else?"

"I think I've said enough," Kurt said, opening the door, stepping out and closing it in her face.

She snatched the door open. The departing policeman was hurrying in the direction of the police station. She called after him. "Why did you bring up your brother?"

He paused and turned to face her. "Oliver said you had a heart of compassion hidden under that tough exterior. If I wanted to get out of your apartment alive, I needed to find the real you before I delivered his message."

"Why don't you come back inside so we can discuss this? I've still got that half bottle of whiskey."

He hurried into the darkness, his voice fading as he got further away. "Oliver wants you to phone him. I'm not falling for your tricks again."

Trouble

in Triplicate

ᔕ☼ᘓ

Micah 6:8b CG - Do what is good,
act justly, love mercy
and walk humbly with God.

ᔕ☼ᘓ

There was no colourful sunrise to herald Sigrid's second morning in town. A steady downpour blanketed the day, dampening her enthusiasm for the extended run she intended to take before breakfast.

Dressed in figure-hugging lycra, she laced up her running shoes before she rearranged the furniture in the living room. At a squeeze, there would be enough space for an improvised aerobics routine. She was searching for suitable music when someone tapped on the apartment door.

It was not the confident banging that had preceded Kurt's arrival last evening.

"We have a visitor," Sigrid said to the locket. She was wearing it again, a concession following her lengthy conversation with Oliver.

She looked through the peephole. Helena Avery was standing on her doorstep, wearing a hooded spray jacket. What did the young constable want? Sigrid opened the door.

"Excellent!" Helena said. "You're ready. I thought the weather might have sent you back to bed. Hurry up; the Sarge doesn't like waiting."

The young constable ran to a shiny pink Mercedes parked outside Sigrid's apartment. An impractical and expensive vehicle for a rookie policewoman. Grabbing her room key, phone, and water bottle, Sigrid spoke softly to the locket as she closed the apartment door. "I wasn't expecting Helena. Find out if Oliver had anything to do with this." She forced a smile, before sprinting for the car to join Helena. "Thanks for coming to get me."

Helena seemed in no hurry to put the car into gear. "It's the least I could do, especially after we broke into your apartment last night. You were incredibly calm about the whole incident. If it had been me, I'd have screamed and then thrown something at Sergeant Jensen."

"I don't think screaming would have impressed him."

Helena giggled. "You're probably right. But I've yet to see him impressed by any woman, screaming or otherwise. Is it true that he didn't respond when you kissed him the other night?"

Sigrid glanced out the window. "Didn't you say we needed to hurry? I'm already on your sergeant's blacklist. I don't want to make trouble for you, too."

"Don't worry about me," Helena said, finally directing the car out onto the road. But instead of heading towards the station, she turned left. "I'm not going to be here for much longer. Once I leave, Sergeant Jensen's disapproval won't count for anything."

"You've been transferred?" Sigrid asked, mentally reviewing the street layout. Helena should take the next right turn.

"Oh, yeah." Helena ignored the side street and drove on. Her smile brightened. "Nothing's confirmed yet, but I can't wait to be back in Sydney. Have you ever lived there?"

Sigrid pushed aside memories of her grandmother. "For a while. I'm a wanderer, so Sydney's not a place I'd call home."

"What brings you to Meredith Crossing?" Helena turned right at the final corner, outside the Bottom Pub.

"I'm on holiday."

Helena snorted, driving past the next side street. "Nobody comes here for a holiday. Look around you. There's nothing to do."

They went past the supermarket. If the car continued moving in this direction, they would leave the business district and arrive at a row of riverside cottages.

"The Kidman wedding," Helena said, turning right into the street which led to the hardware store. "You were a member of the security team that came with the Melbourne guests. But they're staying at the homestead, which is locked down tighter than a fortress. So your services aren't required. The rest of your team went to Newcastle. I want to know why they left *you* behind?"

Sigrid smiled. "You already have a theory?"

"Gav and Des think you're being punished. But after last night, I think your jealous boyfriend didn't want you partying in the city."

"I have a boyfriend?"

"Oliver, that guy who phoned last night and spoke to the Sarge. He was upset that you weren't wearing your locket, so I bet there's some kind of GPS tracker inside it. He's trying to keep you on a very short leash."

Sigrid's hand flew to her throat. "The only thing hiding in this locket is a photograph of my Gran."

Helena brought the car to a stop outside the police station. "Then Oliver won't mind if you come with me to Brumby's Run on Thursday night. Des and Gav also have the evening off. Dinner first, and then we've booked a B&B. I'll let you choose who you want, or we can switch partners as the mood takes us."

"Oliver *will* mind," Sigrid muttered, "but not because he's my boyfriend." She unbuckled her seatbelt and stepped into the rain. "Des *and* Gav? Shouldn't you talk to them before you invite me along on your date?"

Helena ran towards the station. "It was their idea!"

Sigrid caught up to her at the gate. "What if I say no?"

"Then I'll have to keep them both entertained. Oh, look at you! I didn't expect you to be shocked. Don't worry, it wouldn't be the first time. Come on. I told the guys that I'd ask you on the way. Only be careful not to say anything in front of the Sarge. And keep away from old Ben. Gav thinks he's worked out that I'm seeing them both because he's warned them to be careful."

  ဆ ✿ ℭ౩

After a restless night, Kurt had dragged himself out of bed to organise the morning exercise session. He'd lingered in the shower before consuming a quick fruit and yoghurt smoothie. A heartier breakfast would have to wait. He rechecked the outside deck, even though it had been raining for hours. The mats pulled out for Sigrid were soaked. The heavy rain seemed to have settled in for the day, but this did not justify his lethargy.

Everything seemed to take longer this morning, and Kurt was still writing up the activity schedule when his team began to arrive. They were content to talk among themselves while he pushed on with his task, so he tuned out their conversation. It was a quarter past six when he was finally ready.

"We're still waiting for Helena," Gavin Mallory said. "She messaged to say she's collected Sigrid."

As if on cue, Helena appeared at the door, with Sigrid.

"Sorry we're late, Sarge," Helena said, throwing off her spray jacket and hanging it on a hook.

Sigrid stood inside the doorway, dripping water onto the mat. She was not wearing any wet-weather clothes. She shrugged at his raised eyebrows. Kurt found a towel and tossed it to her.

"Thanks, Sarge," she said, mopping her face. When she began wiping the water from her lycra-clad body, Kurt dragged his eyes away. He wasn't the only one fascinated by her actions.

"Time to get started," he announced.

After the preliminary group warm-up routine, Kurt introduced his session plan. It involved paired activities designed to give him insight into any problems within his team. Sigrid's presence would add a new complication. He left the participants to work out how to proceed.

As he predicted, Sigrid was a popular choice. Helena strategically placed herself next to Sigrid before the first paired opportunity, beating everyone else. Gavin and Des, both unmarried constables, had a light-hearted shoving competition to be her partner for the second activity. Des won, but Gavin claimed her at the changeover.

The instant the buzzer signalled the end of that activity, Sigrid shook off Gavin's attentive arm and strode towards Kurt. "Save me," she whispered with her back to the room. Walking to the medicine balls, she stalked back towards him with a heavier one. "The sergeant's mine for this activity!" she shouted, heaving the ball at him. "He. Owes. Me."

He struggled to catch it. The others laughed.

"You're in trouble now, Sarge," Gavin said, passing a ball to Des. "Come here, Helena. The three of us get to play."

While Kurt contemplated this interaction, Sigrid stepped into his space, wrestling the ball from him. "Hey!" he said.

"Hey, yourself!" she muttered, striding back to her mark. "You're supposed to throw it back to me."

Before he could reply, she hurled the medicine ball again. Propelled backwards, he landed heavily on his rear. He blinked away the pain and struggled to his feet. Sigrid appeared in front of him, and he passed her the ball.

"I surrender," he said.

"Best of three," she replied, preparing to launch the ball again. "I'll go easy on you this time. If you catch it and return it to me, I'll buy you breakfast."

"Fifty dollars says he doesn't even try," Gavin said.

"You're on," Des replied. "Come on, Sarge! Don't let a girl beat you."

"It's never a good idea to make fun of your senior officer," Kurt said, keeping his eyes on Sigrid. "Remember who works out the rosters."

"Ready?" Sigrid asked, swinging the ball towards him, but she did not let it go. She repeated the action, her smile fixed on her face. Then, as she repeated the process a third time, she winked at him in the instant before she released it.

The ball soared through the air towards him. Kurt adjusted his feet to maintain his balance, allowing his arms to follow through with the momentum of the ball. When he was sure he had control, he threw the ball back to her. Someone cheered.

"You can rest now," Sigrid said, dumping the ball into his hands as the timer buzzed to mark the end of the activity. "I'm going to walk back to my motel as my cool-down. I'll expect you in the dining room at eight."

While everyone was putting away the equipment, Ben King sidled up to Kurt. "What was that about?"

"I'm not sure. She's angry about something."

"She chose an interesting way to make an appointment with you."

Ben's words echoed in Kurt's mind long after he had left.

A Small Triumph

ઽⓄ ☼ ⓒઽ

Exodus 14:14 CG -
The Lord will fight for you;
you need only to stand still.

ઽⓄ ☼ ⓒઽ

Unsure what to expect, Kurt entered the dining room at seven fifty-five. Sigrid sat at a table on the furthest side of the room. She gracefully rose to her full height. Her blue dress was a heart-stopper – short skirt and a plunging neckline, and then he registered the lacy black stockings and heels. She appeared to have dressed for a rendezvous with an ardent lover instead of a casual breakfast.

He swallowed, attempting a smile. He removed his spray jacket, shaking off the raindrops as he crossed the room. Her welcoming smile disappeared as she glared at his comfortable shirt and well-worn jeans. "I thought you'd be in uniform."

"I'm off duty. Is that a problem?"

After a moment's silent deliberation, she shook her head. Kurt draped his wet jacket over a spare chair and sat opposite Sigrid.

She pointed to two juice carafes in the centre of the table. "Orange or apple?"

"You decide," Kurt said, watching her face.

Sigrid selected the orange juice and filled his small glass.

"Thanks." He took a sip, marvelling that her attitude towards him had dropped another few degrees. Any colder, and he'd be in danger of frostbite.

She poured orange juice for herself. When her glass was full, she stared at the drink for a moment before swallowing the contents in three noisy gulps. Her eyes challenged him to say something.

His mind scrambled for a conversation starter. "You were thirsty." What an idiotic thing to say!

"One point to the policeman," she said, her eyes on her glass. "What else can you deduce?"

He watched the manicured tips of her fingers pursue droplets around the rim. Sigrid lifted her eyes in a silent challenge, and he almost drowned in the depths of her pain. He was shaken by how vulnerable, tormented, and desperate she seemed. Her protective mask had slipped. He took a deep breath and threw off his caution. "If there was vodka in that carafe, you'd already be pouring your third drink."

Sigrid frowned. "I've promised Oliver no alcohol before midday."

Kurt considered that comment. He swallowed, knowing he was again about to say the obvious thing. "Oliver's not here."

The corners of Sigrid's mouth turned up, but the sorrow in her eyes remained the same. "A promise is a promise."

So far, so good. He took a hint from her phrase and spoke again. "What else did you promise him?"

"No drinking alone." This time, she tipped her chin towards him.

Kurt nodded. "I agree with Oliver. Drinking by yourself is the fastest way to ruin your life. Is that why I'm here?"

"No." Sigrid picked up the carafe again and refilled her glass, and then she offered to top up his drink. "I promised Oliver I would ask for help when I needed it."

Kurt gazed across the table. The cold voice of reason interrupted his racing thoughts. He must be reading this situation wrong. Sigrid was no damsel in distress and he'd be an idiot if he dropped his guard. He leaned back in his chair.

An uncomfortable truth exploded in his mind. He'd only known her for a few days but he had lost his heart from the first moment he saw her in the bar. But what of the promises he'd made to himself? At forty-five, he was too set in his ways to make room for anyone else in his life...

Perhaps it was not too late to leave? He visualised himself walking away and imagined how she would react. His experience as a police officer supplied more than enough suggestions. An abusive tantrum or a drunken rampage? But what if he was walking away from a genuine cry for help.

A childhood memory about a favourite television show lurched onto centrestage. Now would be a good time to "phone a friend". Who would he call? A recent conversation with Samson replayed in his mind: "When you find yourself struggling with a difficult decision, turn to God..."

What had Sigrid told him last evening? Oliver always prayed when he was with Sigrid. Was this the kind of situation that drove her supervisor to his knees?

Kurt shuffled his feet. Even if God was interested in helping him with Sigrid, there was no time to work out how to ask—

As if miraculously summoned, Harry appeared at their table with their breakfast order. "One Drover's Breakfast for you, Sigrid, with an extra slice of wholemeal toast and a double serve of bacon, and the same for you, Kurt. I'll leave you to enjoy your meals. Ring the bell on the counter if there's anything else you need."

The smile she flashed towards the proprietor was sunshine and warmth. "Thank you, Harry."

As suddenly as he appeared, Harry was gone. Kurt glanced across the table. An unsmiling Sigrid was shovelling food into her mouth as if she hadn't eaten in days.

"I know what you're thinking," she said, between mouthfuls. "I'm almost as hungry as I am thirsty. Start eating, because if there's anything left when my plate is empty I'm going to steal yours." To emphasise her point, she reached across and grabbed a rasher of bacon from his plate.

His fork was in his hand before he realised what he was doing. Sigrid's action transported him back in time to when he had duelled with his younger brother at the kitchen table. If his brother had stolen his bacon, that would have been a signal. Kurt smiled. "*En garde!*" he cried, waving the fork towards her like a sword.

An amused twinkle appeared in her eyes. Her fingers darted forwards. Kurt smacked them soundly with his fork.

"Ouch!"

"My trusty fork is more than a match for your tricky fingers."

"But I have a fork of my own," Sigrid said. The clang of metal on metal rang out as he countered her attack. It was hard to stay focused when her face lit up with a genuine smile. The sound of her laughter blasted away residual doubts about whether he should stay.

"Oh, foolish maiden," Kurt cried. "Put down your weapon and concede. This plate of food belongs to me."

"Why should I concede to you? The battle has only just begun."

In the heat of his mock battle, Kurt finally admitted a secret regret. It had been a mistake to always allow his younger brother victory in their childhood conflicts. The cheeky boy had grown into a selfish, arrogant teenager. Kurt's fingers tightened on his fork as he remembered the last words Johnny had ever said to him: "I always get what I want, and there's nothing you can do to stop me." Two hours later, his brother was dead.

"Hey!" Sigrid's cry brought him back to reality.

He practised his best smile. "Hunger has weakened you, fair maid. But I'll offer you sustenance if you surrender." He stabbed another slice of bacon and waved it in front of her.

Sigrid's hand darted towards the rasher.

"Not so fast," he said, pulling the bacon back to his side of the table. "First, you must promise not to smite the hand that feeds you."

"I think you mean 'bite'," Sigrid said, and gnashed her teeth. "I promise not to bite you. Now give me the bacon."

"Promise not to *smite*," Kurt repeated, stretching forward and catching her hand. "No attacking me. No hitting, no kicking, no punching, no heaving medicine balls, no knocking me to the ground—"

"All that for a rasher of bacon?" Sigrid asked, wriggling her fingers free from his grasp.

"It's very good bacon, and I'm prepared to give you all of mine to seal the deal." He added the rest of the bacon to his fork.

"Then I promise!" Sigrid stood and leaned across the table. She almost upset the juice carafes in her haste to stuff the bacon into her mouth. She grinned at him as she kept his fork captive, daring him to retaliate. What would happen if he seized her by the shoulders and pulled her closer. A tremor of fear ran down his spine, and common sense prevailed.

When she returned to her side of the table, she attacked her meal while he ate at a more leisurely pace. When he had eaten more than enough, he finished his juice, gazing at her in fascination.

"What?" she asked as she reached across to take the remaining slice of toast from his plate.

"Now I know why you go for a long run every day. You need to burn off the kilojoules."

"Zing. Wrong this time, Mr Know Everything Policeman. I run so that there's room for dessert."

Trying
a New Menu

ॐ ☼ ॐ

*Job 23:6 WEB - Would He contend with me,
in the greatness of His power?
No, but He would listen to me.*

ॐ ☼ ॐ

Breaking the stolen slice of toast into manageable pieces, Sigrid wiped her plate clean. Keeping her eyes downcast, she chewed thoughtfully. Her phone buzzed on the tabletop, but she continued eating.

"Are you going to answer that?" Kurt asked.

"It's Oliver. He should know better than to interrupt me while I'm eating."

"How would he kn— Never mind."

After wiping her fingers on the serviette, Sigrid tapped on the screen to accept the call, stretching her mouth into a smile. "Good morning, Oliver. It's so *nice* to hear your voice."

"Morning to you, too," Oliver said. "I want to talk to Kurt."

"It's for you," she said, passing the phone across the table. "I'm going to order coffee."

Kurt frowned, but he brought the device towards his ear.

Sigrid gathered the empty plates and crossed the dining room to place them beside the register. Knowing that Kurt might be watching should have brought some satisfaction, but instead, she longed to pull down the hem of her skirt. With her hands empty, she smacked the bell. Harry appeared through the doors that led to the kitchen.

"Breakfast was perfect," she said. "I've brought you the plates. Kurt's on the phone, so I'm here to order two coffees. Long black espresso, double shot, extra hot. I'll wait."

Walking to the window that overlooked the car park, Sigrid glared at the continuing rain. When the drinks were ready, she thanked him and picked them up.

On the way back to the table, Sigrid studied Kurt. Would this conversation with her supervisor be a help or a hindrance to her plan? His frown intensified, but before she was near enough to hear anything, Kurt placed her phone face up on the table. He waited while she set one of the coffees in front of him and seated herself.

"Careful," Sigrid said. "It's hot."

"Thanks for the warning." He wrapped his hands around his mug.

What was behind that expression on his face? She couldn't read him.

Silence reigned.

Sigrid sipped her coffee, refusing to reach for her phone when it pinged with an intrusive message notification. Kurt held up the screen for her to read. The hairs on the back of her neck bristled. Those raised eyebrows might be a warning. Was he impatient to leave?

"It's from Oliver," Kurt said. "The message begins: You're too stubb— I can't read the rest. Your phone wants a password."

Snatching the phone from his hand, Sigrid's fingers tapped on the device to unlock the rest of the message. She tossed the phone to him.

Kurt read the message aloud. "You're too stubborn for your own good, Sigrid. You have thirty minutes with nobody listening. Don't waste it."

A dozen uncomplimentary phrases flashed into her mind. She drank deeply from her mug before remembering her own warning. She grimaced, the hot coffee burning her throat as she swallowed. Oliver understood her too well. She transferred her anger from her distant supervisor to the man across the table.

"What did you say to Oliver?" she demanded.

Kurt shrugged, placing the phone on the table. "He did the talking. If you ask the right questions, I'm permitted to tell you what he said."

"Why didn't he tell me himself?"

"I'm only the messenger."

"Then deliver the message." Sigrid glared at Kurt, her fingers throbbing from the urge to smack him.

One of his eyebrows twitched as if he could read her mind. He watched her over the rim of his coffee mug and continued to sip the hot beverage.

"Why are you the messenger?" she asked. "Why didn't he send Jenny?"

"She's coming later this morning, but he wants confirmation that you've accepted the new chain of command before she arrives."

This statement almost threw her onto her feet. "What new chain of command?"

With deliberate care, Kurt put down the coffee mug and steepled his fingers. "From today, you report to me instead of Oliver." He studied her for a reaction.

She sipped her coffee, determined to make him wait. Why would Oliver delegate his authority to someone outside their organisation? One question after another tumbled into her mind. Was there some clue hidden in Oliver's recent text message? Sigrid picked up her phone, confirming that the flashing red icon was off. She puzzled over the words before she noticed the timestamp. Thirteen minutes had already elapsed since Oliver deactivated the locket camera.

A wave of fear washed over her. Those precious minutes of privacy were slipping away. In her panic, she opened her mouth and asked an uncensored question. "Why would Oliver think I'd *cooperate* with *you*?" She cringed at the contempt in her tone.

Kurt nodded. "I asked him the same question. He said you became my responsibility when I was foolish enough to feed you. He said you'd explain."

Sigrid pursed her lips, refusing to reveal any information. Dozens of shared meals with Oliver had cemented their close connection. When their team bonding was complete, Sigrid met his mother. If Oliver was an expert strategist, then his mother, Lisa-Jane, was his greatest inspiration.

Lisa-Jane had welcomed Sigrid as if she were a long-lost daughter, and that undeserved love found expression through offerings of food. The older woman's philosophy was simple: a wandering adventurer remembered where they belonged when they were hungry.

A deep longing sharpened Sigrid's tongue. "Oliver's placing a lot of importance on a few scraps of bacon."

Try

and Make Me

ಐ ☼ ಚ

*Ephesians 6:12 CG - For we wrestle not against flesh and blood,
but against the principalities, the powers,
the world's rulers of the darkness of this age,
and the spiritual forces of wickedness.*

ಐ ☼ ಚ

Sigrid frowned. Kurt remained quiet, keeping his eyes on her face while the clock continued to count down. She was no closer to satisfying her curiosity.

Kurt's pocket beeped. He placed his phone facedown on the table.

Sigrid's hand twitched. "Aren't you going to look at that?"

His pocket beeped again, and he brought out a second phone. He put that device beside the first one. "I already know what it says. While you enjoy this thirty-minute interlude and complain to me about the injustice, Oliver's finalising the paperwork. That first notification was from my duty officer. The second one was also from him to my private phone. Oliver's court order is above the security clearance of anyone else at the station. I won't bore you with the details. You only need to know that three restrictions affect your movement.

"Number one: You report to the Meredith Crossing Police Station twice a day. If you fail to show, I'll issue a warrant for your arrest. Two: You give me a detailed report on all your movements and a list of significant conversations – both will be matched with the surveillance records in Melbourne. And three: you're not going more than a kilometre outside the town limit without permission from me."

Wasn't it enough that her movements and conversations were being recorded? Now they wanted to keep her chained to Meredith Crossing.

"Anything else?" she asked.

"I've added another condition: No inviting anyone without security clearance back to your motel room."

This was *Kurt's* condition, not something Oliver had come up with? Why did *he* care who entered her room? Her heart pounded a little faster, and she took a calming breath. This contest was not over yet. "What did I do to warrant these 'restrictions'?"

Kurt leaned closer and gazed into her eyes. "You asked me to save you."

Sigrid flinched and almost looked away. Only Oliver could justify the loss of her freedom because of a chance remark made under stress.

"I thought you were bored," Kurt continued, "but Oliver read more into that throwaway remark. Of course, he had the advantage of knowing that three of my constables invited you on a group date, and he heard what they said as they applied pressure."

"You know about that?" Sigrid's stomach cramped, and she dropped her eyes to the table. Did that make it easier or harder to ask hi—

"You're not going," Kurt snapped.

A rebuttal flew from her lips as her cheeks reddened. "I would have found some excuse—"

Kurt shook his head. "You've surrendered to temptation too often and need saving from your addictions. That's why you asked me for help. Why else would Oliver have given me this assignment?"

Sigrid folded her arms.

"If anything happens to you, Oliver will fly here to deal with the fallout. He's promised to have me demoted to constable and sent to the back of beyond."

"He wouldn't do that!"

"Tell that to those constables who propositioned you this morning. Oliver wouldn't tell me what Des and Gavin said, but he's already organised their transfers. Both men will be gone by the end of the month."

"What about Helena?"

"She's staying where I can keep an eye on her. It's debatable whether she was drawn into this by the others or if their little game was her idea."

"Why is Oliver doing this? I'm not an innocent. I can take care of myself."

"You think you're safe here, but somebody's spending a lot of money trying to find you. They've already recruited your mother—"

"My moth—" Sigrid choked on that word. "I don't have anything to do with her."

"That didn't stop your mother turning up in Melbourne, asking to see your 'cousin' Freddie. She's been to his workplace. Romano's employees knew better than to speak to her."

"But she also went to his apartment," Kurt said. "Some of Freddie's neighbours spoke to her before the concierge turned her away. She knows you live there – you can't go back."

She folded her arms, ready to answer him, but he wasn't finished yet.

"If that was all, it would be sufficient justification for these restrictions, but you've become very popular. Oliver has been blocking your calls and deleting messages from persistent lovers who want to know where you are."

"So I'm popular! How does that make me a security risk?" Sigrid fought the growing panic.

"There's a money trail back to a wealthy crime family. Oliver promised to do whatever's necessary to keep Gina Gregorio from finding you."

"Oh." Sigrid closed her eyes. The mention of that traitorous woman destroyed her last defences. Wave after wave of recrimination smashed into her soul.

Sigrid had gone undercover to protect Sara, the sweet lawyer who first introduced her to Gina. Sigrid's mistakes had helped lead Sara into a web of psychological, sexual and physical abuse. Oliver was in love with Sara. It had taken him months to organise her rescue. Perhaps the victim would never trust anyone again?

The abusers must want their pawn back. Gina couldn't rely on Oliver to lead him to Sara – he was too careful. But he was also intensely loyal. Gina must be counting on him to come to Sigrid's rescue – which explained why Sigrid had been banished from his presence. She was the bait in the trap Gina was setting for Oliver.

Would she never learn? Sigrid deserved whatever punishment Oliver prescribed. Even here in Meredith Crossing, she had continued to put her trust in the wrong people. She had spurned Kurt's wise advice and fallen in with the younger constables.

"Oliver's about to turn that listening device back on."

Sigrid's heart leapt. Kurt's voice came from beside her. He was crouching next to her chair, concern in his eyes. He passed her a serviette. She stared at the folded fabric. He wiped tears from her cheeks. She never cried! Her hand touched the strange wetness.

"When you invited me for breakfast," Kurt said, "you wanted something from me."

"It doesn't matter now," she said. She turned her face towards the wall. *What a disaster!* She stumbled to her feet, and the off-duty policeman rose with her.

"Sigrid," Kurt said, his body blocking her escape. "You can't run."

"Try and stop me," she muttered, clenching her fists. She moved back to get around him, but she was too close to the wall. She glared at him. It would be his fault if she broke her promise. He already knew she was dangerous.

A phone on the table beeped. She didn't need to read the notification. But she looked anyway when Kurt passed the phone to her.

Time's up.

Sigrid prepared to hurl the phone across the room, and Kurt wrapped his fingers around her hand. "Stop letting your emotions make the decisions for you." His voice was low, and his breath warm on her face. She could smell his aftershave, and memories from their first encounter reminded her that she still had a weapon she could use. With her eyes on his lips, she leaned towards him.

"No!" His hand pushed her against the wall as he took a step away. "Don't kiss me when you're angry."

Her mind responded to the authority behind those words. A flicker of hope ignited, but then something dark shifted inside her and smothered it.

FOOL! TROUBLE ALWAYS CATCHES UP WITH YOU.
YOU HAVE TO LEAVE BEFORE YOU RUIN MORE LIVES.
YOU'RE WICKED AND RESOURCEFUL.
DON'T YOU KNOW
THERE'S MORE THAN ONE WAY TO ESCAPE...

A plan to trick Kurt unfolded with a clarity that had eluded her all morning. "Right, Sarge. You've made yourself perfectly clear. Any other orders before I have your permission to leave?"

Nothing
Trivial Here

ജ ✧ ଔ

1 John 4:18b WEB -
Perfect love casts out fear.

ജ ✧ ଔ

Kurt marvelled at her transformation. With a tilt of her chin, Sigrid switched from furious to compliant in the time it took him to remember to breathe. Every nerve in his body went on high alert. He adjusted his stance, confirming that both feet were still planted on the floor.

A charming smile replaced Sigrid's scowl, changing her from a warrior princess into an enchanting minx. A battle erupted within him. This dangerous woman was going to break his heart. He should let her leave. No matter what Oliver had said, she was *not* his responsibility.

But Kurt's arms ached to hold her. Now was the perfect opportunity to satisfy his awakening desire. If he kept her wrapped in his embrace, his love might be enough—

Love? His knees weakened, but he straightened to his full height. Hadn't he lectured Sigrid about allowing her emotions to take control? Yet, here he was making the same mistake. What did he know about love? He needed time to process this revelation, and that was the one precious resource he lacked.

A list of his responsibilities flashed into his mind. He had to visit the station – and his mother was expecting him...

Kurt brought a phone from his pocket. "I need your phone number." While Sigrid entered her number into the contacts list, he retrieved his second phone and repeated the process. "That's my on-duty phone, and this is my private one. I'll send you a message, and you can save both my numbers."

When she had finished, Kurt sent a message from each device and waited for the corresponding pings on her phone. After stashing both devices into his jean pockets, he beckoned for Sigrid to accompany him to the door. On the threshold, he draped his spray jacket around her shoulders and raised the hood to cover her hair.

"I don't want your jacket."

"I don't have time to argue. Jenny will be here soon. There's barely time for you to change out of that dre—"

"What's wrong with what I'm wearing?" Sigrid posed with her hands on her hips.

A slow heat began to rise through his body. Kurt nudged her in the direction of her apartment. "Message me as soon as Jenny leaves, and I'll collect you."

The rain dripped from his jacket as she held it loosely around her. The longer she delayed, the wetter he became. She smiled sweetly, her eyes lingering on his wet shirt. The fabric was already plastered to his chest. "Jenny won't mind if I'm wearing this dress. If you're coming back, you can help me get changed."

"There won't be time," he said again. "Get changed while you're waiting for Jenny. I want you wearing more than half a dress when you meet my mother." Kurt sloshed through the puddles towards a Toyota Hilux 4x4.

"Why am I meeting your mother?"

He paused with the Toyota door open. *Good question!* If only he knew the answer.

This madness would probably inspire an unfounded hope in his mother. Sigrid would seem like the first instalment towards another grandchild. His mother would chastise him for the lack of notice, yet she would already have enough food prepared to feed an army.

More than enough to win the heart of a warrior princess.

Instead of increasing his distress, the intrusive voice calmed his soul. When this was over, he would make up his mind whether God had really spoken.

Despite the water dripping from his face, Kurt grinned as he called out to Sigrid. "Morning tea. The best homemade scones you've ever tasted, with whipped cream and raspberry jam. There'll be a roast for lunch, a mountain of veggies, and delicious gravy you'll want to drink straight from the jug. And if you're still hungry, there should be at least two choices for dessert."

Without waiting to see her response, he threw himself into the Toyota and made his escape.

ᏹ ✡ Ꮳ

Sigrid stood in the rain, watching Kurt's 4x4 roar out of the car park. He raced up the road towards the police station. Chastising herself, she took a step forward to take a shortcut. Cold water seeped over the strappy toe of her expensive high-heeled shoe. She swore as she extricated herself from a deep puddle. The heavy rain had created tiny rivers which raced each other towards the curb. Navigating the wet car park would be a challenge. She shook her head, trying to banish

Kurt's final words. What was it about that conversation which had triggered the confusion within her?

Kurt was taking her to meet his mother.

The invitation was unexpected, but that did not excuse her reaction. No way could "meet my mother" mean what she first thought it implied. Dozens of possible reinterpretations ran through her mind as she replayed the scene over and over. The process was not unlike the mental confusion she remembered from being too close to an exploding bomb.

Anchoring her thoughts on a distant battlefield brought clarity. She stomped her foot. *Idiot!* Water splashed around her.

Kurt's words had flown across the car park like a well-directed hand grenade. The actual invitation was not important. Oliver must have betrayed her trust! Kurt's hasty escape confirmed that both men saw her as an easy target. Denying her an opportunity to respond intensified the emotional damage. Did Kurt expect to pick up the pieces on his return and find her gratefully submissive?

This strategy might have worked when she had met Oliver's mother, but she wasn't falling for that ploy a second time. She would eat the food and enjoy the country hospitality, but she would not allow a family welcome to distract her from her plan.

It would be easy to defend her heart. Kurt's mother would be a poor substitute for Lisa-Jane, Oliver's mother. There couldn't possibly be two women in the world who would open their hearts to a stranger, especially one rejected by their son. Once his mother saw the way Kurt spurned Sigrid's amorous attention, the trap would be disarmed.

For a moment, she considered disobeying Kurt's demand that she change out of this dress. She played that scenario several times in her mind. Unsatisfied because she came off second-best in all of them, she set aside that rebellion.

"Why are you standing in the rain?" The voice belonged to Jennifer Prescott, Piper's second-in-command. Jenny was the one who had overseen Sigrid's training and certified her readiness for active duty. This woman had the authority to overturn Oliver's restrictions. But Jenny was a difficult taskmaster, continually testing her agents and reviewing their performance. Jenny didn't tolerate fools.

Sigrid blinked and looked for the owner of the voice.

When did that car arrive? Three other people emerged from the car and hurried towards the awning over the apartment door. They wore long coats and broad-brimmed hats. What manner of delegation was this?

Sigrid marched towards them. Her concern escalated as she identified the others: Romano's diminutive wife, Evie; her outspoken sister, Sofia; and Samson's wife, who called herself Ruth, but to Sigrid, this devious woman was always Evie's enemy, Jezebel. Sigrid pushed away the awful memory: Evie lying on the pavement in a pool of blood. Jezebel's actions had caused the early delivery of Evie's twins.

Sigrid remembered Romano's fury when he found out what had happened. She cast an anxious look behind her for that zealous husband. Since the birth of the twins, it was rare to see Evie without him. Sigrid frowned. Why had Romano allowed Jezebel to accompany Evie into town?

"Romano's not with you?" Sigrid asked, flashing her key-card to unlock the door.

"Secret women's business," Jenny said, pushing past her into the room.

When everyone was inside, they busied themselves finding somewhere to hang their dripping coats.

"I wasn't expecting visitors," Sigrid mumbled. It had been a mistake not to tidy the apartment after shoving the furniture aside that morning. "The dining room might be better—"

"Nonsense," Jenny said. "Ruth and I will sort out this mess. I don't know *why* you needed an indoor space when you have the training facility at the police station."

"It's raining." That excuse sounded like a childish complaint. Sigrid tried again. "The motel gym is a glorified broom cupboard, and I don't have all-hours access at the station."

Jenny snorted, already wrestling with the furniture. Jezebel hurried to assist her.

"Excuses!" Jenny said. "This wouldn't be a problem if you hadn't alienated the local sergeant." One of the sofas lurched back into place with a thud. Jenny put her hands on her slender hips and turned towards Sigrid. "That dress tells me you haven't learned anything from your mistake. Kurt Jensen is not going to ruin his reputation over someone like *you*."

Sigrid blinked, refusing to give in to the threatening tears. "I'll make coffee."

Waiting beside the coffee machine in the kitchen, Sigrid took deep breaths. She was careful not to acknowledge the quiet footsteps that approached from behind.

Evie Romano appeared beside her. Her husband might be an intimidating giant, but there was nothing in this woman's physical appearance that suggested she was a threat. And yet Sigrid trembled in her presence.

Tribal
Unrest

ༀ ☼ ༁

*Psalm 85:2 WEB - You have forgiven
the iniquity of Your people.
You have covered all their sin.*

ༀ ☼ ༁

Kurt came to a screeching halt in his driveway. By the time he had the door open, Constable Clifford Briggs was waiting for him under the covered walkway that connected the house to the police station.

"What happened to you?" Briggs asked.

"I don't have time to explain," Kurt said, untucking his wet shirt as he headed towards his house. "What's so urgent that you came to meet me?" He unlocked the door but had to brush dripping water from his face before he could operate the security keypad. Briggs followed him into the house.

"I'm not sure which message to show first. Considering your current mood, perhaps I should hold off telling you about the one that refers to your breakfast date?"

Snatching a towel from the hall cupboard, Kurt vigorously dried his hair. "It was *not* a breakfast date." He paused in the doorway to his bedroom and looked back to Briggs, who stood further along the hallway. "Hang on. Are you telling me that there's more than one message?"

Briggs raised an eyebrow. "One about Sigrid, marked for your eyes only. Is that the one you were expecting? You'll have to log into your computer to access that. I took the liberty of printing the other three." He waved a handful of papers.

"Give me the details while I get changed," Kurt said, disappearing into his room.

"Right, Sarge. There are two from Area Command. There's a specialist task force coming to Meredith Crossing, please await further orders, etcetera. Nothing requires your immediate attention. Half an hour later, the Superintendent wrote again, asking you to 'comply with all reasonable requests' from the taskforce leader while 'not neglecting day-to-day operations'."

"Does it say who the team leader is?" Kurt asked as he peeled off his wet jeans and found a dry pair.

"Inspector Tobias Lester-Angevin. I've not heard his name before. Do you know him?"

"No."

"The third message is from Lester-Angevin. When I saw his accommodation requirements, I sent him the link to Harry's website. Afterwards, I realised he'd already seen it. 'Self-contained and fully serviced apartments, air-conditioned and heated. Indoor and outdoor living areas suitable for private meetings. Fast internet, satellite television', and, of course, 'in-house catering'."

"How many officers are in this task force?" Kurt asked, buckling his belt as he emerged from his room.

"Twelve," Briggs said. "He contacted me almost immediately, asking me to book all four apartments. I haven't replied. You can tell him there aren't four because Sigrid is in one."

"Remind me to thank you when all this is over." Kurt went to the laundry, dumped his wet clothes in the tub before retrieving his heavier coat and his battered Akubra hat. "What else did he want?"

"Between now and the taskforce's arrival on Thursday, he expects us to doorknock every property in the immediate area and perform full background checks on all the occupants and their guests. He wants a detailed map in our operations room, complete with colour-coded pins to confirm the status of our investigation."

"He's not asking for much," Kurt muttered, locking his front door and following Briggs towards the station. "You'd better call in the team—"

"Already have, Sarge. They're waiting for you in our 'operations room'. I've left them preparing the map. I took the liberty of warning them to cancel any immediate plans. Des and Gav weren't pleased. Sounds like they had something special planned for their two-day break."

An unwelcome urge to hit something – or two specific *someones* – was accompanied by a sharp pain at his temples. "I'll check that message about Sigrid first," Kurt said, moving past the front desk and slamming his office door behind him. While he waited for the computer screen to load, he brought out his phone and found Oliver's number.

Oliver answered immediately. "You've phoned to ask me about Taskforce Nine? Nothing for you to worry about. It's a training exercise. But make sure you keep Sigrid on a tight rein while they're there."

Oliver ended the call. Kurt frowned at the phone before refocusing on the computer. He was curious about how Oliver had managed to procure an official police order. The opened message revealed the logo for one of the Sydney-based

Command Centres. There was a flashing clickable link beneath it:

single access only

That link took Kurt to an encrypted site. The letter opened with a personal greeting from a Chief Superintendent Kurt knew only by reputation. The details were outlined in three sparse paragraphs.

Major Sigrid Ericson belonged to a "joint-multi-force international operation". She was under Kurt's "personal protection". Additional officers would be transferred to the Meredith Crossing Station "soon" to provide "more flexibility" for the roster. When they arrived, he was to spend every evening with Major Ericson.

He rubbed his temples and rummaged in his desk drawer for painkillers. After swallowing them without water, he returned to the document.

Information about her mission was above his security classification. There were unspecified allegations about a security breach, but it was uncertain whether her cover was compromised. For that reason, he was not to discuss the details of this request with anyone else. Not his junior officers, no-one at Area Command, nor—

Kurt sat up straight, reading the sentence twice. If he was "approached" by an officer of higher rank, he was to "deny all knowledge" of this assignment.

At the end of the message, there was another link to his "log-in portal" where he could access "further instructions". He must confirm receipt of this email by clicking the link, and when prompted, create a password.

After reading the information several times, Kurt took a screenshot of the original message. He opened a new document, saved the image, and then uploaded the file to his private cloud account. He knew how to track a deleted document. Kurt made this one difficult for anyone else to find. Then he clicked the link, and a blank log-in screen appeared. His name automatically appeared in the top box. He reset his password, and a message popped up:

Welcome Kurt Jensen
This system will shut down in 30 seconds
When you restart your computer, there will be a new app in the
start-up menu
Have a nice day.

The digital countdown moved to zero while Kurt stood at his desk. When the screen went blank, he willed the trembling in his hands to cease and went to face his team.

ߍ ✿ ⳹

The coffee machine hissed and gurgled. Sigrid set aside the first mug and prepared to fill a second one. The remaining cups were lined up on the counter, ready for their turn. Sigrid became increasingly uncomfortable under Evie's silent gaze. There were rumours that Romano's wife had a direct line to God.

Sigrid blinked. She kept her hands busy while dreading what Evie had to say.

LOOK AT HER, YOU FOOL! YOU'RE STRONG ENOUGH TO
SILENCE HER FOREVER.

The mug slipped from Sigrid's hand, smashing on the granite bench. A dark river flowed over the edge, dripping onto the white tiles near Evie's feet. The gentle woman did not move as the liquid oozed towards her. A vision of Evie surrounded by a pool of blood appeared in Sigrid's mind, a nightmare that seemed so real. With a trembling hand, Sigrid grabbed a tea towel and dealt with the spill before it reached Evie.

As she worked, Sigrid's heart rejected ownership of that violent thought. *No! I'd rather rip out my own heart than hurt Evie!*

Taking a deep breath, Sigrid dispatched the damp towel to the sink. "I'm sorry," she said, with her head bowed. *Evie is not my enemy!*

Evie put one small hand on Sigrid's arm. "You're forgiven." A tingling sensation began in Sigrid's fingers and toes which crept up her limbs. A long-forgotten memory of a fainting spell came as a warning. Swirling darkness loomed at the edge of her vision. Then that voice – the one that had told her to hurt Evie – called to her from that mist.

DON'T LISTEN. WHAT RIGHT DOES SHE HAVE TO INTERFERE?
YOU DON'T NEED FORGIVENESS. IT'S YOUR LIFE!

Words of hatred filled her mind, along with a powerful compulsion to curse Evie and reject the compassion on offer. It was a struggle not to speak them into existence.

Sigrid froze. The contrast between Evie and herself had never been more obvious. Evie's strength was in her character. The tiny woman was virtuous and honourable. A truth seeker. An advocate for all that was right and good. A wise woman of faith with an uncanny ability to identify the heart of a problem.

With a single glance, Evie could silence Romano and defuse an angry situation. Sigrid had been there when Evie told Romano he had to forgive Jezebel. The evidence of his promise had played out in recent days. Not only did Romano allow Jezebel to live, he now permitted her inclusion in Evie's close circle of friends...

The silence in the room grew heavy. At any moment, Evie would say something significant. Too many times, Sigrid had witnessed what happened after Evie spoke: unchangeable certainties began to unravel. Even Piper Maxwell, the proud and mighty *Maximum Security* commander, would bow his head in submission to one of Evie's requests.

An atmosphere of intense peace flowed from this woman, wrapping Sigrid in its warm embrace. Sigrid glanced towards the kitchen window. The sun must be breaking through the clouds—

The gloomy darkness outside stole her breath away. It was untouched by the glow that flooded this room. Blood pounded in Sigrid's ears as a different kind of fear awoke.

Sigrid stood her ground as Evie stepped closer and hugged her. A litany of regrets bubbled into Sigrid's mind, accompanied by shameful memories that made her squirm.

TELL HER EVERYTHING.
SHOW HER THE EVIL YOU'VE HIDDEN IN YOUR HEART.
THIS INNOCENT WOMAN WILL NOT WANT TO BE
CONTAMINATED BY YOUR CORRUPTION.

Evie tightened her embrace and rested her head against Sigrid.

TELL HER SHE'S TOO LATE – YOU'VE ALREADY SOLD
YOUR SOUL—

"God knows." Evie's voice was no more than a whisper. Sigrid's head jerked as a blinding light flashed around them. Beads of sweat formed on her forehead, and then a cooling breeze blew over her face. She held her breath, unable to glance away from Evie.

"God has already forgiven you."

The dark despair inside her quivered.

"God has answered your prayers. The time of His favour has arrived—"

A tendril of darkness snaked from the shadows and whacked her. Sigrid shook her head. "I haven't been praying."

Evie smiled. "God hears the cries of your heart."

Sigrid clutched the counter with both hands.

"God has prepared a family for you."

Those words smashed against her defences.

"A mother who will cherish you."

A tear rolled down Sigrid's cheek.

"A father who will be proud of you."

Sigrid gasped as Evie's words scored another direct hit. An excruciating pain awoke in her chest.

"A husband who will hold you in his arms. His love will be a shield against the darkness."

A heavy silence filled the room as Evie released Sigrid and stepped away. Focusing on her breathing, Sigrid waited for the spinning room to settle before she rubbed her eyes and reached for a replacement mug.

"That was very moving," Jenny said from behind them. "But Sofia urgently needs the bathroom. The smell of coffee is making her sick again."

CHAPTER 20
(Tuesday 29th May)

Trifecta
of Warnings

ॐ ☼ ෙ

John 14:27a WEB - Peace I leave with you.
My peace I give to you;
not as the world gives, I give to you.

ॐ ☼ ෙ

After taking one look at Sofia's greenish complexion, Sigrid dashed along the connecting hallway to open the bathroom door. Evie's sister made it with seconds to spare.

"The doctor will be here any minute," Jenny said. "Sigrid, take Evie upstairs so she can choose a room for Sofia's consultation."

"Why is the doctor coming?" Sigrid asked Evie at the top of the stairs. "What's wrong with Sofia?"

Evie smiled. "This will do." She stepped into the first bedroom. "There's nothing wrong with Sofia, but she wants confirmation before she makes a public announcement."

"Confirmation?" Sigrid's eyes widened. She glanced towards the stairs. "But that's—"

"Impossible?" Evie asked.

Sigrid nodded. "Sofia has always said three fatherless teenagers is more than enough trouble."

"This baby won't be fatherless," Evie said. "And has a determined big brother. Marco's been praying for this miracle since he found out I was pregnant."

"Don't remind me," Sofia said, appearing in the doorway. "That's why I came here to see the doctor. There are too many eyes and ears at *Mountain Rise*."

"Marco already suspects," Evie said.

Jenny shouted from below. "Evie, the doctor's arrived. Ruth is letting him in now. Send Sigrid down."

Sigrid was at the top of the stairs when Sofia called to her from the bedroom doorway. "I know it's none of my business, but I hope you're being careful."

Sofia's hand rested on her abdomen as she spoke, and her smile gave more meaning to her comment.

Escaping downstairs, Sigrid tried to shake off Sofia's warning. She nodded to Tim Chappell as Jenny led him towards the stairs. Needing a strong drink, Sigrid made the kitchen her destination. But Jezebel – Ruth – was there, on the wrong side of the breakfast bar. "I've made coffee. You look as if you need one."

"I don't have time," Sigrid said, spinning on her heels. "I have to change out of this dress."

Jezebel picked up both mugs and followed Sigrid into her downstairs bedroom.

"Breakfast with Kurt didn't go the way you planned?" asked the unwelcome visitor.

Sigrid bristled. She clenched her jaws and took a deep breath. With Jenny in the apartment, voicing her hatred for this woman would be foolish.

"Kurt's a good man," Jezebel said.

Hearing those words from that woman's mouth was almost enough to make Sigrid lose her breakfast. Was Kurt one of Jezebel's conquests? She dismissed the possibility immediately, reminded again of his rejection. Jezebel was right. Kurt was too good for either of them.

"He despises me," Sigrid said, wriggling out of the offensive dress. She stomped to the adjoining room and tossed it into the bath. "He's tolerating my company to prevent me from causing trouble for anyone else."

Retrieving the dress, Jezebel found a hanger in the wardrobe. "You were wearing his jacket."

Sigrid snatched the hanger from her antagonist's hands and hung the dress in the shower. "What if I was?"

"A jacketless man doesn't stand in torrential rain for someone he despises."

"Why should I listen to anything you say?"

"You're familiar with my history." Jezebel smiled, making herself comfortable on a padded chair. "I know men. They've paid me for what you give away for free. I've met amateurs like you before. You'll never be satisfied. If you don't stop, the games you play will become increasingly dangerous until they cost you everything. God knows you deserve better than that."

"Don't bring God into this!" Sigrid went to the window. It was still raining. She spun, grabbing the arms of Jezebel's chair. "How long are you going to continue this farce?"

Without flinching, Jezebel slipped from the chair and ducked under Sigrid's arm. "You think I'm conning everyone?" Jezebel walked towards the door, where she leaned against the doorpost. "You won't call me Ruth because you can't accept that I've rejected my old life. Nothing I say will convince you, but consider this: Evie knows the truth. Her acceptance is proof that Jezebel is dead and gone. Evie's forgiven me because I'm free of my addictions and no longer a slave to my demons. My evil past is dealt with, and I'm a new person."

Sigrid sat, refusing to respond. She removed her wet stockings.

"You think I've tricked Evie," Jezebel said. "You believe she's too naive to recognise the truth. But you can't say that about her husband. He's not blind to this world's darkness. Do you think Romano would allow me anywhere near Evie if Jezebel still lurked inside me? He wouldn't tolerate my deception, and I'd be dead."

Begrudgingly, Sigrid conceded that this woman was presenting her argument well. But that didn't mean she had to give her any acknowledgment. Walking to the wardrobe, Sigrid considered her limited options.

Jezebel remained near the door. "The old me didn't care about anyone but herself. Yet the new me stands here, asking you to listen. Take a good look at yourself and flee from the gates of hell before it's too late."

"How much of this 'new me' is a ploy to keep Samson?" Sigrid sneered. "Butch told me that his uncle wouldn't let the 'old you' seduce him. He made you prove that you'd changed before he'd let you anywhere near him."

"Butch is half-right. Samson didn't consummate our relationship until my heart was pure, but not because he despised me. He wanted our love to be untarnished by guilt and regret. Which brings me back to what I need to say to you."

Jezebel returned to the bathroom and retrieved the damp dress. "I can't believe you wore this to breakfast. He deserves better from you. He's not interested in a one night stand, and he doesn't sneak off to visit prostitutes in the city. If you want his respect, show him the real you: the hardworking, selfless soldier who defends those under her protection; the loyal and trustworthy friend. Then when you have his attention, be honest about your vulnerability."

"That's good advice, Ruth," Jenny said, walking into the room. "Leave us. I need to talk to Sigrid alone."

When the other woman had retreated, Jenny shut the door and sat on the edge of the bed. Sigrid waited.

"Why are you standing there in your underwear?" Jenny asked. "It's a workday. I shouldn't have to remind you to wear your uniform. Get dressed."

Sigrid selected the items she needed and put them on, careful to face her superior with a neutral expression.

Jenny crossed her arms, locking eyes with Sigrid. "Remember what the psychologist told you at your first assessment? You weren't ready to listen then. You're too good an agent to throw everything away."

Sigrid dropped into the chair, gritting her teeth as she bowed her head to put on her socks.

"You didn't grow up with your father's approval," Jenny said. "That's an unchangeable fact. You've been trying to cancel out the pain with the wrong things. It doesn't have to be that way. Start listening to advice from people who care."

考 ☼ α

The assembled team turned towards Kurt when he entered the briefing room. They shuffled to accommodate him. On the wall behind them was a high-resolution map, a montage of A3 printed sheets divided into four by a grid of black lines. An alpha-numeric code ran around the outer boundaries.

The Meredith Crossing Police Station was in the centre of this map, and a scattering of coloured pins had already been added. There was a lonely green one for the station house. *That's me.* At least three more pins could fit in that spot.

A colour-coded key was located in a blank space.

Green =	Identity confirmed, clean background check, NO security concerns
Blue =	Identity known, background check incomplete
Red =	Identity known, criminal record AND/OR security concerns
Black =	Identity unknown, further action required
Yellow =	Child or juvenile

White =   Property vacant

In the space next to the key, a handwritten label marked where the rescue helicopter could land at the recreation ground. Kurt scanned the map. Other labels identified the ambulance station, the volunteer fire brigade and the doctor's surgery.

He surveyed the map, noting how each officer had identified their place of residence with a green pin. Helena Avery lived in a cottage on a farm to the north of the town. Gavin Mallory and Des Wilmot, Helena's co-conspirators, shared a unit near the Bottom Pub. Clifford Briggs, and his wife and two children lived beside the river. Ben King and his wife lived with his wife's parents on an outlying farm to the west.

"You've made a good start," Kurt said. "How are you collating the information?"

"Separate tables for each grid quadrant on these clipboards," King said. "Every officer is adding their associates: names and street addresses, blue pins unless we already know they have a police record, or they've been cleared."

"Are there any unassigned colours?" Kurt asked.

"There are a few purple pins," Gavin said.

"Stick some up at Mountain Rise."

"Okay, Sarge," Gavin said. "What are they for?"

"Write: Interstate visitors," Kurt said. "Security clearance confirmed."

"What about Sigrid?" Helena asked.

Helena's hand hovered over the pins. Kurt frowned at her eagerness. "Does she get a red pin?"

Everyone stared at Kurt, waiting for his answer. "I'm tempted to make it red, but why stir up trouble?"

"Purple, then," Helena said.

"That's enough talk about coloured pins. We're here to discuss Taskforce Nine. Twelve officers will be arriving in Meredith Crossing on Thursday. You already know that they want us to door knock the district. I don't have any information about their investigation, but I've had an email from the team leader. Does anyone know Inspector Tobias Lester-Angevin?"

There was a lengthy pause. Most of them shook their heads.

"Is he from Sydney?" Helena asked. "There was an officer with an unusual name at a fundraising dinner I attended. My parents introduced me to him, but I don't remember if that was his name."

"Did you talk to him about Meredith Crossing?" Kurt asked.

Helena gazed into the distance for a moment. When she refocused on Kurt, she shrugged. "Um, I'm not sure, Sarge. I talked to a lot of people that night. I know Dad mentioned my assignment to the Meredith Crossing station to several senior officers."

"Is there a problem?" Ben asked.

"I don't know," Kurt said. "Usually, there's a longer delay between first correspondence and having a task force descend on a station. Two days' notice is not enough, especially when they want us to do a lot of preliminary leg work." His phone buzzed in his pocket, and he retrieved it. A message from Sigrid:

Jenny leaving

Placing the phone on the table beside him, Kurt noted the speculation in the room. He had nothing to hide. "Let's reconvene this discussion in the morning. Sigrid's getting impatient—"

Gavin interrupted him. "Clifford said we had to reschedule our rostered days off. Why doesn't that apply to you?"

"The rescheduling starts when the task force arrives," Kurt said, attempting to mask his anger. His eyes travelled around the group. "The current roster will be updated when I know more. If you're not rostered on this morning, log the time you've been here and go home." He walked towards the door and faced them again. "We've been ordered to maintain normal operations, but be clever about where you go and who you talk to. Use your notebooks, and keep your eyes and ears open. If you're out in the patrol cars, take the less-frequented roads, keep in contact with the duty officer and have him fill in the map information."

Kurt's phone buzzed again.

Where RU

The tension in Kurt's shoulders intensified. Was Sigrid already marching through the storm to find him? Her arrival would only make things worse. But he couldn't leave yet.

"Constable Mallory," Kurt said, "you asked why I'm taking the day off. That implies I'm abusing my rank for personal benefit. Before you leave the station, ask the duty officer to show you the rosters for the past three months. I haven't had a full day off since Easter. Can anyone else in the team match that claim?"

"I meant no offence," Gavin muttered.

"I'd be lying if I said I believed you," Kurt said. The words hung in the air. "I expect your transfer request on my desk in the morning."

Kurt slammed the door behind him. He grabbed his coat and hat from his office and went outside.

The steady rain was the perfect accompaniment for his mood.

Try

This

For Size

଼ ☼ ଼

Psalm 139:7 WEB - Where could I go from Your Spirit,
Or where could I flee
from Your presence?

଼ ☼ ଼

Backing the Toyota onto the road, Kurt drove from the station to the Top Pub. He slowed down in front of her apartment. Sigrid appeared at the passenger side of the ute and had the door open before the vehicle stopped.

"What took you so long?" Sigrid asked, unwrapping his spray jacket from her shoulders. She thrust it towards him, reluctant to admit that she was grateful for it. It wasn't his fault the wet weather gear and some other essentials were missing from yesterday's parcel. But her frustration needed an outlet, and he was here.

Kurt tossed the jacket behind his seat.

"Your meeting with Jenny didn't go well."

Her hands wrenched at the seat belt, which refused to budge. "What makes you say that?"

"Her visit did nothing to improve your temper. And you're wearing your uniform. The hat I can understand, but camouflage gear and heavy boots?"

Kurt undid his seatbelt and reached across to help.

"I'm on active duty," Sigrid muttered, shrinking back into the seat as he dealt with her restraint.

He stayed silent, and the atmosphere in the confined space sizzled with an intensity that gave him goose bumps.

She waited until the Toyota rolled out onto the road before she replied. "Jenny wasn't alone. Evie and Sofia came too, with Jezebel as their driver."

From her tone, Kurt guessed that all four women had contributed to her mood. Which woman was responsible for the greater offence? He took an educated guess. "I've read Piper's reports about Samson's wife, Ruth. Why do you still call her Jezebel?"

Instead of responding to his question, Sigrid stared out the window. "Why are we stopping outside the hardware store?"

"I'm going to buy you a coat. But first, tell me about Ruth. If we're going to work together, I have to know everything. Especially if you've already decided I'm going to disagree with you. Nobody listened to your concerns?"

"I'm not the only one who doesn't trust her," Sigrid said, lifting her chin and staring into his eyes. "Piper says she'll return to her old ways after he catches the people pursuing her. She'll get bored pretending to be a saint, and then he'll be vindicated when she runs back to her old life."

"I hope he's wrong. Samson was devastated the last time she disappeared."

"You made a grand speech about listening to my opinion," Sigrid said, "so give me yours. Why didn't you arrest her before she dug her claws into your friend?"

"There were no outstanding charges, and Samson's a grown man. I couldn't prevent him from falling in love."

"That's another thing I don't understand. How did an uncompromising Christian like Samson fall in love with such a wicked woman?"

"I only know what he told me."

"That story about God sending him to Sydney to find her? You don't believe that, do you?"

"Stranger things have happened." Kurt held back the rest of his comment when he saw the warning flash in her eyes. Instead, he opened the door. "Time to buy that coat."

ଛ ☼ ଓ

Sigrid narrowed her eyes as Kurt leapt from the Toyota. She fumbled with her seatbelt, and he had the door open beside her by the time she was free.

"I don't need your help."

He backed away, both hands raised as if in surrender. His eyes crinkled at the corners, but he turned towards the entrance to the store before she could confirm that he was laughing at her.

With long strides, Sigrid caught up to him as he pushed open the door. She was close enough that she was inside before the door swung shut again. Kurt headed through the maze of shelves, plunging into the shadowy depths of the store. He didn't wait to see if she followed him.

Brum appeared from nowhere. "Uncle Kurt!"

Kurt walked past him with a nod.

The teenager turned his attention to her. "Sigrid! Cool uniform. What's Uncle Kurt looking for?"

"A coat." Kurt disappeared around a corner. "Sigrid, come here and try this on."

When she arrived, Kurt tossed a long coat towards her. The heavy garment was a dark chocolate brown colour.

Brum took it from her and moved behind her, holding it up so she could insert her arms in the sleeves. "No manners, my uncle," the teenager said. "He should know that a gentleman always helps a lady into her coat."

"I'm no lady," Sigrid said. "And he's already learned not to stand behind me. If you don't want an undignified tumble, back off."

Brum danced out of her way. His smile faltered for a moment. He looked at Kurt. The older man reached across and adjusted the coat about her shoulders.

She flapped the long sleeves at him. "You overestimated my size."

"Roll up the sleeves," Kurt said. "You need the extra shoulder width to give you room to manoeuvre. If it was any smaller, you wouldn't be able to fulfil your threat to throw Brum to the floor."

"Are you sure this one wouldn't be a better option?" Brum asked, holding out a blue coat. "Women usually choose this style. It doesn't have the weight across the shoulders and is more fashionable. It comes in brighter colours, and it's half the price."

"The cost is not an issue," Kurt said. "And don't suggest she can't carry the extra weight, or you *will* end up on the floor."

"Oh, that's right," Brum said. "I forgot Sigrid could put her purchases on the account Samson set up yesterday. You could get her more than one coat, so she has options—"

"She only needs one coat," Kurt said, striding towards the front counter. "And I'm paying. No debate. I might not have Sigrid's ninja abilities, but I can still make you regret arguing with me."

ᔓ ☼ ᘒ

They were back in Kurt's ute, heading out of town. He turned right at the intersection that led into the hills. Sigrid had not uttered a word since the hardware store.

"What did Jenny and the others say to you?" Kurt asked after he navigated a sharp corner. "You've been quiet since we left town."

She held the locket towards him. "You can always contact Melbourne and ask to listen to the recordings."

"I'd rather hear from you. I told Oliver I'm not happy with this surveillance."

"Oliver never does anything without a good reason," Sigrid said. "I'm testing this camera's efficiency. *Maximum Security* already employs tracking devices for their female clients. But there are times when it would be 'helpful to see and hear what is happening'. Evie, Sofia, and Freddie's new wife, Alixanda, have each been targeted by kidnappers."

"Only an idiot would try to kidnap you."

"That doesn't make me immune. The invitation I had from Helena and her boyfriends proves that. Promise me a few drinks, and trapping me is easy."

"You don't have to worry about my constables," Kurt said. "Their plan for a little *romantic* getaway has been torpedoed. I'm not sure how Oliver managed it, but all personal leave has been cancelled for the immediate future. There's a special task force coming to town."

135

"Tell me about this task force." Sigrid smiled, her eyes inviting him to tell her everything.

Kurt blinked. "Not so fast, young lady. You still haven't told me what Jenny said."

CHAPTER 22
(Tuesday 29th May)

Road Trip

ℰ ☼ ℭ

Matthew 4:4b WEB - "It is written,
'Man shall not live by bread alone,
but by every word that proceeds
out of God's mouth'".

ℰ ☼ ℭ

Sigrid stared out the Toyota window. How patient was her new "supervisor"?

The native trees flashed past as the off-duty policeman navigated each tight corner with the reckless abandon of an experienced rally driver. His speed on the sweeping stretches set her heart racing as the trees rushed towards her. She revised her assessment of his character. Kurt made Jenny's dangerous city manoeuvres seem tame by comparison.

After the *Mountain Rise* turnoff flashed past, the road climbed steadily into the hills. Where were they going? She glanced at the driver as her hand slipped into her coat pocket. If she used her phone to access a map, would Kurt think this was another act of insubordination?

Better to rely on her memories from the recent Melbourne briefing.

Visualising the topographical map, her mind chose Jenny's voice for the narration:

The Kidman property, *Mountain Rise,* is one of three spread across the mountain. The Kidmans also hold the deeds to the Cassidy homestead, *Valley View.* Old Jack Kidman purchased it from the Cassidys when they fled from the mountain.

In the same way that the Kidman and Cassidy properties pass from father to son, *Forest Heights,* the third property on the mountain, has been home to Kurt's family for generations. That is about to end. Despite being the Jensen heir, he has rejected his inheritance.

The Kidmans are purchasing the Jensen land with financial assistance from Romano, and Evie's sister, Sofia. The investors are acting under Piper's instructions, but the isolation is not the only reason Piper Maxwell wants this mountain.

Dismissing Jenny's voice, Sigrid reviewed what she knew. The access road to *Mountain Rise* crossed the river over a narrow bridge. This river wrapped around the mountain's forested foothills like the coils of a lazy snake. The dense scrub that grew on both sides of the waterway formed an impenetrable barrier.

Samson Kidman's defensive proficiency made him a valuable addition to Piper's team. The ex-combat engineer had abandoned his military career to care for his mother. Now, his expertise had transformed *Mountain Rise* into a sanctuary for his new wife.

Samson had installed hidden cameras on the approach road to give him time to prepare for unwanted visitors. When a Sydney-based criminal organisation attempted an incursion to capture his wife, Samson had locked down the mountain and single-handedly kept her safe.

Without Jezebel, Samson would have no reason to defend the mountain. Sigrid squirmed in her seat, recalling the accidental encounter that first involved her in the case. If only she had known Piper was looking for Jezebel that day! She would never have helped Samson get that *wicked* woman out of Sydney. She shoved aside her regrets.

Jezebel was the only surviving conspirator in the kidnapping of Evie Romano. If Jezebel had fled to a different city, Samson would never have met her, and she would be dead. Without Samson's help, the men chasing Jezebel would have caught her.

Jenny blamed Piper for failing to circulate an alert for Jezebel's capture. Even now, only a handful of agents knew the despicable woman had been involved in Evie's kidnapping. The details were shrouded in secrecy. Jenny would only say that Evie's rescue was a "miracle".

Sigrid diverted her thoughts to Samson, the mountain man who protected Jezebel. The faithful Christian was an unlikely defender for this evil woman. He remained true to every promise he made, but he was no fool. Yet it was *Evie's* intervention that continued to guarantee Jezebel's survival.

Evie, again. Protecting Evie had been Sigrid's primary role for months, and would be again – if Sigrid could redeem her reputation.

Hmmph! If she'd known that Piper would limit her involvement in his paramilitary organisation to babysitting one little woman, Sigrid would have told him what to do with his job offer—

That thought caught her by surprise, and she straightened in her seat.

This annoyance she felt was temporary. Sigrid was committed to Evie's protection. That truth was indisputable.

Sigrid reviewed her recent assignments. Romano was under constant threat because more than one criminal organisation saw his wife as an exploitable weakness.

How many times had those threats left Sigrid on the sidelines, stuck with some mundane task? And yet, when the real danger revealed itself, hadn't she been right where she needed to be?

She was not the only one to be drawn into adventure through an association with Evie. The sequence of events that brought Jezeb— *Hmmph!* that brought *Ruth* and Samson together was only the beginning.

Without Samson, Alixanda and *Ruth* would never have known they were sisters. Freddie and Alixanda would not have moved their wedding to New South Wales. Evie would be in Melbourne, and Sigrid—

She risked a glance towards Kurt. If she had refused to leave Melbourne, she would not be *here* with this man. Her orders would not include wearing *this* uniform.

She would be clueless about Piper's new mountain base, and her biggest challenge would be boredom from being stuck behind a desk.

Sigrid focused on the rushing water in the ditch beside the road. Where did all this water go? Her thoughts skipped back to the river.

When Jez— When *Ruth* was baptised on Saturday, Sigrid had stood on the high bridge that straddled Kidman Road, the perfect place for Melbourne guests to watch the unfamiliar religious ceremony.

Rippling water flowed peacefully beneath them. Evie and her family leaned on the rail while Piper, Jenny and the other security operatives formed a second row.

The river was waist-deep where Jez— where *Ruth* entered for her baptism. Freddie had said this was a favourite swimming hole.

But the water must have been deeper on the other side of the bridge where Piper fell in. Sigrid had been distracted by the crowd, only realising her commander was in the water when other team members shouted in alarm.

According to their testimony, Evie – patient, gentle Evie – had pushed Piper off the bridge.

What did Piper say to incite this uncharacteristic violence from Evie? She had never reacted like this before, despite Piper's frequent taunts about her religious beliefs.

Piper was a big man, and Evie was not renowned for her strength. How did she shove him hard enough to break the bridge rail he was leaning against? And why didn't he defend himself?

When Piper hit the water, he disappeared beneath the surface. The surging waves flattened, yet he did not resurface for a long time.

A murmur of concern rippled through the crowd.

Then he burst from the river with a mighty shout, storming up the riverbank as spectators hurried out of his way. Piper then stole Samson's vehicle and drove away from the mountain with screeching tyres.

Sigrid had not seen her commander since. She had tried discussing her concerns with Jenny.

"Sigrid, drop it. If you want to keep your job, forget about the river."

That had been the beginning of the difficulties between them...

You are frustrated by Jenny's refusal to talk to you. How does that differ from the way you are treating Kurt?

A
Flooded Tributary

ɞ ☼ ʒ

Isaiah 33:21a CG -
God will be with us,
in a place
of wide rivers and streams.

ɞ ☼ ʒ

With a jolt, Sigrid lurched upright. She must have dropped off to sleep! That was the only logical explanation for that voice. Her heart pounded in her chest.

"You asked me what Jenny and the others said," Sigrid began, wriggling to stretch her neck and shoulders. "I don't want to tell you."

She studied her companion. Kurt kept his eyes on the road ahead, but the fingers that gripped the steering wheel turned white.

Massaging her temples, Sigrid inhaled deeply. "Jenny and the others are concerned about my behaviour towards you. Everyone has presumed that I've already seduced you. Evie said God has forgiven me and promises me a brighter future. Sofia warned me to be careful – today she found out she's pregnant, which is supposed to be a medical impossibility."

Nothing is impossible...

She ignored that whispering voice. "Sofia's worried that Evie's miracles are contagious, and if my contraceptive implant fails then everyone will think you're the father—"

Her face grew hot, and she stared out the side window. "Jez— *Ruth*— She said I should try to earn your respect. And Jenny—"

It hurt to breathe, and her vision blurred. *One – breathe in. Two – breathe out. Three...*

The silent count reached ninety-nine before Kurt spoke. "What did Jenny say?"

"Jenny brought up an old psych evaluation."

"Relevant to your current situation?"

Was it her imagination, or had he decreased his speed?

"Here's the short version." Sigrid took a deep breath and focused on the passing landscape. "I was an only child." That was an indisputable truth. "My father wanted a son." When she was born, her father had made no secret of his disappointment. Both her mother and her father's mother had confirmed this. "He died before I could prove that a girl was as tough and strong as any boy."

Sigrid raised her clenched fist. "I got into a lot of fights at school."

"My moth—" She tried again. "My mother chased after anyone who would buy her a drink. I promised myself I would never be like her." A bitter taste filled her mouth, and Sigrid swiped her arm across her eyes.

Kurt's hand appeared in front of her, offering a handkerchief.

She shoved it away. "I compensated for her absence by idolising my father and vowing to follow in his footsteps. But it wasn't enough to be part of an elite military strike force."

Sigrid took another deep breath. "He died on the battlefield."

Another indisputable fact, so why did her chest hurt? It was harder to continue. "The lives I saved didn't matter. The commendations and campaign ribbons increased my self-loathing. I failed him every time I returned to base. And if – somebody else – died—"

The Toyota jerked to a stop in the middle of the road, and Kurt turned off the engine.

Sigrid closed her eyes.

Against a background of pounding rain on the roof, she heard his door open. His boots crunched on the wet gravel, and then the door beside her swung out of the way. Only then did she open her eyes.

Kurt stood beside her, water dripping from his bare head, adding to the tiny rivers that raced down his coat. He leaned closer until she could feel his breath on her cheek. "With your permission, I'm going to give you a hug," Kurt said.

Sigrid stared at him, unable to find the words to reply. When was the last time a man asked permission...

Kurt must have taken her silence as agreement because his arms wrapped around her upper body. The awkward embrace was brief. After he released her, Kurt returned to the driver's seat and started the engine. The journey through the rain continued. Sigrid waited, but he did not explain his actions.

"What just happened?" she asked.

"You needed a hug," Kurt said, keeping his eyes on the road ahead. "Friends do that for each other."

"We've been ordered to work together," Sigrid said. "That doesn't make us friends."

"Would you rather be my enemy?"

"No-o."

"Then we're friends." He glanced towards her. "That's why I bought you the coat."

He fell silent again, focusing on a series of hairpin turns in the road ahead. The rain petered out to a light drizzle and then stopped.

The passing cliffs beside the road provided a distraction. Sigrid admired the tenacity of the overhanging shrubs as they clung to the sheer rock wall. Tiny waterfalls fell from above, joining the gurgling torrent racing down the ditch that kept it from the road. But the magnificent natural show couldn't hold her attention.

Apart from Oliver, Sigrid didn't have any male friends. Ex-lovers or passing acquaintances, but not friends. She should have refused his gift...

"You're worried about what I expect from a friend," Kurt said. "I'm going to be blunt – I need a friend even more than you do. I'm tired of walking into a room and silencing conversations. Most people don't see beyond my uniform. I thought things would be different here because this is where I grew up. But I've been back in Meredith Crossing for sixteen months, and the loneliness is killing me."

Sigrid wrestled with his confession. If he was lonely, why did he push her away last night?

The 4x4 utility rushed around a corner, and the road ahead fell away towards a wide valley far below. Sigrid gasped at the sudden change of scenery. A majestic river spread across the land.

After a few winding turns, the road plummeted straight for the water. Kurt did not attempt to slow, and the Toyota became airborne on the crest of a rolling hill. The tyres made contact with the road again, only to take off at the brow of the next hill. Finally, at the bottom of the rollercoaster ride, the road seemed to end. Sigrid's hands grabbed the armrest.

Kurt swung the steering wheel at the last minute, taking a sharp right turn. "Whoo-hoo!" he shouted, slapping the steering wheel.

Now the road ran parallel to the flood for a while, and then a bridge came into view. Kurt lined up the ute to prepare for the crossing.

Sigrid stared at him in disbelief as he zoomed towards the flimsy wooden structure. This river, wild and ferocious, bore no resemblance to the peaceful stream she had envisaged. Waves smashed against the supports. "Stop!"

ʬ ☼ ʬ

It had been a long time since Kurt felt so alive. Surviving his first tentative overture towards Sigrid seemed to have kindled a fire within him. Surely, nothing this stormy day might throw at him could put out these flames.

He promised himself that the chemistry between them would help him make it through this anniversary. He did not want a repeat of last year's ignoble conclusion, where he had made his escape from the homestead only to drink himself into solitary oblivion.

After all these years, the dark clouds seemed to be lifting, and he felt invincible.

This was not the first flooded river he'd ever crossed. He did not need to hesitate – the rushing torrent presented no immediate danger. It was true that the water level was higher than he expected, but he was confident that the bridge was under no threat.

Kurt slammed his foot on the brake when Sigrid shouted for him to stop. The engine stalled as the vehicle jerked to a halt. "What?"

The knuckles on her closed fists were alarmingly white. Then he noticed the intensity of her green eyes as the colour drained from her face. For a moment, he feared she was about to faint. Was she afraid of the river?

He shook his head in disbelief, and her eyes widened.

"I'm driving," she said, fumbling with her seatbelt and throwing herself out of the Toyota.

He unbuckled his belt and opened his door. "You're not driving," he said, stretching to his full height to meet her challenge.

Sigrid placed a hand on his arm and applied pressure. "This is what *friends* do for each other. You drive like a lunatic. If there's going to be an accident, I want it to be my fault."

That made perfect sense. But letting her drive would complicate everything. "You don't know the road."

Thrusting him aside, Sigrid settled into the driver's seat. "You can navigate. Or you can walk." She started the engine, and the ute took off. When the vehicle came to a stop a few metres further on, he ran to catch up. She grinned at him while he fastened his seatbelt, and then the Toyota crawled forward. Just before the bridge, she shifted out of gear and stopped again. She leaned forward and stared through the windshield.

"Are you worried that the bridge isn't safe?" Kurt asked. "I've crossed this river safely with the water higher than this. We had engineers inspect the supports after last year's flood, and they declared it structurally sound."

The Toyota moved forward, but Sigrid stopped halfway across the bridge and wound the window down. A blast of cold air blew into the cabin. The roar of the water drowned out the engine.

"Can you hear anything?" she asked.

Winding down his window, Kurt stuck his head out into the rain. "Water – the wind in the trees. What am I listening for?"

"I thought I heard a voice."

In an instant, Kurt was standing on the bridge, straining to see if someone was floundering in the floodwaters.

"What are you doing?" Sigrid asked. "Get back in the ute. There's nobody in the river."

"But you said—"

"No, I didn't." She revved the engine, and he leapt back into the vehicle. "I asked if you could hear anything. There's a difference."

Kurt tried again. "What did the voice say?"

"Ha! I knew it. Now that you know about that psych report, you think I'm crazy."

"I'm sure there's a rational explanation."

She stared at him for a moment. "I heard someone calling my name. I usually ignore things that other people *say* they can't hear, but this time I recognised the voice."

It was his turn to stare. "Whose voice did you recognise?"

"Not now!" She pressed her foot on the accelerator, and the vehicle responded. The Toyota rushed across the bridge, increasing in speed as she tackled the gravel road that climbed through the trees on the other side. She laughed. "I've remembered when I first heard that voice, and it changes everything."

The ute swung too far to the left, but before he could grab the steering wheel, she corrected in time to avoid the ditch.

"You said *I* drive like a lunatic," Kurt said.

"You're supposed to be navigating." Sigrid threw the 4x4 ute into the approaching corner.

"Try second gear," he said, "then keep the speed below forty until you come to a sharp left."

They continued in this manner for the next two kilometres. He gave her advance warning of the dangers, and she executed his instructions with precision. Kurt began to relax. "It's relatively easy from here, so I'm going to sit back and enjoy the scenery."

Triggered Memory

ॐ ✿ ☾

*Isaiah 51:11 WEB - They will obtain gladness and joy,
and sorrow and sighing
will flee away.*

ॐ ✿ ☾

Through the trees, Kurt caught the first glimpse of the homestead high on a far hill. Lazy smoke drifted from the kitchen chimney. A shiver ran down his spine. Bringing Sigrid here today would have consequences. Was he ready?

"How far is it?" Sigrid asked, pointing in the direction of the house, as the road veered away to the right. Trees closed in beside the narrow road, blocking the house from view. Sigrid swerved to avoid a pothole.

"Far enough. Can we talk about what happened on the bridge?"

"Take my phone out of my pocket," Sigrid said, shoving the flap of her coat towards him. "There's a photo you need to see. And don't pretend Oliver didn't tell you my password."

Kurt did as he was told. He clicked on the icon for her photo gallery. There were only five images. The first one was a photo of a woman asleep under a green tree. She was dressed in ancient armour, similar in style to the hero on the cover of a novel he had recently read. That story had been set in Genghis Khan's Mongolian Empire. He glanced at Sigrid. Was cosplay one of her passions?

The second photo was black and white. The same dark-skinned stocky woman, holding a sword high in the air. The photographer had applied a filter to suggest there were bolts of lightning emanating from the weapon. Beside the woman stood a terrified man, wearing a modern business suit. The furniture in the foreground matched the man's height. Which meant the warrior princess was impossibly tall.

Kurt swallowed his questions and brought the third photo onto the screen. It was the same woman, a close-up this time. "Wisdom" was written across her breastplate. He studied her expression, almost losing himself in those dark eyes. His heart warned him this woman could unmask all his secrets with a single glare. He glanced towards Sigrid, but her focus remained on the road ahead.

He recognised the two women in the fourth photo: Sigrid standing next to Freddie's wife, Alixanda. Between them was a movie-poster-sized enlargement of the previous image. Kurt frowned. Alixanda held a pen in her hand. He flicked back through the other photos, looking for clues. "Is the warrior princess one of Alixanda's creations?"

"You haven't seen the last drawing yet."

Photo number five almost stopped his heart. Sigrid was the artist's subject this time. Her scantily dressed figure seemed to leap out at him from the screen. Her hair was free of the usual braids, blown by the wind in the fashion of a graphic novel's heroine. She was wearing a Viking-style horned helmet, a sculpted breastplate, and the briefest leather skirt which flapped around her hips. With a round shield strapped to her back, she wielded a massive sword in each hand. Behind her stood the warrior princess from the previous photos. They were both knee-deep in a raging river. Kurt could almost hear the slap of the waves.

"C-can I have a copy of this?" Kurt asked.

Sigrid laughed. "The look on your face is priceless. If Alixanda were here, I'd get her to capture it. Don't try to convince me you're not interested in my body. You asked before you engaged your brain, and you immediately regretted it. And if you don't send it to yourself right away, you'll probably chicken out."

"Alixanda drew this?" His fingers were already sending the image to himself while his mind sought a safer topic. "She has an amazing talent."

"How much do you know about her gift?"

"She's an artist who specialises in realism," Kurt said, "and she has a photographic memory. When Piper interviewed Ruth for the first time, I was there. Afterwards, Alixanda recreated the meeting in a series of detailed drawings. She drew each scene as if she was copying from a photo."

"Alixanda sees things. It's like she's dreaming but with her eyes open. Evie calls these dreams 'visions'."

"Oh-k-ay—" Kurt looked at the photo on the phone screen again. "So, this is from her imagination?" The costume maybe, but he had already seen Sigrid in enough figure-hugging outfits... He took a deep breath and closed the photo app.

"Dismiss it as imagination if you like. But I'm convinced I just heard Wisdom's voice calling to me from that river." She paused, almost as if she was daring him to dispute her claim. "And the first time I heard her calling to me was years before I met the owner of that voice."

Did she expect him to *believe* that? He took his time choosing a safer question. "Wisdom is a *real* person?"

"It's hard to explain," Sigrid said. "I had a friend who looked like her, but... she... died. At first, I thought her ghost had come back, but Alixanda and Evie convinced me that Wisdom only *looks* like my dead friend. She chose that form to catch our attention. But you're distracting me from what I'm trying to tell you."

"Sorry. Keep going."

After squinting through the windscreen for a long time, Sigrid spoke again. "The psych report said I had selective amnesia. The doctors tried hypnosis to unlock my memory. I had read the eyewitness accounts, so I had their version of what happened, but my memories were missing until today. Driving across the bridge must have triggered something, and now I have the whole story. I can't afford to forget again."

Kurt pushed aside a dozen questions. "I'm listening."

"Before I tell you, go to the home screen on my phone and click the icon in the bottom corner, next to the flashing red circle."

He followed her instructions. A password request popped up.

"It's the same password," she said.

He typed quickly, and a new window opened.

"Select 'Privacy – 15 minutes' from the drop-down menu."

"Done," Kurt said.

"Good. I'm turning off the locket camera and if the red circle reappears on the home screen, throw my phone out the window." Sigrid's hand reached for the locket, and she addressed her next comment towards it. "Operator in Melbourne, tell Oliver this is no idle threat. I'm fed up with the camera turning itself back on."

Kurt's hand trembled as he waited for the flashing red icon to disappear. "It's off."

"First, promise me you won't tell anyone else what I'm about to say. This stays between us."

"I can't make an unconditional promise," Kurt said. "I have a responsibility for your safety as well as the welfare of others."

"This is about something that happened to me a long time ago. There's no danger to anyone. Can you accept my assurance and make the promise?"

He considered a variety of scenarios and evaluated the possible consequences before nodding. "I can live with that."

"Some of the details are classified, so I won't tell you where or when. My squad was about fifty clicks behind enemy lines. A strike force of twenty. Four vehicles, no heavy artillery."

She slowed for the corner. "It hadn't rained for months, and it was hotter than hell. But this was our final mission for the tour, so no-one complained. We had seats allocated on a flight out of the country the next day."

Kurt watched her closely, his hand ready to grab the steering wheel. The look on her face suggested she might be seeing a different terrain.

Sigrid blinked, glanced at his outstretched hand and adjusted her grip on the steering wheel. Shaking her head, she continued her story. "On paper, it was a straightforward mission. A quick dash across the border, confirm the intel, get out again. We had a member of a local guerrilla group as our guide. He said we wouldn't encounter any hostile forces."

She frowned. "The major insisted on driving. That was my role, but I didn't challenge her. I was her second – it was my job to follow her orders and ensure the others knew what to do. She asked me to ride in the back, so the local man had the front passenger seat. We were the lead vehicle in our convoy."

His Toyota Hilux stopped moving.

Kurt frowned. The homestead was in full view on the crest of the next hill.

She gazed at him with her green eyes. "I said, left or right?"

He looked out the window again. An overgrown track disappeared between the trees on the right. On the left, a meandering trail went across open pasture towards a small waterhole. "Straight ahead. It's the obvious choice."

Sigrid changed gear, and the vehicle took off again. "That's what I thought, too. The guide told the major, 'go left'. A voice whispered in my ear that I should challenge that decision. Why not straight ahead, I asked. The guide ignored me, and I leaned forward to the major, but she waved me back to my seat. The voice became more insistent: 'Look at the map. Tell her to stop. Danger ahead.' My silence delivered us into an ambush."

Distracted by the intensity of her story, Kurt held his breath as he waited for Sigrid to continue.

"Aren't you going to open the gate?" she asked.

With a jolt, he realised that the ute was stationary again, and now he could hear the cattle dogs barking their welcome. He went to open the gate, and Sigrid drove through as soon as the gap was wide enough. She parked beside the other vehicles in the compound. While he was talking to the dogs, Kurt heard the homestead door open. He looked up in time to see his mother appear.

His mistake hit him hard as he remembered the things he should have said to Sigrid before they arrived. She would have no clue about the significance of this day for his family. But that was not his biggest concern. She was about to be ambushed by his mother, who would presume the newcomer was much more than a friend.

Trying to Forget

ဇာ ✿ ကြ

Psalm 16:11a WEB - You will show me the path of life.
In Your presence is fullness of joy.

ဇာ ✿ ကြ

Sigrid's awakened memory was difficult to set aside. She silently urged Kurt to hurry back to her so she could finish her story. Why was he playing with the dogs?

A figure appeared beside the Toyota. Sigrid looked out at an older woman wearing a spotted apron. Medium height and build, with short, curly, grey hair. Her fingers fiddled with the frill on the apron, and the hint of uncertainty in the woman's eyes did not match her smile.

Stepping from the vehicle, Sigrid extended her hand. "Hi, I'm Sigrid. You must be Kurt's mother."

Mrs Jensen grabbed her hand and came closer, wrapping her arms around Sigrid as if she would never let her go. The world began to turn upside down, but it righted itself when Kurt appeared beside them. She could breathe again now his mother had transferred her attention to him.

The same intense embrace kept Kurt prisoner for an eternity.

When she released him, Mrs Jensen seized Sigrid's hand to lead her into the house. "Kurt didn't tell me you were coming, Sigrid."

They marched up a set of wooden steps. Mrs Jensen opened the screen door and ushered her inside. "The kettle's on, and the scones are about to come out of the oven. By the time you've hung up your coat and freshened up, morning tea will be ready. Kurt will take you to the washroom, and then you can meet the rest of the family."

The covered veranda was long and narrow with a rough wooden floor. Glass panels kept out the rain and allowed a full view of the parked cars in the compound. Windows on the inner wall let light into the house. The sloping roof extended to the distant corners of the house at either end, covering the veranda as it continued around the dwelling. A few well-worn armchairs were the only furnishings.

"What's going on?" Sigrid whispered when Kurt appeared at her elbow. He had already removed his coat. "You didn't say I was meeting anyone other than your mother, and why did she hug me?"

"I was going to warn you, but you kept distracting me." He was standing too close.

"Come on, you two," a voice called from the kitchen door. "The scones are ready."

Sigrid spun towards the speaker. Kurt's sister, Eliza, stood watching them. Remembering yesterday's conversation in the chemist shop, Sigrid backed away from Kurt. She slipped out of her coat, raising an eyebrow when he extended his hand to take the garment from her. "Show me where to hang it."

He nodded. "Here, outside the washroom." He hung his coat on a high hook, and she copied him. "There's a sink in here."

She followed him into an old-fashioned laundry. Along one wall was a row of waist-high concrete sinks. Kurt turned on a brass tap and began to wash his hands with a cake of yellow soap.

While she waited, Sigrid examined the room. Well-stocked shelves lined the other walls: jars of preserved fruits and vegetables and an assortment of larger boxes and cans. An enormous chest freezer sat beside an industrial-sized washing machine.

Through a doorway, she spotted an old-fashioned toilet with an overhead cistern, complete with a pull chain. She walked towards that tiny room, tempted to drag Kurt in and force him to explain himself. Instead, she entered alone.

"Are you okay?" Kurt asked a few minutes later. He sounded as if he was outside the door.

"I'm coming," she said, rising to pull the flush chain and checking that her uniform was tidy.

He hovered while she washed her hands. The water from the tap was freezing. When she could no longer tolerate the icy chill, she took the fluffy towel from him.

"Let's get this over with," she hissed, preceding him from the washroom.

He raced ahead to open the door for her.

℞ ✧ ℅

When Sigrid entered the kitchen, she paused to appreciate the welcome heat. The high ceiling was impressive. She could have stood on one of the sturdy bentwood chairs and it would still be out of reach. As she gazed upward, Kurt's hand appeared on her shoulder, and a hush descended on the room.

"This is a surprise," a familiar voice said. It was Old Jack Kidman – Freddie's father and Samson's stepfather. His weathered face grinned at her from a chair beside an open wood fire. "Young lady, I've heard stories about you that would make your poor grandmother turn in her grave."

"So this is your long-lost relative," the man seated on the opposite side of the fireplace said to Old Jack. "Welcome to our humble home, Sigrid. It might not be as fancy as the Kidman spread, but there's always a warm fire and a pot of tea when ya need it."

"Thank you, Mr Jensen," Sigrid said, walking across to shake his hand.

He remained seated, looking up at her. "Call me KJ. Mr Jensen was my father." He leaned across to Old Jack and laughed. "The old man would have been gobsmacked if a girlie dressed as a soldier came to visit."

"She's a *real* soldier," Old Jack said. "Even more useful than Samson, who likes blowing things up. Your ol' man would have taken her out shooting roos, an' she'd have taught him a thing or two about what a 'girlie' can do with proper training. Your son needs to man up if he expects to keep her. There's a helicopter pilot from Melbourne who's already marked her dance card."

"Enough of that," Kurt's mother said, taking Sigrid by the elbow and moving her towards an empty chair. "Sigrid, dear, sit next to Muriel while I pour you a cup of tea. Kurt, get your guest a scone."

Sigrid forced a smile as she sat beside the pub owner Harry McHenry's feisty mother. This woman's presence was another surprise. Enduring Muriel's inspection, Sigrid was thankful she had not worn *that* dress. On their earlier encounter at the Top Pub, she had learned to address this woman as Mrs Mac. Here, Muriel seemed a more appropriate choice.

Kurt's mother *had* said "meet the family"? The briefing notes said Mrs Mac was related to the Kidmans, but there was no mention of a connection with Kurt's family. And why was Old Jack here? As she tried to put the puzzle pieces together, Sigrid surveyed the room.

The kitchen table captivated her attention. An embroidered tablecloth lay draped over one end. There were old-fashioned teacups and saucers, with matching plates and folded serviettes beside each setting. Pride of place belonged to a mound of freshly-baked scones. An assortment of preserves in fancy dishes surrounded the overflowing platter. An antique glass and silver bowl held whipped cream. Sigrid leaned closer. The serving spoon was also polished silver.

Kurt's sister sat opposite Muriel. There were two empty chairs beside Eliza. One would be for Kurt's mother. Were they expecting another guest?

"How are you enjoying the apartment?" Muriel asked.

Caught off guard, Sigrid said, "It's very... um..."

"Comfortable?" the older woman suggested.

"Big was what I had in mind, but I was searching for a better word."

Muriel chuckled. "Big it is. Harry calls those apartments my folly, but we'll see who has the last laugh. First, you're booked in for an extended stay, and now there's a large group arriving on Thursday to take the other three apartments. There's no end date on their booking either. I don't suppose you're allowed to say anything about why everyone's coming to Meredith Crossing?"

"Top secret," Old Jack called from his fireside seat. "She'll be court marshalled if she lets anything slip. That's why they've given her a police watchdog."

"Ignore them," Muriel said, patting Sigrid's hand. "The two old coots have made a wager on whether you'll storm out before lunch or simply take Kurt outside and toss him in the mud for bringing you here. If this were *my* kitchen, I'd banish them to the veranda where they could have a quiet smoke and a drink, but Missie won't let me."

"Here's your tea," Kurt's mother said, placing a cup and saucer on the table in front of Sigrid. "You're confusing the girl, Muriel. You're the only one who calls me Missie anymore. To everyone else, I'm either Mrs J or *Mum*."

"Thanks for the tea, M—" Sigrid began.

A plate of scones appeared in her hands. "Eat them while they're hot," Kurt said before he dropped onto the chair beside her. "I promised you prize-winning scones, and Mum has delivered. I've given you two scones, to begin with, split in half. I wasn't sure which jam you'd prefer. I've given you strawberry, that one's apricot. The other two are raspberry and blackberry. Let me know if I haven't given you enough cream."

"Stop fussing," Muriel said to Kurt. "The poor girl will think you're nervous about introducing her to your family."

"Nervous is an understatement," Kurt said, selecting a scone from the plate he had prepared for himself and filling his mouth. He licked the cream from his fingers and gestured with his head towards the two men at the hearth. "*This* is why I'm careful not to bring new friends home with me."

"You've never brought a 'girlie' of *any* kind home before," Eliza said. "Mum's already planning the wedding reception in her head. If you didn't want them making a fuss, you should have left your *friend* back at the motel. The whole town's talking about how you slept with her the first night you met her. Didn't you learn anything after the fuss Kimmy Kidman made last year when you were stalking her?"

"Kimmy was lying," Old Jack said. "We all know that. Your brother isn't a stalker, and I'm sure he'll be a lot happier with Sigrid warming his bed."

Sigrid choked on her scone.

Muriel took the plate while Kurt patted her back and shoved her teacup into her hand.

When the emergency was over, Sigrid wiped the back of her hand across her eyes. "Fresh air," she gasped, fleeing from the kitchen.

Try a
Little Kindness

৪০ ✿ ୦୪

*Isaiah 26:4 CG - Trust in God forever;
the Lord is an everlasting Rock.*

৪০ ✿ ୦୪

Outside the house, Sigrid stood on the steps. She wrapped her arms across her body, too stubborn to go back for her coat. She waited for Kurt to arrive and apologise for not defending her reputation.

Two of the older farm dogs were staring at her from a safe distance. "You're no help," she said to them. "All friendly 'come play with me' when you see Kurt, and with me, you're too frightened by my size twelve boots to come anywhere near."

"Don't be too hard on yourself," Muriel McHenry said, appearing at her side. "If Kurt says you're his friend, then he's telling the truth. He's not going to throw away a lifetime of being careful for a quick fling."

"So why do *you* think I'm here?"

"You're here because God called you. Your size twelve boots are perfect for the job. Any smaller, and you'd be too weak and feeble for the challenge. Stand your ground, and don't let anything stop you from succeeding with your mission."

An interesting choice of words. "What do you know about my mission?" Sigrid asked.

"Absolutely nothing, but it must be important if God's throwing one of his best into the battle."

Sigrid snorted. Her now-dead grandmother was the only person who had ever thought she was "God's best". Gran was probably sitting up in heaven, looking down at this mess...

The pain in her chest intensified. Sigrid blinked, refusing to give in. Changing direction, she went back to her first question. "So why doesn't God tell *me* what my mission is?"

"Would you listen if He did?" Muriel asked.

"Good point," Sigrid said, finding unexpected comfort from this exchange. She relaxed her fists as she looked to the horizon. "First, He'd have to convince me that He was real, that He was God. Then I'd have to convince myself I wasn't crazy, listening to strange voices." She turned to Muriel. "Have you ever heard the voice of God?"

"God speaks to his children in many ways."

What kind of answer was that?

"Have you been talking to Oliver?" Sigrid asked, her suspicions about this woman increasing. Had Harry's mother also been recruited to keep tabs on her? "That's what he says."

"I don't know anyone called Oliver," Muriel said. She met Sigrid's glare without blinking. "But he sounds like a wise man."

"He also took me home to meet his mother," Sigrid said, waiting for some kind of reaction. Then she surprised herself by continuing to reveal the truth. "Oliver made sure she knew we weren't lovers, so she never jumped to the wrong conclusion."

She smiled at the memories. So many lonely afternoons when she had found solace in that Melbourne kitchen. Generous servings of delicious food that helped push back the emptiness. She shook herself, alert to the eagerness in Muriel's eyes.

"He told his mother not to feed me," Sigrid said, "or I'd be impossible to get rid of. She said he should get used to having a sister."

Muriel nodded. She glanced back at the house. "Kurt already has a sister."

"She wasn't very nice to him," Sigrid said, surprised by her outrage. "I wouldn't rip into him with false accusations. I like to settle my disagreements with my fists." She paused to catch her breath. "I can probably outshoot him, outrun him – and drink him under the table."

"He had a brother who could do all that, and it wasn't enough to keep Kurt here."

There was something in the older woman's statement that made it past Sigrid's defences. "Is that what you expect me to do?" she snapped. "Keep him from straying back to the big, bad world?"

"He chose to return, but he's not happy. He needs a good woman—"

"I'm a good *soldier*," Sigrid said.

"A good soldier follows her commander's orders."

"What's that supposed to mean?"

"That, my dear, is a question for another time." Muriel walked up the steps and opened the door. "Come back and have some more scones. Before you and Kurt arrived, we were debating whether to postpone the visit to the cemetery until after lunch. The sky has cleared, and we'll be going soon. Missie will be fretting that you haven't eaten enough before that ordeal."

"Cemetery?" Sigrid asked. *I don't do memorial services.*

"Kurt didn't tell you?"

Sigrid struggled not to put her hands over her ears. *No! Don't tell me!*

"Today is the anniversary of his brother's death," Muriel said. "Every year, we go to the cemetery. It's been seventeen years since Johnny and his cousin, Jack Junior, were killed."

"I shouldn't be here."

Muriel took hold of Sigrid's arm and squeezed hard. Sigrid stared at that weathered hand before gazing into the stern face. The light in the older woman's eyes silenced Sigrid's argument.

"This is exactly where you should be, young lady." Muriel reinforced her statement by poking Sigrid in the chest with her finger. "Kurt needs someone to lean on today, and he's chosen you. That man blames himself for not being here. He thinks he could have stopped those boys from joining Michael Cassidy in robbing the bank. Did he tell you he walked away from a promising legal career to join the police force? No, I didn't think so. He's still paying penance."

Muriel frowned. "And he's not the only one who threw his life away. Samson came home from overseas when Ol' Jack sent for him. And Kimberley's still running. She abandoned her two children, and she's blaming everyone else for ruining her life. The families on this mountain have reaped a bitter harvest, and it's time it stopped."

℣✲℥

His mother had prevented Kurt from following Sigrid out the door. She pulled him onto the empty seat beside her and refused to let him go. He saw the distress in her eyes, and he lingered to reassure her.

While he was distracted, Muriel had slipped outside. She was the last person he would have sent after Sigrid.

"Don't you worry, boy," Old Jack said. "Muriel won't let her leave without giving you a chance to make things right."

"Eliza, apologise to your brother," Kurt's father said from his fireside chair.

"Why should I?" Eliza said, her head bowed over her drink. "He shouldn't have brought a stranger—"

"It's not me she should be apologising to," Kurt said, abandoning his mother to take a position at the window. He gazed out to the veranda. Sigrid was engaged in an animated conversation with Muriel. Perhaps this disaster could be averted?

His mother approached with his teacup, and Kurt sipped from the cooling beverage as he waited. He glanced over his shoulder and caught Eliza watching him, but she shrugged and turned away. His mother whispered to his sister, and Eliza shook her head. When the older woman busied herself with the final preparations for the luncheon meal, his sister went to help her.

Meanwhile, the two older men were renegotiating their wager from beside the fireplace. He blocked out their muffled words. The conversation he wanted to hear was outside, beyond the veranda.

He slipped his hand into his jeans pocket, where his phone pressed against his thigh. When this misadventure was over, Kurt would do something he thought he'd never do. He'd contact Sigrid's friend, Oliver, and ask for the transcript of this conversation.

He tried to guess what Muriel was saying. When Sigrid rose to her full height, Kurt held his breath. The older woman grabbed the athletic redhead's arm and then followed that provocation by poking the agent in the chest. The colour drained from his face, and he reached for the door.

Instead of the violence he had envisaged, both women looked towards the house. He pulled back, not wanting to hinder the truce Muriel was negotiating.

Muriel retraced her steps to the kitchen with a subdued Sigrid at her heels. Kurt's mother hurried to take her guest by the hand and lead her to her seat.

"I'm sorry," Sigrid said to Kurt's mother. "I didn't mean to make a fuss."

"No need to apologise," Missie said. "None of us are at our best today."

She glanced at Eliza, who opened her mouth as if she was going to make a half-hearted attempt to redeem herself, but Sigrid waved her into silence. "Not. Necessary."

Muriel shook her head towards Eliza and put a warning finger to her lips. Kurt's mother nodded before continuing with the meal preparations. His sister assisted by carrying the baking trays to the wood-burning oven while Muriel spoke quietly to the two men at the fire.

With everyone gainfully occupied, Sigrid returned to her seat with only Kurt in attendance. He studied her carefully. There was so much he should say, but where to begin?

"Would you like some more scones?"

The corners of her mouth twitched. "No, thank you."

He wasn't certain that he had heard her correctly, so he leaned closer. "Are you sure?"

Sigrid pressed him against the back of his seat with a hand. "You promised me a big lunch," she said in a clear voice.

Her smile widened, yet there was no accompanying sparkle in her eyes. The hairs on the back of Kurt's neck rose. After she withdrew her hand, he could still feel the pressure on his chest.

She straightened his collar. "I don't want to ruin my appetite."

Trial

Run

ᏨᏫ☼ᏨᏃ

Jeremiah 29:13 WEB - You shall seek Me,
and find Me, when you search for Me
with all your heart.

ᏨᏫ☼ᏨᏃ

Resting her head against the passenger window, Sigrid closed her eyes. Kurt was in the driver's seat, and they were crossing the bridge. He was keeping his thoughts to himself.

The scone-choking incident had changed everything. The rest of her visit to *Forest Heights* had been endured through a haze of conflicting emotions. She dimly remembered the journey to the family cemetery. Row upon row of headstones and memorials to generations from the three families who settled on the mountain. The first Kidmans, Jensens and Cassidys must have thought that they would live here forever...

Muriel had taken Sigrid on a tour of the cemetery, pointing out where important relatives were buried, and describing the complicated history of intermarriage between the three families. Muriel, and Kurt's mother, Missie, had both been Cassidy girls – cousins, whose mutual grandmother had been a Kidman.

While attending a family event on the mountain, Missie Cassidy had fallen in love with Kurt Jensen Junior, KJ for short. Everyone had thought Missie too young to marry the rugged mountain man. She was a city girl, unfamiliar with the isolated country life, and he was a determined bachelor. He shared the homestead with his parents and grandparents and had been in no hurry to settle down.

There followed a lengthy courtship under the watchful eye of Missie's older, unmarried cousin, Muriel. Nobody had expected the family-appointed chaperone, prim and proper Muriel Cassidy, also a city girl, to elope with the disreputable publican of the inn where the two Cassidy maidens frequently stayed.

There were gaps in Sigrid's recollection between the family arriving at the cemetery and returning to the homestead. At some point, the rain had resumed, which brought the time at the cemetery to a welcome close. When they returned to the homestead, the atmosphere was solemn and subdued. But the delicious aroma of a slow-cooked meal greeted them in the kitchen, and after Missie Jensen's feast was served, the mood improved.

Sigrid sighed. The bountiful spread had exceeded her imaginings. Kurt's mother piled her plate high, but Sigrid could not do the meal justice. She toyed with her food, and another helping was never offered.

Afterwards, an unlabelled bottle of golden liquid was passed around the table. Kurt's mother and his sister opted for wine instead, but Muriel and Kurt filled their glasses. Kurt nodded his approval when Old Jack taunted Sigrid to give the strong spirit a try.

Sigrid sighed again. That first sip of the homemade brew seared her tongue and cleaned out her sinuses. It felt like a liquid fire that spread to her extremities, endangering her frozen heart with its heat. She downed the rest of the drink with enthusiasm, seeking to satisfy a greater thirst. Despite that initial reaction, the chill returned. When the bottle passed her way again, she shook her head. "One drink is enough today."

The disbelieving look that appeared on Kurt's face remained etched in her mind. She blinked to dispel that image, but it didn't work. The same expression was still evident on his face now. Her stomach cramped, and she jerked upright.

"Stop the car! I have to get out!"

Her door was open, and Sigrid stood on the road, her heart racing as she wrestled her arms free from her coat. Kurt opened his door, watching her awkward dance from across the roof of his ute.

"I'm going to run the rest of the way back," she said. "If I don't get some air, I'm going to be sick. I'll collect my coat and hat from you when I get into town."

She tossed her coat into the Toyota, but she was still too hot. "Take my shirt, too." Frantically, she fought with the buttons on her uniform shirt, until she had stripped it off. She was thankful for the camisole that she was wearing underneath.

Without waiting for him to reply, Sigrid slammed the door and began running down the road. The cooling rain was refreshing, and the pounding of her feet on the ground took her back to a long-forgotten training day. She worked with the memory to fix the marching chant in her mind. She spoke the words under her breath, making her feet keep time.

The Hilux rolled along beside her, and Kurt opened his window. "How far do you intend to run? I'll wait for you up ahead."

"Don't," she said, concentrating on the rhythm. "I need this."

"Talk to me. I want to understand."

"I'm no good at long-term relationships."

"What do you call long-term?"

"Three dates, maybe four. The first hint that a lover wants more, and I'm gone."

"Of all the things my sister said, you're upset that she mentioned marriage?" Kurt said, rubbing his hand over his eyes. "You're running down the road – in the rain – because you think—" He swore and brought the ute to a stop.

Sigrid ran back and leaned in his open window. "Evie gave me a prophecy this morning. Apparently, God has promised me a family. Seeing you with your family helped me join the dots."

He closed his eyes as if she had delivered a knockout blow.

Jogging on the spot, she continued. "Either you let me run until my head stops threatening to explode. Or I get back in your ute, and I run when you take your eyes off me. You decide."

"Run now," Kurt said, rummaging behind his seat. "But take this water bottle. You can refill it from one of the waterfalls coming from the rocks."

She accepted the shiny blue bottle with a smile and took a step back from the Toyota. She sipped the water as he drove away. When he was no longer in sight, she resumed her marching chant, following his fading tyre tracks across the wet gravel.

ॐ☼ॐ

"What was I supposed to do?" Kurt asked. Sigrid was still visible in his rear vision mirror when Oliver contacted him by phone. "I know you have eyes and ears on her every movement, so she's as safe running on this road as she would be anywhere else."

He focused on the next corner while he waited for Oliver to reply. The silence lingered, and he frowned. Reception shouldn't be a problem. Kurt glared at the signal booster, which had never failed him. "Are you still there?"

"I'm here," the disembodied voice said. "I was praying. I already have more than enough on my plate without Sigrid going rogue."

"I'll turn off and visit Samson," Kurt said, "and then give her a call when I think she's ready to be rescued. It's raining heavily. I'm hopeful that will help her cool down."

"You don't know her very well."

Kurt tightened his grip on the wheel.

"I was going to call you anyway," Oliver said. "Evie phoned to ask me to pray for Sigrid."

"Why would Evie do that?"

"I don't have time to explain the mystery that surrounds Evie. My mother says she's a prophet. But experience has taught me to pay attention when Evie calls for prayer. It always precedes an emergency."

Kurt searched for somewhere to turn around. "Should I go back and get Sigrid now?"

There was another long pause. "No," Oliver said. "I've checked the audio. She's shouting at herself and making good progress. Stick with your plan."

"I'm approaching the turnoff to Kidman's Road now."

"Over and out."

Click.

For a moment, Kurt contemplated spinning the Hilux around and racing back to Sigrid. Oliver's assurance was not enough.

But then he remembered the determination in her eyes when she challenged him to deny her request. He rested his head on the steering wheel after he slowed for the turn. "God. Don't let this be my biggest mistake."

Tribunal
Judgement

ஐ ☼ ⊰

Psalm 59:16b WEB - You have been my high tower,
a refuge
in the day of my distress.

ஐ ☼ ⊰

When Kurt arrived at *Mountain Rise*, his longed-for private conversation with Samson was impossible. The continuing rain had kept the children confined to the house.

They must have viewed his arrival as fresh entertainment because there were frequent interruptions. His coffee mug was almost empty before the pandemonium ceased in the kitchen.

The babies were finally asleep. Romano made it clear that there would be "consequences" for anyone who disturbed them.

The two teenage boys – Samson's nephew, Butch, and Sofia's son, Marco – seized the advantage, escaping outside to one of the sheds. Half a chocolate cake was the bounty they claimed to guarantee their absence.

Sofia's step-sons, Matt and Peter, protested, but their father, John, managed to whisk them to the lounge room to watch a movie. The biscuit barrel tucked under his arm was their bribe. Butch's twelve-year-old sister, Nikki, went with them.

Evie, Sofia and Ruth had already disappeared upstairs to the rooftop tower. Kurt puzzled over Evie's assertion that they were "going to pray".

Were the three women really having a prayer meeting overhead, or was that code for some other child-free activity? Oliver's words ran around and around in his mind. Evie had said to pray for Sigrid.

What did that mean, and what was he supposed to do?

"You look like you need answers," Samson said. He and Romano were now the only others seated at the kitchen table.

"I'm not sure where to begin," Kurt said, but then a door behind him opened, and footsteps announced an intruder emerging from the guest wing.

"The twins are still asleep," Jenny said. She closed the door with exaggerated care. "I need coffee. I don't suppose those locusts have left me any cake?"

"Will you accept some of Ruth's ginger cream biscuits instead?" Samson asked. "There's a stash on the top shelf in the pantry. I told Butch they were Romano's favourites, and if they went missing, he would answer to him."

"Thanks," Jenny said, helping herself. "Anyone else hungry?"

The others shook their heads.

"I'll be glad when the weather clears," Jenny said, joining the three men at the table.

"I didn't realise," Jenny continued, "how dependent we'd become on sending the kids outside. This household is enough to put anyone off having a big family. If John's boys aren't whining or arguing, Butch and Marco are orchestrating some melodrama."

Jenny directed her next comment to Kurt. "Did Samson tell you he caught them setting up an indoor mini-golf course in the formal dining room?"

Kurt shook his head, swallowing the last of his coffee. He could not ask Samson for advice while Sigrid's supervisor was in the room.

But Jenny was not finished with Kurt. "Sigrid was supposed to help with the children. I told Piper she was an unsuitable nanny, but he wouldn't listen. He knew she had trouble with family assignments and that she struggled with communal living. It was the younger boys who tipped her over the edge."

"If Butch hadn't told them she was a ninja," Samson said, "Matt and Peter wouldn't have followed her everywhere. *They* were the ones who wanted her to teach them how to fly."

Kurt's imagination supplied the details.

"Is that what they were doing?" Jenny asked. "Nikki said the game was called 'The Noble Art of Leprechaun Launching'."

"Be fair," Romano said, "Sigrid didn't target the smaller boys, and Butch was a willing volunteer. Matt and Peter were delighted when she tossed him over the fence."

"He wasn't supposed to go over the fence," Jenny said. "Tell me there was no malice in overshooting her target by three metres? Nikki's screams brought everyone running. The poor kid's convinced Sigrid tried to kill her brother."

Kurt grew more uncomfortable as the story unfolded.

"Butch was in on the joke," Samson said. "The plan was to convince John's boys to give her some breathing space. It wasn't supposed to get her banished."

The temperature in the room chilled as Jenny glared at Samson.

"I'd better go," Kurt said.

He took the mug to the kitchen sink and gazed out the window towards the forested hills. "It's still raining heavily, and Sigrid will be soaked."

"Why are you fretting over Sigrid?" Jenny asked, directing her anger towards Kurt. "Don't expect her to thank you."

"Enough," said Romano, rising to his feet. "Kurt wasn't asking for your permission, Jenny. He came for Samson's advice, and instead, we've shown him why it was impossible for Sigrid to remain here. If we'd taken better care of her, she wouldn't be out there, punishing herself in the rain."

Jenny opened her mouth, but Romano held up his hand.

"Kurt," Romano said. "When Sigrid came out of hospital after her – ah – *accident* – she wore out two treadmills before the doctors would agree that she could go to the gym. Freddie found her collapsed from exhaustion on more than one occasion. She doesn't know how to stop."

Kurt hesitated, halfway towards the exit. The compulsion to leave had become a physical pain in his chest, yet he needed answers.

While he was trying to work out his response to Romano, the phone in his pocket rang. He froze: Oliver again.

Something strange happened. Everyone seemed to be moving in slow motion.

As Kurt accepted the incoming call, Evie appeared in the kitchen, her dark eyes troubled.

Sofia and Ruth were behind her, visibly upset. All three were windblown and dishevelled from visiting the tower.

The air crackled with energy. Romano took a step in Evie's direction, opening his arms to receive her into his embrace.

Evie looked towards Kurt and said, "You have to go. Sigrid's headed for the river."

The kitchen around him blurred and before him appeared a wide river, the water a brilliant blue. A warm wind ruffled his hair. He stood on the riverbank. Sigrid, dressed in her Viking armour, was wading away from him towards the deeper water. The breaking waves crashed about her thighs. Further out in the river, a giant warrior called for Sigrid to join her.

Fragments of Sigrid's revelations about her photos battled for his attention. What he was seeing couldn't be real. Wisdom was only a figment of Alixanda's artistic mind.

But Sigrid had said: "Alixanda sees visions."

Is this what was happening to him?

The river image shimmered and faded.

Ping. Ping.

From opposite sides of the table, Jenny and Samson reached for their phones.

The kitchen door burst open behind him. Butch stormed in from the mudroom, waving a phone in his hand. "Kurt, your coat pocket was ringing. Why do you have Sigrid's phone? Where is she?"

"She's looking for the river," Evie said.

Butch's eyes widened. He swore, and then he said, "I'll get your coat, Kurt."

The bulky teenager spun back the way he came, shouting to his unseen companion. "Marco, get the gate. Sigrid's in the river."

Triangulate

a Position

ಬಿ ✿ ೞ

Galatians 6:9 WEB - Let's not be weary in doing good,
for we will reap in due season,
if we don't give up.

ಬಿ ✿ ೞ

The trees that grew beside the road had kept Sigrid from the raging river. The roaring water sounded close – the whole landscape trembled with its presence. Yet, she could find no way through the undergrowth to catch a glimpse of it.

Frustrated by her efforts, she put one boot in front of the other, a heavy shuffle that was a poor substitute for the earlier frenzied pace that had devoured her strength. Her chest burned, and her throat was parched. She could no longer ignore the screaming leg muscles. Each step became an agonised complaint, but she kept going.

As the realisation dawned that she had overstretched her capabilities, another forgotten memory awakened. In horrified fascination, she relived her final hours as a officer.

After a sleepless night, she had risen to watch a military convoy roll out to welcome another futile day. The sound of the tanks had shaken the building. The sensation lingered in her chest long after the convoy disappeared into the pre-dawn gloom. She recognised it now – a deep vibration that left her knees weak and her heart racing. It lived on in her nightmares.

Later, she had gone through the motions, shouting orders and forcing the other members of her squad to abandon their lethargy. The loss of the Major was a raw wound for everyone, making their safe repatriation the only thing that mattered.

Until today, Sigrid had never questioned how the responsibility for the ambush survivors had fallen to her. She already knew she had shepherded the squad onto the military transport plane. She had read the eyewitness accounts relating to her missing thirty-six hours. Now she understood that the absence of memory had only granted her the illusion of distance.

These awakened memories were so vivid she could taste the desert sand. After confirming the squad members were strapped in – she was not going to lose anyone else – she had checked that the single coffin was secure.

She saluted the base commander through the closing hatch, then locked her eyes on the precious cargo and remained standing. With her fingers clutching an overhead support, she fought the gravitational forces during take-off. Her muscles screamed. The pain had torn the oxygen from her lungs and the hope from her heart...

With a jolt, Sigrid came back to reality. She was on her knees in a muddy puddle, thirsty and cold. Kurt's bottle was safe in one of the deep trouser pockets. She turned it upside down, longing for a final drop of water. She chastised herself with vulgar hate-filled words because she had forgotten to refill the bottle while she was running beside the cliffs. An empty road stretched before her, nothing but dripping trees on either side.

Her hand dipped into the puddle. The gritty clay sludge oozed between her fingers. Before she could bring the moisture to her lips, she gagged. An attempt to spit out the taste of the long-ago sand failed.

Pulling herself back onto her feet, Sigrid took one step and then another, searching the road ahead for a landmark she could make an immediate goal. Through the rain, she saw a signpost. Here in the middle of nowhere, this must be a good omen. There had not been another vehicle in either direction since Kurt had driven away.

If it wasn't a mirage, then the signpost pointed in the direction of the elusive river. The awakened thirst grew more insistent. She held out her hand to the rain and sucked moisture from her skin. This did nothing but increase the intensity of her longing. Without pausing to read the writing on the sign, Sigrid abandoned her lonely road for the narrower track.

This new road was little more than a double row of wheel ruts, winding through the native vegetation. Progress slowed as the road's condition deteriorated. There were flooded potholes to avoid. To keep herself moving forward, she set herself a step challenge. On a good day, she could hold the numbers in her head into the thousands.

Today was *not* a good day.

She could not get past twenty before she forgot her tally and had to start again. The afternoon light began to fade as the trees loomed closer and closer. How much further before she conceded defeat? *You've come the wrong way...*

The accusation became a taunting refrain, and she chanted the words in time with her feet: "You have come the wro-ong way. You-ou have to tur-urn back. This road is a dea-ead end. It's your fault that you are lost—"

୫୦ ✿ ୧୪

Drumming his hands on the steering wheel, Kurt waited for Samson to open the next gate. The road that descended from the *Mountain Rise* homestead had always been a winding challenge, but the journey between the three gates seemed endless this afternoon.

Oliver's voice came from the dashboard speaker. The operative in Melbourne had kept the phone line open. "Romano's right. Automated gates are essential in an emergency. Samson made the property secure from unwanted visitors, but they make leaving difficult."

"Are you still receiving video from Sigrid?" Kurt asked. "Has she reached the turn-off yet?"

"The rain is a problem, but the tech guy's trying his best. The audio's better. I can hear her voice through my headphones. She's trying to find the river."

Samson waved, and Kurt let the ute roll forward. A glance in the mirror confirmed that Samson's LandCruiser was not far behind them. Romano must be driving it.

"Only two more gates," Samson said. Kurt stomped on the accelerator pedal as his friend landed in the passenger seat. The door slammed as the tyres spun on the slushy gravel, and the 4x4 surged forward.

"Samson," Oliver said. "Can you check your surveillance cameras again? Sigrid should be coming into view soon."

Kurt forced his eyes back to the road.

"I'll let you know when I see her," Samson said, studying his phone screen. "I'm adjusting the cameras to give me a better angle. Piper wants to add more relay stations to speed up the process. The signal has to transmit from here to the control tower and then back to the bridge."

Kurt rushed the next corner, taking a calculated risk. His passenger hissed as the rear of the vehicle swung too close to the scrub beside the road. *Bang!*

Samson stuck his head out the window to check the damage. "The panel beater will be delighted. He expected to make a fortune from your reckless driving."

"I'm not reckless," Kurt said. He eased his foot from the accelerator and took a deep breath. The untamed bush pressed close on both sides of the gravel track. It was broader than an ordinary access road, but that did not allow for over-steering on the corners. He rammed his foot on the brake as the next gate appeared in front of him.

Samson went to open it.

"If there's spare money," Kurt said to the Melbourne operative on the phone, "fixing some of these corners would make my work easier."

"I'll add it to my list," Oliver said.

"About that. Samson said you're paying for the security upgrade. Where's the money coming from?"

"There's a trust fund," Oliver said. "Piper's cousin, Valentino, made provision before his death. He also left Sofia money, which is why she's investing in the mountain."

Kurt frowned at the mention of Sofia. He had already tried investigating the connection between Evie's sister and a notorious Melbourne-based criminal. There were unconfirmed rumours of an engagement between them at the time of that man's death. Piper had shut down Kurt's enquiry before he had confirmation. "Valentino Horatio? I thought he was on the wrong side of the law?"

Oliver hesitated. "I've checked – the money's clean. Valentino took a small inheritance from his grandmother's estate and built himself a legitimate property empire. At the time of his death, he was distancing himself from his family's criminal activities."

Rolling forward again, Kurt collected his passenger, and the ute sped onward.

"So, what's your trust fund for?" Kurt asked.

"There's a lot more I wish I could tell you," Oliver said and fell silent.

"Tell him why everyone's so concerned about Sigrid," Samson said.

"He's your friend," Oliver said. "He's more likely to listen to you."

Samson nodded. Kurt prepared for the next corner. His passenger checked the road ahead and rested his hand on the dashboard.

"Evie's friends dream about a river," Samson said. "Both Ruth and I could describe the river long before Alixanda showed us her drawings. Her illustrations could be photographs of the river in our dreams. I've talked to the others. Freddie and Sofia also had similar dreams."

"Except things took an ominous turn for Sofia," Oliver said. "The river became a real encounter. A living nightmare which culminated with Valentino's death."

Recalling the vision he experienced in Samson's kitchen, Kurt broke out in a cold sweat. "The dream river's real?"

"Romano, John and I were with Piper when he rescued Sofia from a flooded river," Oliver said.

Kurt swung towards his friend for further confirmation.

Samson grabbed the steering wheel. "Watch the road."

"Has Sigrid been dreaming about the river?" Kurt asked when he had both the car and his tongue back under his control.

"She's never mentioned it," Oliver said. "Why?"

"Sigrid heard a voice calling her when we were crossing the *Forest Heights* bridge. What can you tell me about Wisdom?"

"Wisdom?" Samson and Oliver spoke at the same time.

Kurt waited for them to say something more.

His foot pressed down on the pedal. "Samson, check the cameras again."

"There's noth— No. I see her. Drive faster!"

Trickle

Becomes

a Flood

ஐ ✿ ❦

ஐ ✿ ❦

The road turned a corner, and Sigrid stopped. The neglected track had become a well-maintained double-width road. A grassy verge on both sides pushed the wilderness back. She glanced behind her. The neglected track was still there.

The way ahead looked better; the air fresher, the sky a little brighter. An oppressive heaviness lifted.

Allowing herself a momentary rest, Sigrid summoned the last of her energy reserves to resume her river quest. An elusive whisper insisted that she knew this place. She took a deep breath and set off at a slow jog. The hypnotic rhythm should free her mind to find an answer.

Her soul hungered for a view of the river. The sound of rushing water echoed in the treetops and seemed to vibrate through the ground beneath her boots. When she reached the crest of the final hill, she increased her speed, eager to reach the surging watercourse.

Her body protested, but the warning came too late. A loose stone moved beneath her boot. "Aarrgghh!" Sigrid hit the ground hard. Unable to stop, she rolled down the hill until she slammed into a mud wall. Sprawled in a roadside ditch, she gasped as she dragged her head out of the stormwater. In desperation, she watched the rushing water escaping towards the river.

Finally, the world stopped churning, and she crawled onto the road. Facedown on the gravel surface, Sigrid struggled to breathe. It took the last of her strength to turn her head towards the river. There she lay until her heart settled into a steadier rhythm. Its beat melded with the sounds around her to combine with the river's majestic song.

She pulled herself into a sitting position, rocking and gasping, sobbing with relief. She was only a hundred metres from the river now. Her hand searched for the silver locket around her neck. "Oliver! Oliver! Can you see this?"

Her fingers left muddy smears when she tried to brush away the dirt. She raised the locket towards the flood. "I've found the river. Can you feel its power?"

The river wild and magnificent raced through the valley, unimpeded by the long, narrow bridge that straddled its banks and carried the road into the hills. The gully was deep, too high for the bridge to be threatened by the turbulent water. For a moment, her eyes followed the road uphill until it disappeared among the trees.

Patter, patter, patter. The pounding at her temples synchronised with the raindrops. She licked her cracked lips and attempted a smile. "I'm sorry, Oliver. But I can't sit here wasting time talking to you."

Sigrid struggled to her feet and took a wobbly step. She slipped on the wet gravel and fell. "I haven't had *this* much *fun* since basic training." Sigrid groaned. "Not even I believe that lie. When I get back to the motel, I'm going to spend all night in the spa bath. And then I'm going to sleep until next week."

She lay in the mud, watching the river. "Oliver, remember when you said God has a sense of humour. He must be hysterical now. So much water and I'm *dying* of thirst."

Digging her elbows into the gravel surface, she forced her exhausted body forward. "Tell God I'm not quitting yet."

Finding the path that led to the river was the easy part. She slithered down the bank towards the stairs that had been cut into the massive boulders. Only the first few steps were visible from the road. The river was five metres below the bridge when she began her cautious descent. When she arrived at a wide landing, she rested. From this vantage point, she could see the river lapping at the lowest step.

"Almost there, Oliver. I'm going to sit here and rest." Precariously balanced on a step halfway down, she leaned against the rock. "I wish I hadn't lost my phone, Oliver. You'd know how to get a drink without drowning." She struggled to remove the water bottle from her pocket and cried out in alarm as it slipped from her fingers. "No!" The container bounced off the step and flew through the air until the river claimed it.

She closed her eyes for a moment. "Okay – so my phone's not all I've lost. That was Kurt's water bottle. I've ruined my chances with him, too."

There was no reassuring answer from Oliver.

Instead, in this moment of weakness, the final missing memory revealed itself. Exhausted and vulnerable, Sigrid watched the demise of her military career. It began when she walked off the plane, part of the coffin-bearing honour guard. When they surrendered the precious burden, the base commander dismissed them to the care of their families. Without a family, Sigrid had walked into the nearest bar.

The rest of the story she already knew. The military police guarding her hospital room said she had put up a "hell of a fight" when they tried to restrain her. Three of their companions were in neighbouring rooms.

"Oliver," she whispered. "Tell God I'm ready to see my family now."

ℬ ☼ ℭ

Kurt's Toyota drove onto the single-lane bridge. It had been fifteen minutes since Samson's screen showed a brief glimpse of Sigrid before she disappeared again. His eyes swung from the road ahead to the water which rushed beneath them. Samson was equally occupied, checking the small screen while monitoring his side of the river.

The flood level was still five metres below the road, but the fast-moving water was widening across the flood plain. "I'm going to stop at the edge of the bridge," Kurt said.

He turned off the engine and stepped from the vehicle to get a clearer view of the river. Visibility was growing worse by the minute. Soon it would be impossible to see the river through the gathering gloom. The roaring water echoed from the trees like a freight train rumbling through a city tunnel. Everywhere at once.

To keep the rain from his eyes, Kurt pulled his hat tight on his head. Samson appeared beside him, shouting to make himself heard. "She's still talking to Oliver."

Vibrations through the boards beneath his feet announced the arrival of Samson's LandCruiser. Romano's massive figure emerged from the driver's seat. The giant went to the back of the vehicle.

Butch leapt from the rear passenger compartment, with Marco close on his heels.

"Where is she?" Butch demanded, running to the railing and leaning out over the river.

Marco copied him on the opposite side of the bridge.

Kurt took charge. "She's not in the water," he shouted. "Come into the shelter of the ute, out of the wind. It will be easier to discuss what we're going to do."

Romano arrived with two heavy bags slung over his shoulders. Jenny and Evie huddled beside the Toyota. The security commander had her arm around the smaller woman as if she feared the blustery wind would snatch her charge.

"Can anyone get a signal?" Jenny asked, waving her phone in the air. "I noticed on Saturday that there's no reception here."

"There's a signal booster in Kurt's ute," Samson said. "Oliver is still on the line, but you have to be inside the cabin to talk to him."

"Let Evie talk to Oliver," Romano said. "She'll be safer out of the weather. I only agreed to let her come because we may need her after the rescue."

Jenny flinched while Butch and Marco exchanged troubled glances.

Kurt felt as if the bridge had dropped out from under him. He steadied himself by placing his hand on the bonnet of his Toyota Hilux. He thought about the rescue mission where only Sofia survived. Was Evie here to pray over Sigrid's body if they didn't find her in time?

Samson spoke again. "Sigrid's talking as if she knows Oliver is listening, but she hasn't given him any clues, except to say she's having trouble getting to the river."

"What about your cameras?" Jenny asked.

"I had her at the top of the hill," Samson said, frowning into the mist. "Then she stumbled and dropped out of sight.

By the time the cameras caught up with my new directives, she'd vanished."

"Why are we standing here?" Butch demanded. "Let's go! She can't be too far away."

"Don't go rushing off," Samson said, catching the teenager's arm. "With the light fading, it's too easy to get lost."

"Marco and I will stay together," Butch said. "We've brought the new two-way radios, and Ruth's back at the homestead, listening in on the base station. We can give Evie a handset and share out the other three. Then Evie can let us know if Oliver tells her anything useful."

"Better if the two of you split up, Butch," Samson said. "I'll take Marco, and you can go with Kurt. We'll send Jenny up the hill with a radio to see if she can find where Sigrid left the road."

"Put on these climbing harnesses," Romano said, unzipping one of the bags, "in case we need to use ropes to get you back. Kurt and Samson, here's your gear. I've given each of you a spare harness. Don't wait for backup if your team finds her." He passed Jenny and the teenagers large torches. "Take these. I'll stay to prep the LandCruiser. We have hot water bottles and blankets in the other bag."

"Sigrid's coat is in my ute," Kurt said. "I should never have let her—"

"Don't beat yourself up," Jenny said. "This is Sigrid's mistake." The angry woman grabbed one of the radios and stormed off into the mist, following the road up the hill.

"Jenny needs to take her own advice," Romano said. "Evie will talk to her when the emergency is over."

Triumphant
Rescue

ಎಂ ☼ ಣ

*Luke 6:36 WEB - Therefore be merciful,
even as your Father
is also merciful.*

ಎಂ ☼ ಣ

After fastening his harness, Kurt checked that the ropes would not impede his movement. Romano assisted the teenagers with their equipment.

Samson studied the floodwaters. "I'll check upriver," he said, pointing away from the bridge. "Kurt, you take the rock steps downriver. Tie off your rope to the bridge supports. Getting down is going to be difficult enough in this rain, but the climb back will be treacherous."

"That's why Romano's staying on the bridge," Marco said. "Tell him when Sigrid's tied on, and he'll pull her up. That's what he did when he rescued Mum."

Kurt closed his eyes. He didn't need another reminder about Sofia's river rescue.

"We don't have the right kind of stretcher," Samson said. "This time, we'll rely on the buddy system."

While Samson tied one end of a long rope to the bridge, Butch stayed close to Kurt, playing with the radio. "Hey, Marco, do you copy?"

"Butch, get off the channel," Jenny's voice said.

"We're going over the bank," Butch said into the radio. He took a tentative step. "Aaargghhh!"

Kurt grabbed him before Butch slid off the narrow path into the undergrowth.

"Don't worry," Butch shouted into the radio. "I'm fine."

Throwing a loop of rope towards the teenager, Kurt said, "Here, clip yourself on, and don't move until you're secure."

"Right, Sarge," said Butch. He acted with confidence, confirming Samson's assurance that the teenagers had been doing rope work under his supervision. Kurt checked that the carabiners were securely snapped into place.

"What about you?' Butch asked.

"Don't worry about me," Kurt said.

The teenager remained quiet as they slipped and slithered down the winding path towards the boulders. They were both muddy when they reached the top of the manmade stairs.

"There's no rush to get down," Kurt said, restraining Butch. "The rocks are wide enough that if you lose your balance and slip, I'll be able to keep out of your way until you correct your fall. There's a right-angle turn, halfway down. We should be able to see all the way to the river from there."

When they were almost to the landing, Butch paused to study some etched markings in the rock. "There's graffiti here. Look, my mother's name: Kimberley Kidman. And up there, 'Samson Davidson' and 'Kurt Jensen'. Weird that you and Ma used to go swimming together."

"Samson and I were fourteen when your mother was born," Kurt said. "We were gone by the time she was old enough to swim here."

"Ma came with Jack Junior," Butch said, pointing to another name. "And your brother Johnny. Look, my dad, Michael Cassidy – he was older."

"Enough," Kurt said. "We won't hear Sigrid if you're talking."

"What are the chances that we'll fi—"

"Stop! I'm going to send you back to the bridge if you—"

Butch pointed at a blue object that flew through the air before tumbling towards the river. "What was that?"

"Get on the radio! She's here. That was my drink bottle."

Leaving Butch to carry out that mission, Kurt took the remaining steps two at a time until he reached the landing. He rounded the corner to check the lower stairs. Sigrid lay slumped across a narrow step, about halfway down. Her upper body rested against the rock wall. The water had already covered the lower steps, and foaming waves slapped at the next riser.

Despite the roar of the wind and the rushing water, her voice travelled towards him. It was almost as if she was whispering for him alone. "Oliver, tell God I'm ready to see my family now."

Hadn't she told him her family were dead?

"Sigrid," Kurt shouted as he leapt down. When he reached her, he knelt on the step below. Sigrid's eyes were closed. His heart pounded in his chest. She didn't like surprises. He glanced at the hungry river. Before he placed his hand on her shoulder, he rechecked his connection with the rope. "Sigrid?"

"What took you so long?" she said without opening her eyes. With a sigh, her body fell forward like a lifeless doll. Kurt caught her against his chest, almost overbalancing on the stone step.

Butch wrapped his arms around Sigrid's waist from behind and pulled until Kurt regained his footing. "Hey, Sigrid," the teenager said. "We've saved you. The river's not getting you today."

Sigrid made no response.

While Butch supported her weight, Kurt searched for a pulse. It was a relief to find one, but the coolness of her skin was a warning that the danger was not over yet.

"Unclip the spare harness from my belt and let's get it on her," Kurt said. "Then I'll clip Sigrid onto my harness, so we're both attached to the rope. I'll need you to climb up ahead of me, taking up the slack in the rope if you can."

"Right, Sarge."

"Don't call me 'Sarge'."

"Aye, aye, Cap-tain," Butch said, saluting briefly. He chuckled to himself as he prepared the harness and carabiners.

The process took a few minutes, but before they were ready to start the uphill climb, Samson dropped from above to land on a higher step. He was attached to a rope dangling from the bridge.

"Hey," Butch said, watching his uncle unclip his harness from the rope. "Why didn't we come over the side of the bridge like that?"

"You haven't had enough training," Samson said to his nephew. "And don't think you're going up by rope either. Go back up the steps while I get Kurt and Sigrid attached. Romano's going to pull them up. I've left Marco keeping watch for you, and I'll follow you up as soon as I can."

"Race you to the bridge," Butch said. "I don't want to miss seeing Romano in action." Without further delay, the teenager turned towards the slippery stone steps.

"It would be safer if you took Sigrid," Kurt said to his friend, and he reached for the connecting carabiners. His fingers fumbled with the clips, the self-locking D-shaped variety that required manual unfastening.

"When we were kids," Samson said, pushing Kurt's hand aside, "you were fearless on the ropes." He checked that both harnesses were correctly attached to the new rope. "And I'm sure you've done emergency training since then. Stop wasting time. On three, I'm sending Romano the signal. Three!"

Samson tugged on the rope, and Kurt jerked upward. He wrapped his arms around Sigrid to keep her close to him as they rose through the air.

As soon as they left the ground, the bodies on the end of the rope swung like a pendulum. For a few seconds, Kurt had a dizzying view of the river below their feet. He twisted his head to catch a glimpse of Samson as the mountain man chased Butch up the steps.

The sudden motion sent Kurt and his precious burden spinning perilously close to the rock wall. He used both hands to prevent Sigrid's head from smashing against the boulders. That sent them flying back towards the wooden supports beneath the bridge. After using his feet to propel them away from the first pylon, he had to do the same with another one. By readjusting his position, he attempted an outward swing to determine how much further they had to go.

Above Kurt's head, Romano was heaving on the rope. Jenny wrestled with the excess loops forming behind him, wrapping them around an anchor point on the LandCruiser. The upward momentum slowed. Was the Melbourne man strong enough for the task? Samson appeared beside Romano, with Marco and Butch at his side, adding their efforts to the rescue.

When Kurt finally lay on the bridge decking, Jenny unclipped Sigrid from the rope. She dragged the unconscious woman into the back seat of Samson's LandCruiser while Romano hauled the off-duty policeman to his feet.

"Take off your coat and get in," Romano said. "Jenny needs your help with Sigrid's boots."

Too dazed to protest, Kurt found himself shut inside the LandCruiser. Jenny was peeling off Sigrid's wet top. He refocused on the boot laces, his trembling fingers struggling with the knots. By the time he pulled off the first boot and the accompanying soggy sock, Evie had joined them. She leaned over from the front seat, holding a blanket to shield Sigrid's body from view. Kurt wrestled with the second boot, removing it a few seconds before Jenny dragged Sigrid's wet trousers from her legs and tossed them at him.

"Into the bag," Jenny said.

He caught a glimpse of a tattoo on the unconscious woman's lower leg before the woollen blanket covered her naked form.

The bag Jenny indicated was on the floor between them. Kurt bundled the wet clothes into the bag and followed them with the boots.

"Here," Jenny said, and a blanket-wrapped body was thrust into Kurt's arms. "Hold her tight. We don't want the hot water bottles falling out. When you have the seatbelt secure around both of you, I'll add another blanket."

Floral
Tribute

Ꮹ☼ᏆᏄ

Isaiah 35:1a WEB -
The wilderness and the dry land will be glad,
the desert will rejoice and blossom.

Ꮹ☼ᏆᏄ

Bright sunshine greeted Sigrid when she opened her eyes. The grey clouds, the cold rain, the untamed Australian bush, and the flooded river were gone, replaced by an open meadow filled with flowers. She lay on her back, enjoying the warmth as she waited for reality to return. The sky was too blue, the colours exuberant and bright, like a child's drawing. This was a dream—

But *not* an ordinary dream!

Scrambling to her feet, Sigrid gazed around. This looked like the scene that Alixanda often drew. The meadow spread in every direction, with the hint of a forest in the middle distance. She recognised the small stand of trees nearby. But where was the river? It should be right where she was standing.

"What happened to the river?" Sigrid asked.

"It is not your time," a familiar voice said.

Spinning around, Sigrid stared up at the towering, armour-clad warrior. Wisdom. "I know this is a dream, but I take great comfort knowing that you are not forgotten."

"I am not your dead friend."

"I know that," Sigrid said. "Alixanda told me that your name is Wisdom. Piper thinks these dreams are a form of mass hysteria. Our subconscious minds trying to process information by calling upon a familiar scene. He'd tell me that I've spent too much time in Alixanda's apartment."

"And what do you think?" Wisdom asked, dropping to the ground and picking a long-stemmed daisy. Sigrid's visitor began to detach the petals from the bright flower, one thoughtful pinch at a time.

"I want to believe," Sigrid said, staring at the fluttering shower of yellow petals, "but it's hard. Taking advice from someone who only exists in a dream is crazy."

"Yet here you are," laughed Wisdom, casting aside the bare stem and seizing another delicate bloom. She placed the purple flower lightly across Sigrid's open palm. "What do you want to know?"

Sigrid sat beside Wisdom and folded her legs to match Wisdom's pose. The armoured warrior stared at the floral token that lay in Sigrid's hand. Sigrid extended a finger towards the flower. A tingling sensation buzzed up her arm when she touched a petal. Sigrid pressed her hand over the daisy, and a surge of energy swept through her body. Hastily, she lifted her hand from the flower, and the blast faded, leaving her with a prickly scalp and pins and needles in her toes. Her hair stood out from her head.

Her heart danced to an unfamiliar rhythm. Sigrid took a deep breath and held it, only exhaling when her lungs screamed for air. Her unbound hair took a few minutes to fall back into place about her shoulders, and there was a further delay before she could move her tongue.

Sigrid poked the flower again, but nothing happened.

Wisdom smiled. "What do you want to know?"

"I have a new mission, but no-one will tell me the specifics. Can you tell me anything?"

The dream messenger nodded. "You have been preparing for this mission all your life. That is why you train your body to the extreme. But physical strength and endurance are not enough. You need a sound mind and the ability to control your emotions if you are to succeed."

Those words were like vicious spikes, driven deep into Sigrid's heart. "Then I'm doomed."

If recent events were anything to go by, it was already too late. Wave after wave of regret washed over her, dark threatening clouds that promised greater disappointment.

The colourful meadow began to fade. Sigrid needed no further information. Now she understood why the dream river was absent – she would never be good enough—

Something hot brushed her face and Sigrid recoiled. In an instant, the darkness retreated, and the meadow was present in even brighter glory. Wisdom had not moved.

Sigrid uncurled her clenched fist to reveal the crushed flower. "My mind is broken, and my emotions are out of control. That's why I'm here in this dream."

"You are here," Wisdom said, removing the ruined flower from Sigrid's hand and cradling it as if it were a precious treasure, "to learn to appreciate what you have."

The silence stretched until Sigrid could bear it no longer. "Nothing and nobody?" She cringed as those poisoned words lingered in the air.

Wisdom shook her head. "You've nurtured that lie until it has become your reality. Yet hidden in a corner of your heart lives an undying hope. Are you ready to receive the truth?"

A hot flush surged through Sigrid's body. She wiped her brow. "I'm ready."

Instead of answering immediately, Wisdom held the crushed flower towards the sky, and a stream of brilliant light poured from above. The dazzling brightness rendered Sigrid temporarily blind.

When Sigrid could see again, Wisdom was much closer. The stem of the flower hung from her huge fingers.

"You have been selected." Wisdom punctuated that remark by plucking a single petal from the battered flower and releasing it into the space between them. A gentle breeze caught the fluttering petal, and Sigrid chased it with her fingers. When she had it safely tucked inside her closed fist, she refocused on her companion. A dozen questions demanded attention, but Wisdom had already moved on.

Another petal met the same fate. "You are trained."

This petal almost escaped Sigrid's reach, but she was back in position when Wisdom spoke again.

"You will be ready."

As the words echoed inside her, the third petal floated onto Sigrid's outstretched hand.

With deliberate care, the dream-messenger spoke a different phrase to accompany each new petal falling into Sigrid's waiting hand.

"You have been called – you are precious – you will be equipped – you have been chosen – you are forgiven – you will be delivered – you have been redeemed – you are restored – you will be victorious."

Now all that remained of the flower was the fluffy red centre, still attached to the stem. Wisdom held it up. "Without a central truth, there is nothing to hold these promises together. Are you ready to accept your mission?"

Sigrid nodded.

Wisdom dropped the core of the flower, and Sigrid caught it. Only when the remnant joined the scattered petals did the warrior speak the final words. "You are loved."

Those three words echoed across the landscape, repeating themselves again and again. Every flower in the meadow sang the same song, as the breeze blew across the plain. Sigrid closed her eyes and waited until the words began to fade. When they were no more than a whisper, she opened her hand. The deconstructed flower was whole again, with the perfect petals arranged in their original place.

"How did that happen?"

There was no answer. Sigrid was alone in the meadow. She stood, and the flowers that surrounded her whispered as they brushed against her legs. "You are loved. You are loved. You are loved..."

༄ ✿ ༄

Kurt cradled the unconscious woman in his arms, sweltering beneath the blankets. Sigrid's face was barely visible within her cocoon as she snuggled against him. Her feet extended onto the seat beside him. The LandCruiser's cabin was stuffy, warm air blowing from the dashboard heater. He adjusted his position and glanced at Jenny and Evie, crammed into the remaining passenger space. They had both shed their coats, and their cheeks were flushed.

Samson was leading the way to Meredith Crossing in Kurt's Hilux, with Marco as his passenger, while Romano drove the LandCruiser. Butch sat beside Romano, relaying the driver's questions about the road ahead to the first vehicle using the two-way radio.

"How long until we get to the sealed road?" Jenny asked Kurt.

He leaned sideways for a better view. The LandCruiser's headlights reflected off the raindrops, making the landmarks ahead difficult to identify.

"Once we pass the turnoff to Mrs Mac's, there's only another ten K to the main road. Then maybe another twenty minutes to Meredith Crossing because of the weather."

"Mrs Mac's place is coming up on the left," Butch said from the front passenger seat.

The big man handled the twisting country roads with precision, despite the treacherous conditions. Kurt's admiration for the city driver increased with each passing kilometre, and he privately revised his estimated arrival time.

A more pressing problem was pushed to the forefront of Kurt's mind. The team from *Mountain Rise* would only tarry until the doctor stabilised the patient's condition. Sigrid would require constant supervision, but he needed to prepare for the task force.

Unable to find a solution, Kurt closed his eyes and tried to shut out the world.

Trillions

of Petals

ಏ ✿ ಆ

2 Peter 1:3b WEB - His divine power
has granted to us all things
that pertain to life.

ಏ ✿ ಆ

Something tickled Sigrid's face. Her eyes flew open, and she sat up. She was back in the meadow, surrounded by piles of deconstructed flowers.

"Some people use flowers to tell their fortunes," Wisdom said, releasing a handful of petals over her head. "He loves you... He loves you not... He loves you!"

"You ruined all these flowers because of a childish game?" Sigrid asked. "What a waste!"

"They're only wasted if you reject their message," Wisdom said, handing her a flower. "It's your turn."

"What?"

"When you awaken, you will want to dismiss your time here as a dream, the product of your imagination. You will even doubt your mission. That is why these flowers are a sign for you. They will remind you that you have a destiny. The success of your mission is pre-determined."

"So I'm supposed to look for a flower," Sigrid snapped, "and rip off its petals?"

"There will be no need. You won't return to your reality until you have 'ripped off' enough petals in this place to be certain of the outcome."

Sigrid stared at the petals spread about her. "Are you telling me that every one of these flowers delivered the same answer to the rhyme?"

"What little you value in your life was won through painful trials," Wisdom said. "Unless there is a struggle, you will have difficulty accepting that anyone can love you."

"What kind of love are we talking about?" Sigrid asked.

Wisdom reached down. With a single motion, her massive hand plucked a posy of flowers. A misty haze appeared beside the warrior as she removed the white ones and passed them to Sigrid. "Sister."

From within the mist, a group of women emerged. There was no time for Sigrid to identify them before they disappeared.

"Wait," Sigrid said, but it was too late. The only one she could be confident about was Evie Romano.

Wisdom was already handing her the blue ones. "Brother."

Again a group of figures appeared within the mist. Wisdom continued selecting a different colour and handing them over. "Cousin... Friend... Companion... Mother... Father... Child..."

Sigrid trembled as she accepted the different coloured flowers, overwhelmed by the accompanying visions.

"There's still one more," Wisdom said, holding a single variegated daisy. It was the one that she had held in her hand at the beginning of this conversation. The warrior kept it out of Sigrid's reach. "Only one man will satisfy the requirements."

Sigrid examined the flower. This one had three rows of petals, longer blue ones on the outer edge. The middle row was yellow. The inner circle of red petals was the same colour as the fluffy centre. "Blue for a brother?"

Wisdom nodded.

Sigrid licked her lips and continued. "Yellow is a friend and red is a companion. So that makes this person a brother-friend-companion?"

"You are more familiar with another term," Wisdom said, grinning as she continued to dangle the flower out of Sigrid's reach. "But you have yet to learn the true nature of this kind of relationship. You have settled for the world's transient imitation. Once you have learned to accept this man's love, there will never be another lover."

With a shout, Wisdom threw the precious flower into the air.

Sigrid gasped and dropped the other flowers in her haste to catch the falling bloom. She held it with reverence, waiting for the vision to show her the man.

"You have to pluck the petals," Wisdom said, "to reveal your future."

"But there's only one," Sigrid said, looking at the flowers growing nearby. "What if I make a mistake and the flower tells me that this man doesn't love me?"

"You have a whole meadow of flowers to practice on."

Wisdom sat and crossed her legs. She reached for another flower and pulled off the petals one by one. Sigrid frowned. A heaviness settled around her shoulders, and the lump in her throat almost choked her. Her heartbeat was too fast, and the pounding at her temples matched the throbbing in her fingers and toes.

This is a test, her mind screamed.

What kind of test? What would she risk for happy-ever-after? A relationship like Evie and Romano's, or the match between Sofia and John. She had thought that love between

Freddie and Alixanda was impossible, and hadn't their recent marriage proven her wrong? And what about the transformation that came to Jezebel after Samson promised her his love?

Her voice trembled as she began to pinch off the petals, one by one. "He loves me... he loves me not... he loves me."

Sigrid paused. Something was wrong. She closed her eyes and concentrated, waiting to identify what was missing. As she waited, an array of faces appeared before her. One by one, she considered and rejected the men who had shared her bed. Too many were only represented by a fleeting memory. Some she could not name. That said a lot about her character.

No. The flower represented the man's character. He had to be a brother-friend-companion. Now she reviewed those few who had ever said no to her invitation. It was a short list. Kurt Jensen was the last of them, but instead of fading, his face remained before her. Sigrid made a difficult decision. All or nothing.

"Kurt loves me, Kurt loves me not. Kurt loves me." Three petals fell, one for each phrase. Sigrid stared at the flower. "Who am I kidding? Kurt can't stand me." She wrenched out several petals and threw them into the air. With deliberate care, she selected a single petal. "Kurt loves me."

Waiting until that petal joined the others on the ground, she grabbed the remaining petals and ripped out a few more. "Ha! He only wants me for a friend – that's a good place to start. Kurt loves me. Kurt loves me not – he's been ordered to keep an eye on me. Kurt loves me – he took me to meet his family. Kurt loves me not – he didn't want to be alone at the memorial..."

Abandoning herself to an argument she could never win, Sigrid continued until the flower was destroyed. Shaking and upset, she tore out the final yellow petals. "He loves me not."

What are you left with?

Where did that voice come from?

Is that you, God?

You wanted to hear my voice, and I have granted your request. Look at the flower. What are you left with?

Sigrid glanced down at her hand. The bruised stem still bore the red, fluffy centre. In an instant, the whole meadow broke into song: "You are loved. You are loved. You are loved..."

Wisdom appeared beside her. "Have you learned your lesson?"

"He loves me," Sigrid whispered, and the dream meadow disappeared.

ഌ ✿ beta

With great care, Kurt rested his hand across the casualty's forehead.

"Has Sigrid started to warm up yet?" Jenny asked.

The last time he had touched her cold skin, he shivered. "She's warmer now," he said.

Sigrid stirred, opening her eyes. There was no recognition in those glazed green eyes. The top blanket began to wriggle, and her hand emerged. Sigrid pushed at the wrappings until a bare shoulder appeared from among the folds. Kurt hastily adjusted the fabric, his face glowing at the reminder that she was wearing nothing underneath.

After a few seconds, she stopped wrestling with the covers and stared into his eyes. The most amazing smile spread across her face before her eyelids closed with a flutter. She wriggled again, pressing against him as if she was trying to burrow herself deeper against his chest. He tightened his embrace, and she sighed. When her movement stilled, he glanced around. Jenny was watching him. Kurt turned his head towards the window and pretended to study the passing scenery.

"You're in trouble," Jenny said, "if Sigrid wakes up and remembers any of this."

CHAPTER 34
(Tuesday 29th May)

Trialling
Trust

ঙ ☼ ৎ

Romans 10:9 CG -If you confess with your mouth that Jesus is Lord,
and believe in your heart
that God raised Him from the dead,
you will be saved.

ঙ ☼ ৎ

The small convoy arrived in Meredith Crossing and headed for the motel. Kurt recognised Doctor Chappell's vehicle, parked outside the separate apartment block with a police patrol car beside it. The rain had lessened to an inconvenient shower, and the afternoon light was fading. The floodlit car park seemed unusually crowded, destroying his feeble hope that today's misadventure could be kept quiet.

Kurt closed his eyes for a moment, marshalling his thoughts. It was unproductive to think about anything except the wellbeing of the woman in his arms. The niggling pain behind his eyes had intensified during the journey, competing for attention with the ache in his protesting shoulder muscles. But it was his grieving heart that concerned him most. How could he be mourning her loss while Sigrid was still in his arms?

"I'll do what I can," Samson's voice said over the radio.

Kurt's eyes sprang open. The lead vehicle headed towards the patrol car. Meanwhile, Romano reversed into one of the

211

parking spaces reserved for Sigrid's apartment. Kurt craned his neck to catch a glimpse of Constable Ben King alighting from the patrol car to meet Samson.

"Be quick," Jenny said, unclipping the seatbelt that secured Kurt and his blanket-wrapped burden.

Kurt fumbled for the door latch while the other passengers scrambled from the vehicle. Their voices faded. Romano appeared beside him, and Kurt shoved Sigrid into his outstretched arms. She stirred and began to whimper. Romano took a step back to give Kurt space to get out of his seat. Her cries intensified as she wrestled within the blankets to free her arms. As soon as Kurt was upright, Romano thrust the struggling woman towards him, and he drew her close to his chest. Sigrid's arms snaked around his neck. Clinging to him, she burrowed her head against his shoulder while Romano readjusted the blankets to cover her exposed skin.

The big man shepherded Kurt towards the open apartment door. As soon as they were inside, Tim Chappell appeared at his side. The doctor peeled back the upper blanket and placed a hand on the patient's forehead while reaching for her hand.

"I told you," Jenny said. "Her body's already making a strong recovery. There's no need to evacuate Sigrid to a city hospital."

"It's not her body that I'm concerned about," Tim said. "I'm not satisfied with your explanation about how she came to be in this state."

"Could you save your argument for later?" Kurt asked. "I need to put Sigrid somewhere before I drop her."

"This way," Jenny said, moving towards the archway, but instead of taking the stairs, she pushed open the door to a downstairs bedroom.

Kurt moved past Jenny. Evie was already in the room with the covers turned down on one of the single beds. He lowered

Sigrid's body onto the bed, but he could not disentangle her arms from his neck. She began to whimper again and clung even tighter. A flash of memory robbed him of oxygen, a past occasion where he had removed a hysterical child from her father's arms. He fell forward onto the bed, with Sigrid crushed beneath him.

Jenny swore loudly from the doorway while Evie's quiet voice came closer. Evie spoke in an unfamiliar tongue, and every hair on Kurt's body bristled at the sound. Sigrid froze, and her arms slipped from his neck as she turned her head towards that voice. He pulled himself free and scrambled to his feet.

"Go," Evie said, and gave him a gentle push towards the door.

Jenny grabbed Kurt's arm and dragged him to the dining room, where Romano shoved a cup into his hand. Kurt inhaled the steam from the coffee as he collapsed onto one of the seats beside the table. He stared at a plate of apple pie that materialised before him.

"All she had in the fridge," Butch said, distributing pie to the others. "The cupboards were empty too, except for some potato crisps. Marco and I have already eaten them."

"There's a bottle of whiskey," Marco added, "but Romano said to leave it where we found it."

Kurt shoved the apple pie away from him.

"If you're not going to eat that," Butch said, "can we have it?" Without hesitation, the teenager snatched the plate and shared Kurt's portion with Marco.

Kurt turned towards Jenny.

"Don't ask," Jenny said, between mouthfuls of pie. "Even if I understood Evie's power, my explanation would only leave you with more questions."

"Are you done here, Kurt?" Romano said. "You need to rescue Samson. Your officer has refused to stay outside. He's waiting in the main room."

Taking a quick gulp of his coffee, Kurt left the table and went through the archway to the living room. Samson smiled when Kurt appeared and waved his hand towards two visitors who were seated on separate sofas. Harry McHenry sprang to his feet while Constable Ben King remained where he was.

"Is Sigrid going to be okay?" Harry asked.

"The doctor's with her now," Kurt said.

"Is it true that you pulled her from the river?"

"Why are you asking about the river?" Kurt asked. He glanced at Samson, who shook his head.

"You know how quickly news spreads," Harry said. "Samson's wife phoned Doc Chappell, who ordered a helicopter. They alerted emergency services about a river rescue and then, when nobody knew anything, contacted the station. If she didn't fall in the river, what happened?"

"Is that why you're here, Ben?" Kurt asked.

"I was already on my way to the motel when the call came through," Ben said. "You know that old saying, 'It never rains, but it pours'? The taskforce commander arrived two days early."

"He wanted to know who's staying in this apartment," Harry said. "Sigrid warned me not to talk about her to anyone, so I kept quiet. But—"

"But?"

"There was a crowd outside the pub," Harry said, "when you carried Sigrid into the apartment."

"The inspector wants to talk to you," Ben said, and his eyes conveyed much more.

"It's time you went back to your patrons," Samson said to Harry. "That's the best place for you. The less you know, the better."

"Oh, right," Harry said, hurrying to the door. "Let me know if there's anything else I can do." Then he was gone, with Samson at his heels.

"What's going on?" Ben asked as soon as the door closed.

Kurt narrowed his eyes and searched his heart. Of the officers under his command, Ben King was the one he considered the most trustworthy. But how much information was Kurt free to share?

Bring him into your confidence.

Kurt flinched. What had Sigrid said about hearing voices that were inaudible to anybody else? "Did you hear someone say something?"

"No." Ben studied him. "What did this *someone* say?"

Bring him into your confidence.

That voice again. "Give me a moment," Kurt said. He remembered Sigrid talking about ignoring the warning voice... With his pulse racing, he responded in his mind.

Are you sure?

Yes. Do not carry this burden alone. Here is someone who can watch your back.

"I'm taking a risk telling you anything," Kurt began.

"Nothing will go beyond these walls," Ben said, lowering his voice and leaning forward. "I'm glad you've decided to trust me, and I promise not to mention this conversation to anyone. I've known you a long time, and I'd hate to see you carrying this burden alone."

Hearing that echo of the inner voice gave Kurt the confidence to continue. "Sigrid is an *Operation Phoenix* security operative. They're setting up a facility here – Samson Davidson will be the base commander."

Ben's eyes widened, and he nodded for Kurt to continue as he leaned back in his seat.

"We all thought the base would remain a secret," Kurt said, "but then Sigrid was ordered to wear her new uniform. She thinks this is a test, but I suspect she's the bait in a trap. Sigrid's under constant surveillance, which is how we knew she was in trouble this afternoon."

"What happened?"

"I'm supposed to be gaining her trust, and I blew it big time. She needed space to deal with something that happened, and then I lost her in the rain."

"Don't be hard on yourself," Ben said. "The first time I saw Sigrid, I knew she was like my cousin. He was a Vietnam war veteran. We never knew what would trigger a dangerous episode. He used to act as if he was back in the jungle, and we were the enemy."

Kurt considered that information. "Sigrid's found a different role for me. Her father died when she was young, and she's acting like I'm his replacement."

Trick
or Treat

ಬ ☼ ಛ

Job 23:10b WEB -
When He has tried me,
I will come out like gold.

ಬ ☼ ಛ

Hours earlier, everyone had abandoned Kurt to a solitary vigil. The patient lay silent and motionless. Her earlier mutterings, which included multiple references to Oliver, love, wisdom, and the elusive river, were falling further and further apart. Kurt rose from the chair beside Sigrid's single bed, again pondering her sleeping arrangements. Why wasn't she using one of the luxurious upstairs bedrooms? If Jenny had not led the way, Kurt would have carried the casualty up the stairs.

The overheated room enhanced his drowsiness. Fighting the temptation to close his eyes, Kurt located the remote control for the wall-mounted reverse-cycle air conditioner. The thermostat was set for thirty degrees Celsius. Perfect for a recovering patient but too warm for someone who needed to remain alert.

He longed to unfasten the window and stick out his head to keep himself awake. Instead, he pulled open the sliding door to the shared bathroom until it was wide enough to slip through. Kurt closed the gap behind him to keep the warmth in the bedroom. The bathroom was chilly, and he leaned his back against the white wall tiles until the chill seeped into his core. His reflection in the mirror was still flushed, and he splashed cold water over his face. After tarrying until he started to shiver, he slid the door open again and returned to his chair.

It was not long before the drowsiness tormented him again. His head jerked backwards, awakening him with a jolt. He rose to his feet, pacing the room. The second bed called to him, promising him a comfortable rest, but what if she awoke and slipped away while he slept? The doctor had warned Kurt not to leave Sigrid unsupervised for at least twenty-four hours.

Losing her again would be unforgivable.

His stomach rumbled. Locating his empty coffee mug, Kurt headed for the kitchen. It was only eight pm, and the pub chef should still be on duty. He found the room service menu in a drawer. While he debated his selection, a loud knock from outside the apartment signalled a visitor.

Before Kurt could respond, the front door opened.

"Kurt, it's me." The voice belonged to Muriel McHenry, and she was already heading towards the dining room. She carried a covered tray. "I've brought your dinner, and I'm going to sit with Sigrid while you eat. I'd have been here earlier if that son of mine had let me know what had happened. How is she?"

"Sigrid's asleep," Kurt said, hovering while Muriel unloaded the tray. There were two bowls and a larger plate, each covered with a cloche. He grew tense, wondering if he was awake enough to deflect her curiosity.

Muriel pursed her lips as she adjusted the table setting. "Harry told me not to ask you any questions." She frowned. "Show me which room she's in, and I'll leave you to eat."

A lifetime of obedience to his demanding relative made it easier for Kurt to obey. He settled at the dining room table, raising each cloche: Pumpkin soup with a swirl of sour cream and a sprinkling of chives, roast pork with vegetables, and a generous serve of chocolate self-saucing pudding.

This unexpected act of kindness brought tears to his eyes. He brushed them away. Dipping a spoon into the soup, he savoured the thick, delicious creaminess before he paused. "This is you, isn't it?" he whispered to the room, which no longer felt empty. "You said I shouldn't carry this burden alone. Thank you."

Kurt ate his dinner, enjoying every mouthful. When he finished, he tidied the plates and put them on the tray. He approached the bedroom and Muriel rose from the chair. He backed away and she followed him towards the dining room.

"Thanks for dinner," Kurt said.

"I'll be back in a few hours," Muriel said, collecting the tray and going towards the front door. "I have to go home and get a few things. You look dog-tired, but with a full belly, it should be easier to stay awake until I relieve you." She hesitated on the threshold. "Do you have to work tomorrow?"

"I've put off the city officer for tonight," Kurt said, "but he expects me at the station in the morning."

"That's what I thought. You don't want him sticking his nose into Sigrid's business while she can't defend herself. I must say, Kurt, when you finally went a-courting, you chose a complicated woman."

He mumbled a reply, not wasting time trying to deny he was "a-courting".

"And those Melbourne folk won't be any help," Muriel said. "Not with that 'city officer' snooping around. But I'll figure something out. One way or another, someone trustworthy will be sitting beside her bed until Sigrid's well enough to take care of herself."

ଽଠ ☼ ଔ

(Wednesday 30th May)

Awaking with a start, Kurt cracked his head on the upper bunk. In the half-light, he frowned at the furnishings in the second downstairs bedroom. He slipped from under the covers as he looked at his phone. It was five-thirty. Having slept in his clothes, he hurried through the shared bathroom to tap on the sliding door. Muriel appeared, following him into the hallway and on towards the main exit.

"I know you said I should wake you at five," she said, shoving him out the door. "But you were sleeping soundly. Sigrid's had a quiet night. After the doctor visits this morning, I'll get him to come to the station. Now get going, or you'll be late."

The apartment door closed in his face. Kurt stood on the footpath. His ute keys weren't in his pocket, nor did he have a key-card to the room. His boots were upside down against the wall beside the door. He pulled them on, dodging puddles as he walked up the road towards the police station. Sunrise was officially half an hour away, and the streetlamps lit his path. The crisp pre-dawn air burned his lungs, but he was thankful that the rain had passed. He should have time for a shower and something to eat before his officers arrived for their exercise session.

As Kurt approached the entrance to his flat, Constable Clifford Briggs appeared beside him. "Hey, Sarge. The inspector just phoned to say he's on his way. He's looking forward to *finally* meeting you. Someone must have told him about the morning workout."

Kurt used the spare key and opened his door. "Thanks for the warning," he said, dismissing the officer. In the privacy of his flat, Kurt fought rising irritation. He gathered what he needed for the bathroom. "Okay, God," he said as he turned on the hot water. "I need you to deal with the inspector. There's too much on my plate already."

ഇ ✿ ☯

Kurt refused to be distracted while organising the exercise equipment. The other officers talked with Inspector Tobias Lester-Angevin while they waited. The visiting officer was young, probably in his early thirties, and he wore his branded exercise gear as if he were a professional model.

The newcomer boldly approached the whiteboard and studied the entries before taking a marker and adding his name to the list. Tapping the board, Lester-Angevin asked, "Will Sigrid be joining us this morning?"

"Time to start," Kurt said, pretending not to hear the question. "I've outlined the warm-up exercises on the board. Work through them at your individual pace, and when you get to the end, choose one of the stations in the circuit. The interval timer will signal when you need to move on." He set them an example by beginning immediately.

Helena Avery positioned herself beside the city policeman as everyone began the first stretches. She was wearing more makeup than usual, and she fluttered her eyelashes as she smiled at Lester-Angevin. "Sigrid won't be here today," Helena said. "She'll be out of action for a while because of her little *accident*."

Kurt watched the exchange as a reflection in the window.

Clifford Briggs shook his head in disapproval. "The Inspector isn't interested in idle gossip."

Helena's smile slipped. "It isn't gossip when there's an incident report sitting on the sergeant's desk. The doctor treated Sigrid for hypothermia."

"Officially, Sigrid went for a run and got lost in the rain," Gavin Mallory said, joining the discussion. "Ben was on duty, and he wrote the report."

"And unofficially?" Lester-Angevin asked.

"The sarge's sister said there was an argument," Helena said. "That's why *he* was the one who went looking for her."

"There were plenty of witnesses," Des Wilmot added, "when the Sarge carried her into her apartment. But nobody saw him leave."

"You haven't told them," Lester-Angevin said to Kurt, and his tone brought everyone to a standstill.

"There's nothing to tell," Kurt said, in his best sergeant's voice. "Nothing that can't wait until the eight am briefing."

Team Trials

ஐ ☼ ໕

Isaiah 30:18b CG -
God will show you mercy,
because He is the Lord of justice.

ஐ ☼ ໕

The animated conversation in the meeting room ceased when Kurt pushed through the door. Inspector Lester-Angevin rose to acknowledge his arrival. The younger Meredith Crossing constables who had been hovering around the visiting officer hurried to their seats.

"There you are, Senior Sergeant," Lester-Angevin said. "It would seem we started on the wrong foot. I wasn't implying you were keeping your team in the dark."

And yet you're mentioning it again. Kurt dragged forward an empty chair and settled beside Ben King. "Yesterday, I was on personal leave."

"Ah, the anniversary of your brother's death?" the Inspector said. "He died during a bank robbery."

The three younger officers leaned forward with earnest expressions on their faces.

"My family history has no relevance for this conversation," Kurt said. "With no prior warning of your early arrival, there was no reason for me to check my emails while I was off duty. You're here, so tell us what we don't know."

"Of course." Lester-Angevin's smile swept around the room. "Taskforce Nine is part of a national interagency investigation." The visitor paused as if to reinforce the importance of his statement. "Our mission is to track members of an organised criminal organisation that is allegedly active within regional New South Wales."

"What kind of organised crime?" asked Helena, perched on the edge of her seat.

"Designer drugs," was the quick response, "both the manufacture and distribution. But that's the tip of the iceberg if the earliest allegations are confirmed. There's also fraud, extortion and aggravated assault, abduction, forced prostitution, and human trafficking."

"People smuggling?" Des asked, from beside Helena. "I've been in Meredith Crossing for two-and-a-half years, and Gav's been here for four. There's never been any hint of major crime."

"There was that child abduction case in Brumby's Run last year," Gavin said. "Sarge dealt with that because he knew the Kidman family."

"Nothing came of it," Clifford reminded them. "Butch and his sister Nikki were found within twelve hours."

"So, why is the task force coming here?" asked Gavin.

"An excellent question," Lester-Angevin said. "There is an international organisation investigating the trafficking syndicate. Is anyone familiar with the name *Operation Phoenix*?"

Nobody volunteered any prior knowledge. Kurt watched the silent exchange between Helena and her friends. *What were they hiding?*

The Inspector raised an eyebrow at Kurt, who gestured for him to continue. "Little is known about this paramilitary force, but we do know that Piper Maxwell is the commander. There are unsubstantiated claims that *Operation Phoenix* agents cross international borders with impunity."

"Piper Maxwell?" Helena asked. "Isn't that the man Sigrid works for?"

"Indeed," the Inspector said, rewarding her with a generous smile. "There are rumours that Maxwell has agents working undercover throughout the world. Learning that an active *Operation Phoenix* agent is staying in Meredith Crossing has raised concerns in Sydney."

"Sigrid came here as bodyguard to a Melbourne millionaire's wife and children," Helena said. "They're here for a wedding."

"That's probably a cover story," Lester-Angevin said. "If you could access Sigrid's military record, you'd know that she's overqualified to babysit a wealthy family."

"Why do you think she's here, then?" Helena asked.

"That's what I'm here to find out."

"How can we help?" Gavin asked.

"You can start by telling me what you know."

"Sarge knows her best," Gavin said. "I did think there was something suspicious about the way Sigrid zeroed in on him right from the start."

"I think you'll find that *he* targeted *her*," Lester-Angevin said. Kurt shifted uncomfortably in his seat. "Your sergeant was approached by a senior officer and ordered to get *close* to Major Ericson."

Helena laughed and then covered her mouth with her hand. "I'm sorry, sir," she said. "But our Sarge is the wrong man for that assignment. He's too old and conservative. Gav or Des would be better candidates."

"I appreciate your frank assessment," Lester-Angevin said. "It's been suggested that she might be more amenable to a younger man."

"Not on my watch," Kurt muttered through his teeth. Ben King placed a cautionary hand on his arm.

"Did you say something?" the Inspector asked.

Kurt considered closing the distance between them and knocking the smug expression from Lester-Angevin's face with his fist. That reckless action would end Kurt's career, but if that was what it took to protect Sigrid—

In an instant, he dismissed that folly. Kurt unclenched his fists, smiled at the city officer and spoke clearly. "It's not going to happen on my watch."

"What do you mean by that remark?"

"I'm not sure where you obtained your information," Kurt said, maintaining his seated position. "But you appear to be missing some important facts. If you check the *Operation Phoenix* webpage, you'll see that the organisation offers a variety of services for ex-military personnel, particularly those who are experiencing difficulties reintegrating into civilian life."

"Your point is?" Lester-Angevin asked.

"You accessed Major Ericson's military record? Then you should understand why a decorated special forces officer would need that kind of support. I'm to keep an eye on her and try to steer her away from trouble. Helena's correct about my lack of success. Sigrid's only been in Meredith Crossing a few days, and there have already been three incidents requiring my intervention."

"If Sigrid's such a danger to society, why are there no charges against her name?" asked Gavin.

"How do you know there are no charges?" Ben King asked. "I typed her name into the database, and I didn't have the security clearance to access her file."

Gavin shook his head, keeping his chin up but not meeting the older officer's eye. "I didn't need to access her file. Everyone knows that our Sarge would tell us if a dangerous criminal was in town."

"And he looked as surprised as the rest of us," Des added, "*both* times she attacked him."

"She attacked you?" Lester-Angevin asked. "And you survi—"

Kurt interrupted him. "Attack is too strong a word. I'd call it a warning. She was only establishing her boundaries."

"There's something I don't understand," Helena said, breaking the silence that followed. "Why the interest in Sigrid?"

"An excellent question," the visiting inspector said. "Last November, Sigrid was an eye-witness to the murder of an important Crown witness. There were unanswered questions at the time about why she was with the witness when the attackers stormed the safe house."

"I don't see the connection," Helena said.

"The attackers didn't expect Sigrid to live, and she's been under close watch by her agency since the attack in Melbourne. Then, suddenly, she's out in the open, drawing attention to herself in an unprotected backwater—"

"So either she knows something's about to happen—" said Gavin.

"Or she's bait," Des said. "And your Taskforce Nine is coming to take advantage of either scenario."

The ensuing conversation brought a few suggestions about what the outcome might be. The inspector waited until there was a pause and gestured to Kurt. "Let's hear what your sergeant has to say."

"There's a third option," Kurt said. "Sigrid's presence might have no relevance to the taskforce investigation. Perhaps she came looking for a sanctuary. She's slowly waking up to the reality that the Meredith Crossing welcome has only compounded her problems."

ᘓ ✿ ᘔ

Unsure whether she had entered another dream, Sigrid lay still. She listened to the nearby voices.

"I went through my stash," an unfamiliar voice said. "I found these fat squares that I bought on sale and never used them. You said you wanted strong primary colours for our new project."

"These will be perfect." This voice belonged to Muriel McHenry. What was Harry's mother doing here? "I found a bolt of red to use for the borders."

"You said I should bring these unfinished squares—" That sounded like Kurt's mother, Missie Jensen. "I had six pieced together before Hannah changed her mind and asked for fairies instead."

"I haven't seen this motif before," the first voice said. "And it's unusual to have red circles for the flower centres. The colour's an excellent match for Muriel's border."

Missie laughed. "I used one of Hannah's drawings for the daisy template. She was only six at the time. We made a special trip to the city to choose the fabric."

A door opened. "I've set up the sewing machine in the study," an impatient voice said – Kurt's sister Eliza. "I don't know why you're holding your quilting group here, nor why I had to give up my lunch break to help you."

Sigrid cringed inwardly. Eliza did not sound any friendlier than she had at the homestead.

"You know that it's a family tradition," Missie said. "You only have to stay long enough to help us put together the first square, and then you can go."

"She's not staying in Meredith Crossing," Eliza said. "And even if she does, Sigrid won't appreciate your handiwork."

"Muriel's already explained," Missie said. "God told her that Sigrid and Kurt are soul mates. We're going to start making their wedding quilt."

Whatever else they said was lost in a swirling flood of emotions. Sigrid kept her eyes closed, waiting for the spinning sensation to stop. She must have drifted back to sleep. The next time she resurfaced from the darkness, the voices were gone.

"I know you're awake," Muriel said. "You must be thirsty. I'll get you some water."

Sigrid opened her eyes and searched for her visitor. Muriel rose from a chair and reached for a tumbler on the bedside table.

"Thanks," Sigrid said, shuffling upright to accept the glass. She drank a few sips before sagging back against the pillow. "What are you doing here?"

"Keeping an eye on you. Kurt's gone to the station, and I'm here to make sure you stay in bed."

Her eyes only closed for a moment, but when Sigrid opened them again, Muriel was gone. Missie Jensen occupied the bedside chair. Kurt's mother had a bright square of coloured fabric on her lap. Sigrid watched Missie working with her sewing needle.

"What time is it?" Sigrid asked.

Missie laid the fabric in her lap and smiled. "It's twenty minutes since you asked me last time, half-past two on Wednesday afternoon. I didn't think you were properly awake then. You staggered to the bathroom with my help, but you were asleep on your feet before we made it back again."

Sigrid frowned. "I don't remember." She shuffled upright in the bed, and Missie fussed over her, rearranging pillows and straightening blankets.

"Don't move from there," Missie said. "There's soup warming on the stove, and I'll fetch it."

At the mention of food, Sigrid's stomach rumbled. Missie returned with a large mug. "Doctor Chappell said to start you on clear liquids first, so it's chicken broth."

Wrapping both hands around the mug, Sigrid breathed in the delicious aroma. "It smells wonderful." She took a cautious sip, careful not to burn her tongue, while Missie hovered nearby. With a sigh, Sigrid swallowed and closed her eyes as the hot liquid flowed down her throat. She took another sip and smiled her gratitude. When the soup was gone, Missie took it away and returned with a refill. This time, she resumed her sewing.

Sigrid carefully set the mug aside when it was empty again. "What are you making?"

"I'm putting together squares for an appliquéd quilt," Missie said. "I don't suppose you've ever seen anyone working with appliqué before." She reached for a small pair of golden scissors and snipped the thread before laying aside the needle. "This design is a repeated motif – a daisy, in different colourways. All the smaller pieces must be in the right place before machining. That's why I'm hand stitching the flowers onto the background first."

With a flourish, Missie held up the completed panel. Sigrid sank back onto the pillows, wide-eyed and breathless, as she stared at the blue, yellow and red daisy with the red centre. *That's impossible!* She closed her eyes and waited for the room to stop dancing.

A Tricky
Conversation

∞ ☼ ∽

Romans 1:16a WEB - For I am not ashamed of
the Good News of Christ, because it is
the power of God for salvation
for everyone who believes.

∞ ☼ ∽

When Sigrid reopened her eyes, Kurt – her brother-friend-companion – was seated in the chair. A wave of heat rushed through her, and she wrestled with the covers.

Kurt reached across and tugged on the bedding. "Mum said she 'tucked you in tight'."

With a shove, Sigrid threw off the covers and pushed herself upright. She swung her feet onto the floor and stood, only to sit in a hurry. A wild glance around the room confirmed three things. It was dark outside. Kurt was the only person present. All evidence of the quilting project was gone.

"Take it easy," Kurt said. "If you're that desperate for the bathroom, lean on me, and I'll get you there."

Before he could wrap his arm around her, Sigrid staggered to her feet and lurched towards his vacant chair. "I don't need your help." She stumbled across the space towards the bathroom and slammed the sliding door behind her. She had chosen the worst hiding place. Despite the thick socks she wore, the tiles beneath her feet were icy.

Shivering uncontrollably, she pushed towards the connecting door to the next bedroom. Sigrid fell through as she shoved the barrier aside. The floor loomed towards her, and her shoulder screamed as she grabbed for the bedpost. Catching her breath, she surveyed the room. There was a small suitcase next to this bunk. A police uniform hung from the hook behind the door that led to the hallway. Why was Kurt staying *here?*

Move! Sigrid made it to the dining room before her legs refused to carry her further. She seized a chair and collapsed with her head on the table. It was several minutes before she realised there was bunched fabric beneath her face. Slowly, she lifted her head. Piles of decorated squares covered the table. As she pulled herself upright, she glanced at the blue, yellow and red daisy panel scrunched within her hand.

Before she could fling it from her, Kurt appeared at her side. He pressed her back onto the chair while prising her fingers apart to rescue the square.

"Do you know what this is?" she hissed.

Kurt glanced across the table. "My sister phoned me. She wants me to get Muriel and Mum to abandon their 'new project'. I told her I might as well try and stop the wind." Then he frowned. "How did you know? They said you were asleep."

"I heard enough. Your family still think we're getting married!"

"I've told them you want a long engagement."

🜂☼ɣ

Kurt left Sigrid at the dining table and beat a hasty retreat to the kitchen where he grabbed the counter. After taking several calming breaths, he went to the saucepan on the stove.

"Do you want to eat there, or can you make it to the breakfast bar?"

Busy spooning the thick vegetable soup into two bowls, he waited until he heard the stool dragging on the tiled floor. "If you can keep this soup down, there's stewed apples and hot custard for dessert."

When he turned, Sigrid was already sitting at the bar with her eyes fixed on the bowl he was carrying. She snatched it from his hands and reached for a spoon, but then she hesitated. "I'm starving. Hurry up, or I'll start eating without you."

Hastily he retrieved the hot bread rolls from the oven. After dropping them onto a plate, he carried them over, along with his bowl. Sigrid's green eyes did not leave him. Still, her spoon lay untouched on the counter. Why was she waiting?

"I don't know how to say grace," she muttered.

"Oh – umm – right," Kurt said. "Ah, thanks, God, for this food." He took another breath. "Thank you that Sigrid is well enough to eat it. Please help her to recover her strength—"

"Amen," Sigrid said, snatching a bread roll and dipping it into her soup. "I'm hungry enough to eat yours too, so you'd better keep up."

"Thanks for the warning." The soup was delicious, but it was impossible not to stare as she wolfed down her portion. When she took up a third roll and reached for his half-finished bowl, he leapt to retrieve the saucepan from the stove.

"Wait," she said, taking the saucepan from his hand after he filled her bowl to the brim. She used the bread to wipe all traces of soup from the metal surface before she surrendered the empty vessel to him.

"How long are you staying?" she asked a few minutes later.

He glanced sideways, confirming that her bowl was empty again. Pulling away to protect what remained of his soup, he moved until the counter stood between them. "The doctor made me promise not to leave you alone until you've fully recovered."

"Then why are you sleeping in a separate room?"

"Muriel is coming at eleven to watch you while I get some sleep."

"I don't need anyone to watch me," Sigrid said. "I'm not going anywhere."

"You're not going to be left alone, nor are you going anywhere until you're wearing a replacement locket. I'm expecting a courier delivery before the weekend."

"What happened to the old locket?" Sigrid asked. Her fingers twitched, but she refrained from reaching for the missing ornament.

"The camera failed, but the audio provided enough clues for us to find you before you fell into the river."

Sigrid closed her eyes. A single tear trickled down her cheek. "There was no river."

She staggered to her feet. Kurt followed her through the archway. With a single movement, she swept all the appliquéd squares into her arms. Before he could intervene, Sigrid carried them into the main room. By the time he caught up with her, the carpet was littered with colourful fabric. Sigrid sat on a sofa with her head in her hands. He gingerly stepped between the flowers until he stood beside her. With his heart pounding, he dropped onto the sofa, placing an arm around her shoulder.

With a shudder, Sigrid leaned against him, wrapping both arms around him. Her body shook as she surrendered to her tears. After a few minutes, the weeping woman grew rigid in his arms, and he released her. He handed her the box of tissues from a side table, and she shuffled sideways, pulling the oversized tee-shirt down around her bare knees. This action was her first acknowledgement about what she was, or – more importantly for his quaking heart – what she was *not* wearing.

Kurt retrieved a hand-crocheted rug from the adjacent armchair. After draping it over her legs, he said, "I'll go and reheat the apple." He didn't wait for a response.

Upon his return, he paused in the doorway. Sigrid was on the sofa, examining a selection of squares. He carried across the tray, and when she emptied her hands, he placed it carefully on her lap. After returning with a smaller share of dessert, he lowered himself to her feet, analysing her behaviour while he ate. He shoved his empty bowl aside and reached for one of the flower panels.

"Thank you," Sigrid said, stretching out her hand to take the yellow daisy panel from him. "For dinner – and everything. You're a true friend."

I want to be more than a friend. He squeezed his eyes shut.

"Pass me another one."

Blindly, he scrambled with his fingers, passing the unseen fabric to her.

Her laughter surprised him, as did the fingers that tussled his hair. "I didn't ask for a third one, but your selection has only confirmed what I already knew." First, she waved a blue daisy towards him. "I've never had a brother." Then a red daisy flapped in his upturned face. "I thought I worked better alone, but it looks like I'm stuck with you."

"What are you talking about?"

"While I was sleeping, I had a visit from Wisdom. Each of these flowers represents a relationship. If I'm to recover, I'm going to need them all. I'm not just talking about recovering from this recent trouble. Wisdom said this healing dealt with anything that has ever wounded me: my broken family, the trauma from my military career, my struggles with civilian life. Everything. If I hadn't woken up to this quilt, I'd have written it off as a dream."

While his mind wrestled for a rational explanation for her words, an unplanned question escaped his lips. "Why were you crying?"

"You ask too many questions. I'm going back to my room. While I'm taking a shower, you can clean up this mess."

Trying
to Stay Safe

ℬ ☼ ℭ

Job 23:10a WEB -
But He knows the way I take.

ℬ ☼ ℭ

Sigrid leaned in the window of the patrol car. "Kurt, stop worrying." She gestured at the empty stretch of road ahead of them. "That nosy inspector isn't going to find me in the middle of nowhere."

"It doesn't feel right—" Kurt muttered.

"Tim Chappell said I could go for an extended walk, and you agreed this was the best option. You drop me here, and I'll make my way to the crossroad where you can pick me up on your return."

"How can I be sure that you won't break into a run as soon as I'm out of sight?"

Sigrid shoved the locket camera in his face. "Have you forgotten the Melbourne watchdog will call you if I do that? You phoned him twice before we left. Stop acting like an overprotective big brother, and get to your meeting in Brumby's Run."

When Kurt drove away, Sigrid stood by the side of the road until he disappeared from view. Despite her bold assertion, it was hard to move. Taking out her phone, she checked for a non-existent signal, then accessed the map she had already downloaded. Three options would deliver her to his rendezvous. She had not forgotten her original mission to cover all the access roads into Meredith Crossing. If she paced herself, there would be time for a few *detours.*

"It's not running," Sigrid told the unseen watcher as she broke into a slow trot. "I'm going to keep talking to you to prove that I'm not over-exerting myself. Plus, my watch will beep when my heart rate exceeds the doctor's limit. There's a side road coming up on the right..."

Twenty minutes later, Sigrid came to an intersection that would bring her back to the original road. Until now, she had encountered no traffic, and she stepped onto the verge as the approaching noise behind her grew louder. At first glance, Sigrid thought Kurt had doubled back to check on her, but then she recognised her error. "There are two officers in this patrol car," she told the locket.

The vehicle came to a stop beside her, and the window opened. "Sigrid," Helena said from the passenger seat. "What are you doing out here? You don't have the equipment to be hiking. Can we give you a lift somewhere?"

"Hello, Helena." She bobbed down to smile at the driver. "Hi, Des. No, thanks, I don't need a lift. I'm out for a 'gentle stroll', doctor's orders. Kurt dropped me off, and he's picking me up again soon. I wasn't expecting to see anyone on this goat track."

"Are you sure the task force hasn't recruited you to help with the surveying?" Helena asked.

Sigrid glanced around. "What's there to survey out here? Kurt didn't mention—"

"Forget Helena said anything," Des said, revving the engine. "Enjoy your 'stroll'."

The patrol car pulled away in a cloud of gravel. A few seconds later, the brake lights came on, and the vehicle reversed. Helena opened the window again. "Did Sarge tell you how long he was going to be? Even if his Friday meeting ends on time, it's going to be at least an hour before he gets back from Brumby's Run. Tell us where he's picking you up, and we'll take you there."

Sigrid waited a few seconds and leaned closer, lowering her voice. "Do you know for sure he went to Brumby's Run?" She looked left and right. "If he comes looking for me and I'm not where I'm supposed to be..." With a sigh, she shook her head. "I'm trying to earn his trust after Tuesday's debacle." She took a step back. "Your offer is tempting, but I'd better not."

"Suit yourself," Helena said. "See you back in Meredith Crossing."

"Not if I see you first," Sigrid muttered after the vehicle pulled away. "I have a bad feeling about this," she said to the locket. "Why did she want to know where Kurt would be collecting me? It's obvious which roads I'll be taking if he's coming from Brumby's Run."

Shaking her head, Sigrid turned around, retracing her steps. "If Helena was concerned about me, she must know that I don't have a mobile signal here. So why didn't she offer to use the patrol car's boosted signal to check with him? It's a good thing this locket has a satellite transmitter." Her feet settled into a rhythm, the pace increasing to a slow canter. "I'm heading for that alternate route. The one Kurt dismissed because it crosses the river. I know, I know. I'm supposed to stay away from the river. In case this is another one of my blunders, tell Kurt I'm sorry."

Alternating between jogging and running, Sigrid searched for an elusive intersection. A growing sense of urgency pushed her onward, but she kept a close eye on the readings on her watch. She hadn't dressed for intense exercise, but her feet were comfortable in the lightweight shoes. With her long-sleeved over-shirt tied around her waist, the only discomfort was where the denim jeans rubbed against the scar on her leg.

From Kurt's briefing, she knew the road provided access to a well-patronised forest reserve, so it should be in good condition. Finally, a side road appeared up ahead, and she sprinted to the corner. After confirming there were tracks in the gravel to support his account, Sigrid abandoned the open road for the tree-lined winding track leading into the hills.

Approximately ten kilometres into her detour, Sigrid arrived at the entrance to the reserve. She paused to catch her breath. "Recent tracks – big truck? – maybe a bus?" Leaning down, she scanned an image of the tyre tread with her phone before tracing them with her fingertips to aid her memory. "Came down – that hill. I'd better – start – climbing."

She walked up the middle of the road. With her feet parallel to the wheel marks she was following, Sigrid went up the first hill, jogged down into a shadowy gully and then paced herself to the top of a steeper climb. "Hope I – see – the river – soon."

An observation bay marked where the road touched the sky. It had parking space for a couple of cars. She hurried towards the safety rail and swore. The road snaked down to the valley, all sharp turns and heart-stopping descents. Far below, the narrow bridge straddled a swollen river spread across the floodplain.

"This road was only – a wavy line – on the – map."

蜴☼⁊

The phone concealed in Kurt's pocket buzzed again. He glanced at the clock on the wall. The meeting was due to finish in ten minutes, and they were only halfway through the agenda items. He wrote the time on the paper in front of him.

"Are we keeping you from something, Sergeant Jensen?" Superintendent Bellamy asked, frowning at him across the table. Before Kurt could answer, the door opened, and a red-faced constable burst into the room.

"Excuse the interruption, Sir," the constable said, "but Senior Sergeant Jensen hasn't been responding to his messages. I've had a Chief Superintendent from Sydney on the phone demanding immediate action."

Kurt grabbed his paperwork from the table, nodded a silent apology to his colleagues and left the flustered constable to deal with any questions. He retrieved his phone, frowning at the caller ID before racing to the car park. By the time the phone connected him to Melbourne, his patrol car was zooming away from Brumby's Run with the lights and siren activated.

Without preamble, the *Maximum Security* duty officer launched into his report. "Sigrid is safe but has requested retrieval. I'm sending you the coordinates. I'll call you if anything changes."

Kurt clicked through the backlog of four messages. A photo of Constables Avery and Wilmot accompanied the first.

Sigrid taking evasive action after encounter with known antagonists. Confirming alternate route via forest reserve & river
New rendezvous requested – ETA?
Medical limit exceeded – ETA?

He wove between traffic, accelerating on the straight sections until he neared the side road he needed. After making the turn at speed, he roared along the connector, alert for the next junction. A cloud of dust billowed behind him.

The phone rang, but it was not the Melbourne man.

"What's the emergency, Ben," Kurt asked.

"Where are you?"

"I'm on my way back."

"Is Sigrid with you?"

Ben didn't wait for an answer. "I've had several reports about suspicious vehicles in the vicinity of the forest reserve."

"I'm listening."

"Two dark SUVs with tinted windows almost ran one of the Brumby's Run school buses off the road. I've despatched Avery and Wilmot to investigate, but the suspect vehicles will be long gone by the time they get there."

"Is that all?" Kurt asked, calculating the distance to the next corner, and shifting into a lower gear.

"The bus driver pulled over at the lookout to call it in. He's got a satellite internet connection. While he was on the line, one of the students uploaded a live-stream video of the vehicles. The kid had a zoom lens, and the clarity's amazing – we're watching it now. They're checking the road ahead—"

Ben swore. "A certain redhead is now on centrestage. If the SUVs don't slow, she'll be stranded on the one-lane bridge when they reach her."

"Send me the video link," Kurt said. "I'm putting you on hold."

He waited until the screen registered the incoming message, and then he punched the Melbourne number. The duty officer answered on the second ring. "I'm forwarding a live video link. Does Sigrid know there's traffic approaching?"

"She can hear a vehicle, but she has no visual confirmation. There's no cover. How far away are you?"

"Fifteen minutes."

"I'll notify Piper." *Click.*

Kurt switched back to Ben. "Any change in the situation?"

"The SUVs are slowing down. They must have seen her. Wait, the lead vehicle is driving onto the bridge."

Finger

on

the Trigger

ಖ ☼ ೞ

Isaiah 54:17a WEB -
No weapon that is formed against you
will prevail.

ಖ ☼ ೞ

"I have company," Sigrid said, shrinking against the rail to give herself more room. The bridge was five metres wide, but she wasn't taking any chances. She studied the dark SUV that was roaring towards her. "I hope you can zoom in on that number plate. I don't want to be run over by some anonymous tourist."

The vehicle veered towards her, and she scrambled up the wooden guardrails. The side mirror missed her by a finger's breadth, and then her distorted reflection flashed on the polished surface until the danger passed.

The occupants hid behind tinted windows. She took a breath when the vehicle continued to the end of the bridge. But instead of driving away, the brake lights flashed red, and all momentum ceased.

A woman stepped from the passenger side of the SUV. Distracted by her imminent visitor, Sigrid was taken by surprise when the rails beneath her feet shuddered. She wrenched her head sideways to witness the arrival of a second SUV. This identical vehicle stopped a few metres from her perch.

"I might have to take evasive action," Sigrid said, glancing over her shoulder towards the surging river below.

The doors on the latest arrival remained closed, so Sigrid refocused on the woman. Definitely not a local farmer. Bottle-blonde hair and lots of makeup, a skin-tight dress over a lanky frame, and nightclub-worthy heels. Those bony fingers clutched a cigarette, and smoke rose into the air. When the woman was only a metre away, Sigrid almost toppled from the rail. *My mother!*

"Okay, river," she muttered. "Get ready for me. I might not hang around long enough to hear what she has to say."

Wait.

Wisdom's voice, clear and insistent, came from the opposite side of the bridge yet the dream messenger remained invisible.

"What are you doing here?" Sigrid asked her mother.

"Dar-ling, I was on my way to see you. What a surprise to meet you on the road."

"What do you want?"

"I heard you were ill. Come down from there and meet my friends."

"I don't want anything to do with you – or your friends."

"You always were a stubborn child," her mother said. "You get that from your father. My friends only want to talk to you."

"If you come any closer," Sigrid said, climbing up to the next rail, "I'll jump."

"Come back to the car, Kylie," a voice called from the first SUV.

Kylie walked away without a backwards glance. The woman who spoke stepped out and swaggered towards Sigrid.

"Gina?" Sigrid's stomach cramped. The Melbourne crime family heiress oozed charm, but Sigrid would not be fooled again. "Gina Gregorio?" Oliver's warning that the conspirators were coming after Sigrid had not prepared her for this twist. "How do you know my mother?"

"Kylie's been helping us," the wealthy Melbourne woman said. "You weren't easy to find."

"Why were you looking for me?" Sigrid asked.

"Straight to the point," Gina said. "I like that. Our mutual friend has gone missing, and I believe you're the key to finding her."

"What mutual friend?"

"Don't pretend you know nothing," Gina said. "She always trusted you, and Oliver couldn't have persuaded Sara to run away without your help. Tell me where he's taken her. I only want to confirm her safety."

"Who told you she ran away with Oliver?" Sigrid asked, raising her bottom to the top rail.

Wait!

That voice again.

Perhaps this is a dream? Sigrid wriggled as if to adjust her balance and deliberately pressed her tender leg against the bridge. She frowned as she endured the wave of pain.

"I haven't had any contact with Sara in months, and I've not been talking to Oliver. I don't know anything. You've come all this way for nothing."

"There's more than one way to get information," Gina said. "Which is why I brought reinforcements."

The young woman waved towards the second vehicle. Two dark-haired men, wearing expensive business suits, stepped onto the bridge. Sigrid recognised both their faces. The younger man she had never met. But the scars on her arms and leg were a permanent memorial for Sigrid's past encounter with the other one.

Finally, her enemy was within reach. She silenced the emotional storm as she prepared to attack.

Wait!

The same message but spoken by a different, more powerful voice. The order rumbled from within the clouds and reverberated above the flooded river. Years of submitting to military authority brought an immediate reaction. Glaring at Gina, the red-haired warrior cancelled her planned offensive. The other woman showed no sign that she heard anything.

"Am I supposed to know who these men are?" Sigrid asked.

"You don't recognise me, Sigrid?" the older man said. "I'm disappointed. I was sure Piper would have ordered his agents to watch for me. I'm Ricardo Barononi, but my friends call me Rick."

Sigrid was already familiar with Rick's history, but his physical presence was a significant distraction. There were too many similarities to her employer. She rebuked herself. This man might share the same Italian-Australian heritage, but Piper would never sneer at her like this.

"You look confused, Sigrid. Didn't Piper fully brief you? Or weren't you listening? Let me remedy that. This is my eldest son, Matteus," Rick said, indicating the younger man. "My cousin Cosima, and my youngest son Quin, are also here."

Two men from the first vehicle now stood beside Gina. "As you can see, you are outnumbered again."

"Again?" Sigrid asked, inviting him to implicate himself for the hidden camera.

"You don't remember?" Rick laughed. "Last time, I left you for dead. You carry the scars on your arms—"

There was no longer any need to conceal her hatred after Rick's confession. "Y-you killed my friend!" She calculated the distance between them.

Wait!

Why should I wait? Revenge is within my reach—

There will be more revelations. Obey me and I will reward your patience and multiply your victories.

While she argued with God, she locked her eyes on her adversary. When a handgun appeared in Rick's hand, Sigrid glanced at the other men. They carried similar weapons.

"Cowards!" she hissed. "If you have me outnumbered, why do you need guns?"

Rick laughed. "I've seen you fight. Only a fool would face you without a weapon."

"Shoot me, then," Sigrid said. "I've made my peace with God. I'm not afraid to die."

"It's premature to talk about dying," Gina said. "After we get the information we need about Sara, Rick's going to sell you to the highest bidder."

A

Few

More Tricks

ಬಿ ☼ ಊ

*Isaiah 30:18c CG - Blessed are all
who wait for the Lord.*

ಬಿ ☼ ಊ

Beep! Beep! Beep! The alarm on Sigrid's smartwatch shrieked.

"What is that?" Gina asked. "Make it stop!"

Sigrid ripped the offending technology from her wrist and flung it towards Gina. "My heart rate must have exceeded the doctor's recommendations. You know I've been ill. I'm *supposed* to be taking it easy."

"Throw the watch into the river," Rick said. "It will include a tracking device. Piper doesn't like to lose his agents."

Gina obeyed. Sigrid followed the watch's progress until it disappeared beneath the surging torrent before returning her focus to her enemy.

"What about her phone?" Gina asked.

Sigrid slipped her hand into her pocket and dropped the phone onto the bridge beneath her feet. "Take it. There's no signal anyway, so it's useless to me."

Gina took a step towards the phone, but Cosima held her back. "Come down off the rail," he said to Sigrid, "and kick the phone over here. We all know you're not going to jump. You're afraid of the water."

"I'm not afraid," Sigrid muttered through her teeth. "I'm following orders." She dropped to the deck of the bridge. With precision, her foot flicked the phone into the air, launching it towards him.

Cosima dodged the missile, and it smashed against the side of the bridge behind him. Cosima took a step closer but Rick waved him away.

"Leave her to me," Rick said. "First, I'm going to prepare a message for Piper. Sigrid, do you play chess?"

His free hand dipped into his pocket. When it reappeared, it was full of familiar playing pieces.

Rick tucked his gun into his trousers before sorting through the carved figures to select a white knight. "Sigrid, you are one of Piper's warriors."

He passed the object to Matteus, who sat the ivory chess piece on the riser supporting the wooden rails.

"You may be expendable," Rick said, "but that won't stop him searching the river for your body."

Then he handed a black queen and a white rook to Matteus. "Did Piper think I'd forget that he stole my queen, the woman you call Jezebel? When I retrieve her, I'll also eliminate her protector and destroy Samson's *Mountain Rise* sanctuary."

Sigrid froze, silently praying as the queen and rook came to rest on the bridge below the white knight.

This locket had better be working. There's more than Jez—

Her name is Ruth.

Oh-kay, Ruth is not the only one in danger if he attacks *Mountain Rise.*

Rick considered the remainder in his hand. He dropped the white king onto the bridge and stomped on it with his heel.

Crack!

When he raised his shiny black shoe, the broken fragments fell apart. "Without Piper, his army will scatter." Tossing the other chess pieces aside, Rick waited until Sigrid returned her attention to his hand. He held up the white bishop. "Then the little prophetess will be mine—"

No! Not Evie!

Sigrid pressed against the side of the bridge, calculating how much room she would need to manoeuvre. But before she launched her attack, the door on the closest vehicle opened, and when she saw who stepped out onto the bridge, she grabbed the rail in disbelief. Samson's half sister, Kimberly Kidman!

"I told you to stay in the car," Matteus said, spinning towards the newcomer.

"Your father left me his phone," Kimberley said, waving the device in his face. "There's no signal out here, but the car booster gave me two bars. I have a message for you, Rick, from your police snitch. Kurt Jensen left Brumby's Run early, and he's on his way to rescue her."

"How does he know she needs rescuing?" Matteus asked.

"That school bus stopped at the top of the hill," Kimberley said, pointing behind her.

"Some kid sent a video link to the police. They must have had a zoom lens because Sigrid was easy to identify as she ran onto the bridge. You're lucky, though. The signal failed. They only know that she's got unexpected company."

"This changes everything," Cosima said. "We need to leave now."

"I haven't finished with Sigrid," Rick said. "Quin, give Gina your gun and take Kim to the lead car."

"What about my bags?" Kim asked, trying to free herself from Quin's grip.

"Quin will give you cash to replace what you're leaving behind," Rick said. "Now go. You won't get anything if that policeman catches you with us." Kimberley stopped struggling, and Quin hustled her away. Rick turned to Cosima. "You should have time to get off this road before Jensen makes the turn. Take Kim to the drop-off point, but be careful – don't let anyone see her with you."

"I'm always careful," Cosima muttered, stalking back to the lead SUV and driving away.

"Samson won't let Kim on the mountain," Sigrid said. "She ruined her chances when she sold her kids."

Rick laughed. "She's not going to the mountain. Kurt's sister told Kim you've bewitched him and begged her to come back. She'll be waiting to offer Kurt a shoulder to cry on when you're gone. Once Kim gets her claws into him, all the mountain's secrets will be mine. I win, whether I take you dead or alive."

Now!

"There's a third option," Sigrid said and leapt into the air.

ॐ ✿ ೮

Narrowly avoiding a collision with a guidepost, Kurt slowed the patrol car to negotiate the next bend. His phone chirped, and the Melbourne officer came back on the line.

"Sigrid survived the initial encounter, and she's talking with the occupants of the vehicles. They don't know she's recording them, and their identities have been confirmed.

"We also intercepted the video feed from the kid on the bus, and we're the only ones who can see— Wait, there's another woman. She's delivering a message. They know you're on your way. The suspects are splitting up. One group is trying to get to the intersection before y—"

The duty officer swore.

Kurt's hand jerked the wheel, and he headed for the ditch. As he corrected his angle, he resisted the urge to reduce his speed. His heart pounded in his chest. "What happened?"

"I'm sorry. Suddenly her screen filled with sky, and then muddy water was rushing at me. I rewound the bus kid's video, and it shows Sigrid doing an incredible backwards somersault.

"She cleared the bridge railing by at least a metre before diving into the river. Her captors shot at Sigrid while she was in the air, but I can't tell if she's been hit. Sigrid's screen shows nothing but swirling mud. Two of the shooters are leaning over the rail, firing into the water."

"I'll get the SES—"

"NO!" yelled the Melbourne duty officer.

Kurt rammed his foot on the brake. "Why not?"

"You can't tell anyone you know what's happening. There's a traitor on your team. I'll try and organise reinforcements from this end. While I'm on the other line, I'll connect you to Sigrid's audio—"

The sound of rushing water flowed from the dashboard speaker until it wrapped around him. How long would the locket continue to transmit? Kurt increased his speed, praying for one of "Evie Romano's miracles".

CHAPTER 41
(Friday 1st June)

Try
Anything Once

෨ ✿ ෪

Mark 11:24b CG - Whatever you ask for in prayer,
believe that you have received it,
and what you asked for will be yours.

෨ ✿ ෪

Time seemed to stand still when Sigrid leapt into the air. She filled her lungs, rejoicing in her freedom. When she reached the apex of her trajectory, she caught a glimpse of the surprised expressions on her enemies' faces before she arched her back to fling her body out over the water. She twisted her head so that she could still see what was happening on the bridge.

Sigrid's weight pulled her down, the rushing water ready to possess her. Her adversaries stretched out their hands as if they hoped to halt her progress. Then she saw the fiery flashes, and the worst kind of fear awoke within her. Searing pain exploded across her shoulder. She blocked that part of her mind, refusing to acknowledge her mortality.

The cold water embraced her, and then time sped up to reclaim those reckless moments. Agony from her folly registered everywhere. The rushing torrent tore at her flailing body. Every survival instinct kicked in, compelling her to rise. Yet certain death awaited her if she did so. Forcing herself deeper, she tried to conserve her strength by going with the flow.

Aarrgghh! Sigrid crashed against a submerged tree. Precious bubbles of air escaped from her lungs. She wrapped her arms around the trunk, struggling to see through the murky depths. What looked like a large clump of massed leaves appeared at the limit of her range, and she headed in that direction. It cost her dearly to fight against the current.

God! Where is your promised help?

Suddenly, the river bottom pressed against her feet and a spark of hope drove her forward. The water became brighter, the pull of the current easier to resist. Finally, Sigrid came to the place where a leafy crown rose above the waves. Pushing her body among the extensive foliage, she lifted her eyes out of the water.

In every direction, all she could see was greenery. Clinging to the life-saving branch, Sigrid raised her chin and sucked in air. She had been shot in the back, but was there an exit wound? When she could convince her body to obey, she looked down at her chest. She blinked at the bloody mess – the bullet had passed straight through, shredding her shoulder and leaving a fist-sized open wound. The forbidden pain reawakened.

Gritting her teeth, Sigrid reached for her belt. Instead, her fingers encountered the shirt tied around her waist. After fighting to free the knot, Sigrid grasped part of a sleeve in her teeth. The fabric ripped, and she shoved the scrunched bundle into the exit wound in her flesh. She couldn't reach where the bullet had entered. After binding the bundle in place with the rest of the shirt, she parted the leaves to survey the landscape.

The bridge overshadowed her position. The tree that protected her stuck out from between two boulders at an extreme angle to the surging water. Without realising it, she had taken herself back towards her enemies.

Rick leaned over the rail. "Can you see her?"

"Not yet," a voice replied. Sigrid twisted her head. A hundred metres past her position, Matteus stood on the riverbank surveying the water through a pair of binoculars. "She must have been carried further down."

"Keep looking," a third voice cried. Gina appeared beside Matteus, carrying her spiky-heeled shoes. "She's a military hero, trained to survive. She's probably holding her breath and laughing at us."

"I'm sure I hit her," Matteus muttered. "I expected to find her floating on the surface."

"Wait another five minutes, and then come back," Rick said. "Even a hero can't hold their breath for that long."

ෆ ☼ св

When Kurt reached the intersection, his tyres skidded on the gravel as he wrestled for control after making the turn. The realisation that he'd exceeded his previous top speed by twenty kilometres per hour brought him no comfort. He glanced in the mirror at the spray of mud and gravel that signalled his passage. When he refocused on the straight stretch ahead, he noticed a low cloud approaching. The advancing storm had a black dot at its centre. A speeding vehicle occupied the middle of the road with no indication that it would yield to his flashing lights.

Kurt identified two shadowy figures through the vehicle's windscreen just before he wrenched his steering wheel to the left. His patrol car abandoned the road, launching itself towards a sagging barbed wire fence. The bucking vehicle careened through low scrub into a small clearing.

Without pause, he spun the wheel and headed back to the flattened wooden posts. After surveying the road in both directions, Kurt silenced both his siren and the engine. Sigrid's river transmission flooded his senses as he searched for the mute button. Holding his breath, he wound down the window. It took precious seconds to shut out the pounding at his temples and focus on the real world.

There was no evidence of an approaching second vehicle. Satisfied that he had this stretch of gravel to himself, Kurt drove back onto the road and accelerated again. He left the siren off.

He called the Meredith Crossing Police Station. "Log this call. One of the suspect vehicles ran me off the road. I didn't get the registration number. I'm not sure if the second SUV is ahead of me, so I'm proceeding with caution."

"Do you need backup?" Ben asked.

"I'll let you know after I get to the bridge. Sigrid might be fine. Concentrate your efforts on tracking these SUVs. I want someone charged for damaging my patrol car."

Kurt broke the connection. With the accelerator pedal flat to the floor, his vehicle surged forward. He hated lying to Ben – at this speed, the bridge was only ten minutes away. He wrestled with his conscience as he reactivated Sigrid's transmission. He increased the speaker volume, straining to hear anything other than gurgling water over the roar of his engine.

"Speak to me," he muttered. "I need to know you're alive."

The single-lane bridge lay at the end of a long straight, approximately three kilometres ahead. Kurt could see the outline of the sign that asked drivers to give way to oncoming traffic. The road ahead was empty. So much for his plan to catch Sigrid's attackers unawares.

He attempted to elicit more speed from the labouring engine. About five hundred metres before he reached the signpost, a dark figure stepped out from the trees. The man raised his arm towards the patrol car, and then there was a sudden flash of light. Kurt had no time to take evasive action.

PING! Long cracks like a spider's web spread across the windscreen, fracturing his forward view.

BANG! Ker-chunk-thwak-thwak– BANG! Chunker-chunker-chunker...

The patrol car bucked – the second and third shots must have taken out two tyres. Kurt clung to the steering wheel, fighting to stay away from the protective barrier on the right, as he eased his foot from the accelerator.

CRACK-whee-PING!

The left rear passenger window shattered, and something whistled past his ear. A fist-sized hole appeared in the windscreen's safety glass, surrounded by a blizzard of tiny cracks. Kurt flinched, and the steering wheel jerked to the right, slamming the vehicle into the solid guardrail that preceded the bridge.

BANG! The patrol car leapt into the air as if it were a child's toy in the hands of a giant. The sky was no longer where it should be. The horizon tilted at an impossible angle. Kurt banged his head on the side window, and then the seatbelt grabbed him as his body lurched forward.

POW-phhsssoooo! When the patrol car stopped rocking, Kurt battled the deflating airbag, hoping that the spinning multi-coloured flashes in his vision would cease. His ears were ringing, and as he attempted to raise himself from the driver's-side window, he struggled to breathe.

Please, God. Make the shooter leave...

ଫ ✿ ଓ

How did he get onto the bridge? Kurt pulled himself upright and clung to the wooden rail. He looked around, puzzled about the throbbing sound that filled the air. Only when a violent wind wrenched him off his feet did he look in the right direction.

An approaching helicopter flew low over the bridge, passing him as it followed the flooded river. The machine swung around in a wide arc and came back towards him. After hovering, the aircraft landed in the middle of the road, blocking the bridge.

The rotor blades were still coming to a stop when the pilot opened the door and hurried towards him. A spark of recognition flickered in Kurt's mind. What was Oliver Johnston doing here? Kurt rubbed his hands across his eyes to clear his vision – there was blood on his fingers.

He looked back over his shoulder to where he expected to find his patrol car. Scanning the area, he spotted the rear of the vehicle precariously perched on the wrong side of the safety barrier. Kurt frowned, trying to remember what had happened.

Oliver leaned closer and studied Kurt's face. "You'll live. Let's get Sigrid—"

Kurt drew back and pointed to the helicopter. "You can't park there."

Shaking his head, Oliver frowned up to the sky. "I could do with some help here, Lord. Not that I want to tell You what to do, but if Kurt could come to his senses anytime soon, it would make my job easier. As always, I'm thankful in advance."

"Do you always talk to God like that?" Kurt asked as the fog suddenly lifted. He recalled his primary mission and ran to the rail. "Sigrid's out there somewhere. Why did you land?"

"She's within metres of the bridge," Oliver said, bobbing down to pick up some objects scattered beside the rails. He continued to talk as he stuffed the unseen items into his jumpsuit pockets. "I flew past several times to triangulate her position. She must be hidden within the trees snagged among those boulders."

Together, they made their way to the farther end of the bridge. Clambering down to the river's edge was difficult.

"What are you doing here?" Kurt asked. "Have you flown from Melbourne?"

"No, I was already near. An hour ago, I delivered a guest into Samson's care at *Mountain Rise*. When your SOS came, I turned around."

"Did you see the two SUVs?"

"No. When I arrived, there was only you. I've been talking to the duty officer in Melbourne, and he brought me up to speed. By the way, Sigrid's locket is still transmitting water sounds, but the video's failed."

Oliver had an electronic device in his hand. Pausing on the bank, he pointed towards the tangled trees. "Start there," he said to Kurt. "Unless you have a spare uniform in your car, you'd better strip off. If we're to convince anyone that you couldn't find Sigrid, you can't get your uniform wet. I've got a rope to keep you from being swept away."

Kurt frowned. "I'm still shaky after the crash. Nothing you've said makes sense." His hands fumbled with his uniform. "Why am I going in the water?"

"I can't trust you to be my anchorman," Oliver said. "Besides, you're the one who lost Sigrid, so it makes sense for you to risk your neck fishing her out."

The water flowed too fast for Kurt to maintain his balance. He gave up the plan to wade closer before he tried to swim. With flailing arms, he pushed across the current towards his goal. He was underwater more often than he was afloat. When he came within reach, he grabbed a branch and pulled himself above the flow.

"Sigrid," he called, shoving the leaves aside and searching the shadows for some sign of movement. A pale white limb flapped for a second before disappearing beneath the muddy water. "I've found her," Kurt called out to Oliver.

Trial and Error

꙰ ✿ ꙰

*Psalm 9:1 CG - I will give thanks to the Lord
with my whole heart.
I will tell of all Your marvellous works.*

꙰ ✿ ꙰

Sigrid! Sigrid! Wake up!

Something cold and wet slapped Sigrid's face, and she gasped. Her arms flopped into the air as she tried to release herself from whatever held her captive. A moment later, she remembered where she was, but it was too late. The sudden movement dislodged her from her precarious perch. The swirling brown water pulled her down as she floated free from her sanctuary. With her remaining strength, she pushed up towards the surface, coughing and spluttering.

"Sigrid!"

Her heart leapt, and she searched for her rescuer. "Kurt!" she cried, splashing towards him.

He wrapped his arms around her body as she hugged him with her good arm and nestled her head against his bare shoulder. Then she felt a sideways tug. Glancing towards the riverbank, Sigrid almost wept to see Oliver there, pulling on a taut rope that spanned the distance between them.

When they reached solid ground, Kurt loosened his grip as if he intended to pass her to Oliver. "Don't you dare, Kurt Jensen," she muttered, squeezing him tighter. "I'm not letting *him* carry me. He couldn't wait to be rid of me before. I'm your responsibility. So let me play the damsel in distress for a little longer. I'm going to close my eyes and pretend you're taking me home."

"What do you mean, 'a little longer'?" Kurt asked.

Oliver spoke from behind them. "She has to disappear."

"Then I'll go with her," Kurt said. "I promised to take care of her."

He laboured up the embankment. Sigrid opened her eyes and looked for the helicopter. "You can put me down, Kurt. I can manage the rest of the way." She reached for the rail, and he staggered as she dropped from his arms. "Get dressed while Oliver patches me up."

Without looking back, Sigrid pulled herself along using the bridge rails. Oliver slid the cabin door open, and she threw herself across the gap to grab the doorframe.

"Your shoulder's a mess," Oliver said, hoisting her into the cabin. "It looks like you've lost a lot of blood."

"I'm not dead yet," Sigrid said. "But tell your God I'd like to keep it that way. He promised me victory, and I'm not feeling it."

"Tell Him yourself," Oliver said, rummaging in the first aid kit. She flinched when he applied pressure to her shoulder and then started securing the padded dressing with tape. "And while you're at it, ask Him to deal with Kurt. That man's not letting me take you without a fight."

"Don't hurt hi—" Her protest was derailed by a sudden pain in her uninjured arm.

"You're going to sleep for a while," Oliver said, depressing the plunger on a large syringe attached to the needle in her arm. "You have sixty seconds to say what you need to say to Kurt."

She could already feel the powerful drug affecting her thoughts as she dragged herself towards the open door. Kurt leaned into the cabin. He was fully dressed now, concern written across his face.

"Don't say anything," Sigrid said, reaching for him and pulling herself upright to lean into his arms. "Promise not to forget me." His lips parted, and she silenced his response with a lingering kiss. Already her fingers and toes were tingling, and a heaviness washed over her. She could feel herself slipping away. "I'm sorry," she whispered.

ಬಂ ✿ ಶ

"Sarge! Can you hear me?"

Kurt's eyes fluttered open. He stared into the familiar faces of two of his officers, but he couldn't recall their names. He rubbed his eyes before attempting to stand. Rough hands shoved him back to the ground. "Wait for the ambulance, Sarge. You've banged your head. For the last ten minutes, you've been drifting in and out of consciousness."

"Sigrid?" he said, trying to see past them. "Where's Sigrid?"

They glanced at each other. "We're sorry, Sarge, but she jumped in the river."

"No-o!" He searched his memory. "There was someone else here. He took her—"

"Take it easy, Sarge. We've called out the SES, and they won't stop searching the river until they find her."

"She's not in the river."

"Stay with him," one officer said to the other. "I'll see what's keeping that ambulance."

The next time the darkness lifted, two frowning ambulance officers were tightening the straps that bound Kurt to a stretcher. "Do you know who you are?" one of them asked.

He dutifully recited his full name, rank, station and identification number.

"Do you remember what happened to you?"

Kurt blinked away the image of a helicopter parked on the bridge. *Focus.* "My patrol car left the road – I must have hit my head."

"We're taking you to the hospital in Newcastle."

"Can I talk to one of my officers first?" An ambulance officer left and returned with Constable Briggs.

"You wanted to talk to me?" Clifford asked.

"You said Sigrid went in the river. How do you know that? Was there a witness?"

"One of the Brumby's Run school buses was parked up on the lookout. The students had a clear view of the drama. Those kids saw her jump."

"Were they still there when I arrived?" Kurt asked.

Clifford frowned and shook his head. "The driver turned the bus around and left after Sigrid jumped. He said he received a phone call from the police, but we can't identify who called him."

"What about video?"

"Your body camera's missing. We were hoping you might remember what happened."

Kurt began to shake his head, and pain smashed him into stillness.

"The dashboard camera on your patrol car shows nothing after the crash but the river," Clifford said. "We did think we had a video from the lookout. One of the kids live-streamed the event, but it didn't record like it was supposed to. There was a glitch with the server too, and it didn't save there either. But we don't think it would have helped anyway. The signal cut out before Sigrid jumped."

"So you don't have any evidence other than the witness accounts from the lookout? Nobody knows what happened after the bus left and the first responders arrived to find me?"

"Afraid not."

It was Kurt's turn to frown. "I'm almost certain there was a man with a gun standing near the 'No Passing' sign when I arrived."

"We'll check it out. Any idea who?"

"I don't think Sigrid's attackers left until after I arrived. Find out where they were hiding."

"Right, Sarge." Clifford turned to leave and then came back. "How did they know you were coming?"

"I want to know why they let me live."

⁊ ☯ ∵

Impatient to be released from the Newcastle hospital emergency department, Kurt listened to the conversations buzzing around him. His bed was in a corner cubicle, with the curtains drawn. It had been several hours since he returned from having a scan. The preliminary results confirmed that he was suffering a "mild case of concussion". During the long wait, other patients had arrived. It sounded as if the on-duty resident was too much in demand. But what concerned Kurt the most was that nobody ever seemed to be discharged.

The curtain whooshed aside to admit three people. One of them was the nurse assigned to monitor his vital signs. She swished the curtains closed and stood with her back to the opening. There was something in the way she held herself that reminded him of Sig— Kurt closed down that thought and focused on the two men.

"Sergeant Jensen," said the older doctor, glancing up from the clipboard in his hands. "I'm Douglas Willowfield, Head of General Medicine, and I'll be taking care of you while you're with us. We're waiting for a bed, and then you'll be taken upstairs to the ward."

"I thought I was going home," Kurt said, glaring towards the resident who hovered in the background. "It's *just* a bump to the head. A few hours observation—"

"Ah," Dr Willowfield said. "That prognosis came *before* we got your toxicology results. A police officer is waiting upstairs to interview you."

"Interview me about what?" Kurt asked.

Dr Willowfield rechecked his clipboard before passing it to the resident. "In the notes, Sergeant Jensen said he had pain between his shoulder blades. Let's take a look." Both doctors approached, and Kurt endured their examination. "Ah, yes. Exactly as I predicted. See that circular bruise with the darker spot in the centre? That looks like a puncture mark from an injection."

The junior doctor mumbled something. Kurt closed his eyes to hide his reaction. What had Oliver done to him?

The older man continued, "It takes a few hours for the bruise to develop, so there's no need to apologise for having *overlooked* it." Without waiting for a further response, Dr Willowfield swept from the room. The red-faced resident nodded to Kurt and hurried past the attendant nurse.

"What was that about?" Kurt asked the nurse, reading her nametag. Macy busied herself gathering his possessions.

She turned with his folded uniform in her hands. "The Inspector upstairs is impatient to see you."

Kurt submitted to wheelchair transport towards his "new room" on the fourth floor. The silent nurse hesitated for a few seconds when they emerged from the elevator. "The Inspector," Macy said in a low voice, indicating the plain-clothes officer chatting with the nurses at the ward reception desk, "watch yourself with him." She rolled the chair towards Tobias Lester-Angevin. "He marched into Emergency, issuing orders like he was our lord and master. If Doctor Willowfield hadn't been in the hospital, the Inspector might have whisked you away without a thought for your recovery."

Room 423 was around the corner from the nurses' station. Lester-Angevin followed Kurt into the private room. He leaned against the wall while Macy surrendered her patient into the care of two colleagues. All three threw veiled glances towards the waiting officer.

"Buzz, if you need anything," one of them said, and then the three women retreated.

"A fine mess you've gotten yourself into, Jensen," Lester-Angevin began, dragging a chair close to the bed. "There are holes in your statement large enough to drive a truck through. What are you trying to hide?"

"My statement contains everything I remember," Kurt said.

"But not everything you know. Why was Sigrid Ericson on that road?"

"Only Sigrid can answer that."

The Inspector frowned. "I'll ask her when you tell me where she is."

"I thought the SES were searching the river?"

"You told the first responders someone took her away."

"I was confused. Surviving a car crash can do that."

"Tell me about the drugs."

"What drugs?" Kurt asked.

Rising to pick up Kurt's medical chart, Lester-Angevin tapped an entry with his finger. "Your tox-screen came back positive for the family of drugs Taskforce Nine is investigating. I'm waiting to hear your explanation."

"I don't have one. You're the first to mention these drugs. Do they explain the truck-sized holes in my memory?"

"A convenient excuse," Lester-Angevin said. "I'm awaiting a search warrant for your police residence and Major Ericson's apartment." Before Kurt could reply, the phone in the Inspector's pocket began to ring. "That will be the authorisation now." The officer identified himself to the caller and then fell silent.

His face turned red, and the Taskforce commander stepped towards the window. "Yes, sir. You've made yourself perfectly clear."

The phone returned to his pocket, and Lester-Angevin strode over to the bed. "I don't know how you managed to get a chief superintendent involved, but you haven't seen the last of me." The Inspector stormed from the room, slamming the door behind him.

The encounter with the Taskforce commander gave Kurt plenty to stew over. But he was no closer to unravelling the tangled threads when the door burst open again. His mother and father entered the room with Muriel McHenry behind them.

"Oh, Kurt," Missie Jensen cried, bursting into tears and wrapping her arms around her son. "They wouldn't tell us anything, and we sat in that waiting room for hours."

"In the end, I called Samson," Muriel said. "He said there was nothing he could do, but fifteen minutes later, a nurse came out and told us where to find you."

"What kind of trouble are you in?" KJ asked.

"I'm not in trouble." Kurt exhaled slowly. "But Sigrid's missing."

Everyone stared at him, but it was Muriel who asked the question. "What do you mean, 'missing'?"

"They're searching the river for her body. I can't tell you anything else."

"Can't or won't?" Muriel asked.

Kurt closed his eyes.

Public Trial

ೞ ☼ ೞ

*Isaiah 32:18 WEB - My people will live in
a peaceful habitation, in safe dwellings
and in quiet resting places.*

ೞ ☼ ೞ

Checking his watch for the third time, Kurt stepped from his Hilux. It had been three days since Sigrid's disappearance. He surveyed the streetscape. Except for the hardware store, every property had For Sale signs plastered on the windows. On the nearer corner sat the struggling petrol station. It was the last surviving fuel outlet in Meredith Crossing. The aging owners could not afford much-needed maintenance, and their sons had left to work in the city.

The adjoining mechanic workshop, a converted blacksmith's forge, had been closed for decades. The locals self-serviced their vehicles, or they drove to Brumby's Run, where Eliza's husband, Bruce "Diesel" Callahan, worked for *Henderson and Sons Auto Mechanics.*

Kurt approached the abandoned Art Deco building that squatted between the smithy and the empty block beside the hardware store. The Co-op property had once been the venue for a movie theatre, a weekly farmers market and half a dozen small shops. It had been closed for thirteen years. The windows were boarded over, and he couldn't see inside. A faded 'For Sale' sign served as a lonely sentry beside the padlocked double doors. He was recalling earlier days of prosperity for his home town when a vehicle stopped at the curb behind him.

"Sorry we're late," Samson said. "We had trouble getting away without Butch and Marco. They wanted to avoid the packing mayhem."

"Your Melbourne guests are still leaving this afternoon?" Kurt asked. "They're not staying for Sigrid's send-off tonight?"

"Too many people," Romano said, unfolding himself from the passenger side of Samson's LandCruiser. "Piper wants us well away by the time he makes his public announcement."

"Did you have any trouble getting time off?" Samson asked, producing a key and heading towards the locked Co-op doors.

"I'm on 'light duties'," Kurt said. "The taskforce has left, so nobody's keeping tabs on me."

Samson unlatched the padlock and removed the chain. The additional door locks required separate keys.

"When you said Romano wanted my input about a property he'd bought," Kurt added, "I thought you meant the service station."

"I've bought that too," Romano said, producing a crowbar and freeing the windows from their wooden shrouds. "And the other vacant properties. I offered to invest in the hardware store to ensure it stayed open, but the owner said my patronage had already increased his profit margin."

Kurt followed Romano and Samson inside. "Why did you buy failed businesses in a dying town?"

"Take a look at this," Samson said, pressing a glossy brochure into his hands. "Romano hasn't seen it yet either, so read it aloud."

Moving towards the dusty window, Kurt began reading. "Operation Phoenix – **RE**deem your past. **EN**ergise your present. **TR**ansform Your future. Located in Meredith

Crossing, in regional New South Wales, the OPERATION PHOENIX REENTRY PROJECT offers world-class rehabilitation, retraining and reintegration services for ex-military personnel, in a tranquil rural setting." His voice fell silent as the implications hit him. "*This* is why Sigrid was here? *REENTRY* was her secret mission?"

"It's your mission now," Samson said. "Piper's nominated you as the project manager. He filed the paperwork last week."

"What do I know about project managing?" Kurt asked. His throbbing headache was back with a vengeance.

"You give orders, and people follow them," Romano said. "You earned my vote when you brought Sigrid into line."

For the next hour, Kurt trailed behind the two men, half-listening to their plans. *REENTRY* was only part of a broader vision.

"If we package this enterprise right," Samson said, "Mrs Mac's dream for economic revival will get a boost."

"Why would Piper be interested—"

"It pays not to question Piper's motivation," Samson said. "Just take on the project."

"A mountain of red tape and a workforce to manage will give your heart time to heal," Romano added.

"I only knew Sigrid for a week," Kurt muttered.

Romano slapped Kurt on the shoulder so hard he had to fight to remain upright. "Evie stole my heart within the first hour. Don't underestimate your feelings."

ଚ୦ ✿ ଓଓ

Kurt was haunted by Romano's words as the day slowly crept towards his evening appointment. Still reeling from the recent revelations, he entered the Top Pub barroom and stopped short. The offer of free food and an open bar tab in Sigrid's honour had guaranteed a crowd, but he was unprepared for this. Among the regular community members were clusters of upset Brumby's Run school students, with their concerned parents in the background. A poignant reminder that Sigrid's dramatic exit had been a public performance.

An awkward silence fell, and space opened around Kurt. Samson met him halfway.

"You look like you need a drink," Samson said, steering him towards the bar.

The interrupted conversations resumed. Harry had a drink ready for him on the counter. "Sigrid's favourite brew," the proprietor said.

Kurt focused on the bottle. Samson edged closer and whispered. "Take it. A few beers won't hurt you."

Harry leaned towards him. "Listen to your mate," Harry said. "These people need to know you're not made of stone." Then the proprietor stepped back and spoke in a louder voice, "I'm sorry she's not here to have one with you."

"Thanks, Harry."

Kurt sipped his beer and surveyed the room. His parents sat at a central table, with Muriel and Old Jack for company. Kurt downed half the drink in a rush before closing the distance between them. Samson came too, but after exchanging a polite greeting, his friend abandoned him. Kurt rested his bottle on the table and dropped into an empty chair.

"You're making a good recovery from your injuries," KJ said, "but don't go the way of Ol' Jack and lose yerself in the bottle."

His mother burst into tears, and Muriel wrapped her arms around her cousin.

Old Jack sprang to Kurt's defence. "You know he's a better man than that. And we're gonna make sure he sticks to the straight 'n' narrow."

"You old coots are worried about nothing," Muriel said. "Kurt's not going to drown himself in booze. He knows he's going to see her again."

Kurt locked his eyes on the table and squeezed the beer bottle.

"You and your future resurrection," KJ said. "Cold comfort to a man with empty arms and a lonely bed."

"They've not found her body," Muriel said. "If anyone could survive, it's our girl. One day, Sigrid will come marching through that door and prove you all wrong. And Kurt will be waiting."

Taking no part in the heated debate, Kurt watched the door. Sigrid's employer was not here yet.

Muriel leaned towards Kurt. "Have you thought about what to say? Harry's signalling for you to come to the microphone."

Kurt drained his beer. "Could you come with me? You knew her better than anyone else."

"I was coming anyway, but it's nice to be asked."

Muriel rose to her feet, and he followed her. With each step, the temptation to make a break for the door intensified. The fractured memories tormented him still. Had he dreamed Oliver and the helicopter? The ongoing silence from the Melbourne pilot was not helping...

Piper Maxwell came through the swinging doors as Kurt reached the bar. The imposing commander headed straight to him, extending his hand. Kurt shook it and then stepped back. Piper nodded to Muriel, and she offered him the microphone, but he signalled for her to proceed.

"Friends and neighbours," Muriel began. "First, let me say that Harry and I are pleased to see such a fine crowd. We've gathered here to honour a recent addition to the family, Sigrid Ericson. It would be better if she were here to speak for herself. But then Harry would've needed to order more beer. Sigrid could drink most of you under the table and still be sober enough to carry you out the door."

Awkward laughter broke out at the back of the crowd.

"Don't hold back the laughter," Muriel said. "Sigrid wouldn't want us to be miserable. She went on her own terms, with her head high, unafraid of the adventure ahead."

"Get on with it, Ma," Harry said from behind the bar. More laughter as she shushed him.

"Pay no heed to Harry. I told Sigrid I'd make a speech at her wedding, and while this isn't that happy occasion, you're going to listen. Sigrid thought she was alone in the world, but me and my cousin, Jack Kidman, are determined to prove her wrong. Just because she had the wrong surname doesn't mean we weren't proud of our newly-discovered relative. She would have made Kurt a good wife and kept him from taking himself too seriously."

A few people shouted their agreement. Kurt longed for the floor to open beneath his feet. His mother's loud sobbing carried across the room. Piper Maxwell leaned against the bar, alert and watchful.

"One more thing, before I get Kurt to speak to you," Muriel said. "I'm going to read you something." She reached into her pocket and pulled out a folded piece of paper. "Love is patient. Love is kind... Love bears all things, believes all things, hopes all things, and endures all things. Love never fails."

Without another word, she held the microphone towards Kurt. Before he could accept it, Piper Maxwell grabbed it.

"Thank you for your kind words, Muriel." After a smattering of applause, everyone fell silent. "My name is Piper, and I am— I *was* Sigrid's boss. When I sent her to Meredith Crossing, I never expected her to capture the attention of your senior police officer. I, too, would have made a speech at their wedding." Piper wrapped an arm around Kurt's shoulder, his eyes scanning the crowd. "You've heard that Sigrid's body hasn't been found. Until proven otherwise, she remains alive to those who loved her. Now Kurt is going to say a few words, and afterwards, I have an announcement to make."

If Piper had released the microphone, Kurt would have dropped it.

"Sigrid packed a lot into her short time with us," Kurt said. "Many of you are unaware that she was a decorated military hero who dedicated her life to defending others. Sigrid was strong and brave, and loyal, but she struggled with ghosts from her past. Perhaps some of those ghosts caught up with her on Friday?"

A lump formed in his throat, and Kurt turned towards the bar. Harry already had a fresh beer ready to press into his hand. Kurt took a long drink, and the crowd seemed to hold their breath. "I can't get her final words out of my mind. She asked me to promise not to forget her. I'm going to make a toast." Kurt raised his drink to the ceiling. "To Sigrid, never forgotten."

"To Sigrid!" echoed the crowd.

Kurt tried to escape, but Piper held him in place.

"I've something that may help Kurt keep his promise." Piper reached into his pocket and brought out a rectangular, royal blue velvet box.

Kurt put down his bottle and opened it. Campaign medals and ribbons rested on a white satin lining in both halves. The inscription on the left bore her father's name and rank, while the crowded section on the right bore Sigrid's name.

"Look after these for her," Piper said.

Kurt nodded. Piper removed the box from his trembling hands and held it up for the crowd to see. With tears in her eyes, Muriel reached for the box. She circulated with it among the eager spectators.

"Kurt has been entrusted with Sigrid's treasured medals," Piper said, "but I'm here to announce a more permanent memorial to her dedication and her sacrifice. Sigrid came to Meredith Crossing to represent an organisation committed to supporting ex-military personnel. Your community has been chosen as the home for *Operation Phoenix's* first brick-and-mortar facility. Kurt will be the acting project manager in Sigrid's absence."

An excited buzz rose from the crowd. Piper held up his hand. "Work on refurbishing the Co-op building will begin at the end of this week..."

CHAPTER 44
(Tuesday 5th June)
Tribulation

୫୦ ✿ ୯୫

*Luke 11:13 CG - If even evil people know
how to give good gifts,
how much more will God give to His children?*

୫୦ ✿ ୯୫

The door to Sigrid's hospital room opened, but she could not roll over to face her visitor. After her last escape attempt, the medical staff had strapped her in place. Her restricted movement was "essential" for her shoulder wound to "drain properly". Footsteps approached the bed. She lay still.

"You haven't learned anything since your last hospital stay," Piper said, dropping into the chair near her head.

Sigrid's eyes flew open. "You can't keep me a prisoner."

"If you obeyed the doctor's orders, these restraints would be unnecessary." Piper held her medical charts in his hand. "Three times you've been back to theatre because you won't lie still. If you try to escape again, they will sedate you."

"How long do I have to stay here?"

"Until I'm satisfied you're fit to leave. You're not the first operative to wake up to these restrictions. But I'm hoping you're a fast learner. It took Jenny almost a year. Perhaps it would help if I told you that the only way out of here is by helicopter."

A stream of poisonous words flowed from her mouth.

Her commander set aside the charts and rose to his feet. "Your temper would improve if you'd accept the pain meds. I'll talk to the doctor and get the prescription changed. While you're strapped down, it will be easier to administer them intravenously. When you're in a better mood, I'll come back and tell you about your memorial service."

"What memorial service?"

"The people of Meredith Crossing had a fine community send-off for you. Free beer and refreshments, and I even made a speech."

"But I'm not dead!"

"Outside of this facility, you are."

"What about Kurt?"

Piper smiled. "He's confused, but he's keeping his mouth shut. The rumour is circulating that he's suffering from a broken heart. I did what I could to help by giving him your medals."

"You WHAT?"

"The good people of Meredith Crossing think I've given up hope of finding you alive. Rick's spies will soon tire of watching your policeman and leave him free to complete his mission."

‘☯‛

Grey clouds were gathering overhead. Kurt hurried into the supermarket. He grabbed what he needed and returned to the car park. A woman stepped from the shadows and met him beside the patrol car.

"I heard you were back, Kim," Kurt said. "You're staying with my sister."

"Eliza has been very kind," Kim said, placing her hand on his arm. "If she hadn't asked me to stay, I would have been out on the streets."

Kurt shouldered her out of the way. He placed his groceries on the rear seat. "I can't believe you've come back. Not after what happened to your kids."

"That was a misunderstanding. I've been to the Newcastle police and answered their questions. There are no charges against my name. It's my word against that *woman* Samson married. She fed Butch a bunch of lies."

"Butch was already planning to run away before Ruth met the men you were entertaining in your home." Kurt glanced around.

A changeable wind blew past, and Kim wrapped her arms around her slender frame. The skimpy dress she wore offered limited protection against the elements. "Can we get in your car? I'm freezing."

Kurt stepped back. "The only place I'd take you is the lockup."

"You're supposed to be my friend," Kim whined. "Why won't you believe me? I only want what's best for my kids. They belong with their mother."

"A mother who sold them—"

"Where's your evidence?" Kim snapped, and then softened her tone. "Ruth's lies have poisoned *everyone* against me."

"You only have yourself to blame."

"You could help me. My dad would let me come home if you told him I'd learned my lesson." She reached for the collar of his police shirt and pulled herself closer. "I'd make it worth your while."

Knocking her hand away, Kurt retreated. Speechless, he took in the way she was standing, reinterpreting the low-cut neckline, the too-short skirt and heavy makeup.

As her smile faded, Kim put her hands on her hips. "Take a good look. When you realise what you're missing, come and find me, but don't take too long. I'm not Sigrid. I'm not going to wait forever."

Without another word, Kim stomped across the car park and disappeared from view. Kurt closed his eyes, leaning against his car and waiting for his heart to stop pounding.

"That was an enlightening conversation."

Spinning around, Kurt found Muriel McHenry behind him. "How much did you hear?"

"Enough to suspect that there's more to Kimberley's return than she's told us. Do you think she had something to do with Sigrid's attack?"

"What?"

Muriel frowned. "She talked to her father today. Ol' Jack's never been able to say no to Kimberley. It was a surprise when he said she wasn't welcome at *Mountain Rise*. The Melbourne guests have gone, so it's not like there isn't any room." A strange light came into her eyes. "Unless there's *someone* else staying there—"

"Not Sigrid," Kurt said, a cold certainty holding him upright. "Samson would tell me if he knew where she was."

"You're right," Muriel said, patting his arm. "Not Sigrid. If she were there, that boss of hers wouldn't have asked me to move her luggage to the master bedroom in her apartment. He's had a lock put on the door."

"Why is Piper paying for an empty apartment?"

"I thought you knew. The building crew for the old Co-op building's renovations will be staying there. Harry wanted me to interrogate you about the project, but I'll tell him you're as much in the dark as everyone else."

"I'm talking to the architect next week," Kurt said. "I only found out about this project yesterday. I think things have been brought forward because Sigrid—"

"Don't you worry about Harry. You focus on getting back to full strength, and then we'll talk again." Muriel left him standing there, but then she came back. "Kurt, one last thing and then I'll leave you in peace. I've taken Sigrid's quilt. Your mother's too upset, so don't tell her that I'm going to finish it. You can put it with Sigrid's medals for safekeeping."

CHAPTER 45
(Thursday 14th February)

Tried
and Tested

ॐ ☼ ଓ

Romans 3:24 WEB - Being justified freely by His grace,
through the redemption
that is in Christ Jesus.

ॐ ☼ ଓ

"I've not seen *Mountain Rise* from the air before," Sigrid said to Oliver as the helicopter dropped towards the landing site. "There's been a lot of building work in the eight months since I was last here."

"Piper's put the construction teams to good use," Oliver replied. "It helped that a lot of them had engineering experience. They were trained to construct temporary bases overnight, and it's been a luxury for them to work on something permanent."

"It's strange being back. Are you sure Piper gave the order? I thought he had me permanently chained to the base."

"It wasn't supposed to be a punishment," Oliver said, flicking switches and preparing to disembark. "You're ready – you're stronger than you've ever been. If your enemies come looking for you again, you don't need to hide. But I must confess that I'm praying that your stay here is boring and uneventful."

Sigrid laughed. "Thanks for the vote of confidence."

Oliver grinned at her. "Don't dismiss my prayers. I have a lot invested in your survival. And I'm not saying that because I saved your life. Although it doesn't hurt to remind you why my helicopter was in the area when you jumped off that bridge. If I hadn't flown Sara to *Mountain Rise* that day you would have died in the river."

"I'm not likely to forget. You haven't stopped reminding me that you'd rather be here with the woman you love than keeping an eye on me."

"I'm glad you understand what's at stake," Oliver said. "I'm convinced there's a strong enough *Operation Phoenix* presence in the area to guarantee Sara's security, but before I ask Piper to give her more freedom, I need you to prove that Meredith Crossing is safe."

"I can't make you any promises," Sigrid said. "You're the one who says trouble follows me."

"All I'm asking is for you to stay out of trouble for more than a week. Sara went into hiding the same day that you did, but you've enjoyed more freedom. Sara hasn't set foot off the mountain since the day she arrived."

"I'll do my best. Did anyone warn Kurt that I'm back?"

"What? And ruin your surprise?" Oliver said. "I didn't tell anyone, but I did ask Samson to leave me a vehicle. I'll wait until you're on your way to the first checkpoint, then I'll ask him to unlock the gates."

⁢⁢⁢ ✧ ⁢⁢⁢

"Hi, Harry," Sigrid said when the proprietor appeared behind the reception desk. Her wheeled suitcase rested against the counter.

The colour drained from his face. "Sigrid?" Harry leaned against the shelf behind him.

The temptation to fiddle with her locket was strong, but she resisted. Pasting a brighter smile on her face, Sigrid tried to reassure him. "Don't worry. I'm not a ghost."

"Sigrid!" he said again before shaking himself. A smile split Harry's face. "Sigrid, welcome back. Ma told me you'd come walking through that door one day, but I didn't believe her."

Sigrid laughed. "Yes, Harry, I'm back. I hear there have been some big changes since I left. My uniform won't be out of place?"

Harry nodded. "There are lots of *Operation Phoenix* personnel around. They stayed here for a while, but most of them are living up at the mountain base now."

"Did the Melbourne office book me a room?" Sigrid asked.

"Your old apartment is still reserved in your name. Ma refused to let me change it. Piper had me move your things into the master bedroom. Some of the construction crew stayed in the downstairs rooms, but the apartment's been vacant for a few weeks." He opened the ledger. "I feel foolish now. I should have guessed you were coming. The Melbourne office phoned yesterday to have the pantry restocked. I've put apple pie and ice cream in the freezer."

"Fetch me my room key. I need to freshen up before I go and surprise Kurt."

"He's not expecting—"

"Do you know what day it is, Harry?"

"The fourteenth of Feb— Oh." Harry fetched the key, hovering as she signed her name. "Happy Valentine's Day, Sigrid."

"Thank you, Harry."

Sigrid shoved her hat on her head as Harry followed her to the door.

℘ ☼ ℭ

Tap, tap, tap. Kurt looked up from the files on his computer screen. It had been futile to tell the new constable not to disturb him. Was this the third or fourth interruption? "What's the emergency?"

"Sorry, Sarge. I know you said you're not here, but there's an *Operation Phoenix* officer at the front desk. She won't go away until she sees you." He glanced over his shoulder, and fear flashed across his face.

Kurt rose to his feet as a uniformed figure grabbed the constable by the shoulders and lifted him out of the way. Kurt opened his mouth, outraged that one of Piper Maxwell's private army thought this was appropriate behaviour. But then his unidentified visitor removed her hat, and a pair of long plaits dropped down about her shoulders. He slammed his jaw shut. The red-haired, Amazonian troublemaker put her hands on her hips and glared at him.

"Should I send for reinforcements?" the frightened constable asked, peering around the door.

"No," Kurt said. "I'll take it from here. Sigrid and I are not to be interrupted." He waited for his no-longer-missing friend to explain herself. He wasn't sure of the rules of this game.

"You remember my name," Sigrid said, dragging a chair closer. She adjusted her seated position, so her steel-capped boots rested on his desk.

Kurt continued to gape at her. "Of course, I remember. But it's been eight months—"

"Don't let me distract you from your work," she said. "Your new constable said you were busy. I'll sit here until you're finished. Then you can take me out to dinner."

Kurt clicked the save button. "Why am I taking you out to dinner?"

"Do you know what day it is?" Sigrid asked.

"It's the fourteenth."

"Exactly. Valentine's Day. You're hiding in your office because you don't have a date."

"I don't have a date," Kurt said, "because I promised my maybe-she's-not-dead fiancée I'd save myself for her. Besides, I'm not hiding. I have more than enough work to keep me here until after midnight."

"I've spent the last few months drowning in paperwork," she said, examining her knuckles. "I can give you the perfect reason to leave your paperwork behind." Sigrid pulled her boots off his desk and gracefully straightened to her full height. "If you don't, there'll be even more paperwork. I feel the strong urge to break something – or someone."

"Why are you angry with me?" Kurt asked.

"You made me promise not to kiss you while I'm angry."

Sigrid marched out the door, slamming it hard enough to crack the glass. Kurt sat frozen at his desk, replaying the conversation.

"Are you okay, Sarge?" the constable asked, pushing the door open.

"Which way did she go?"

"She didn't go anywhere. I can see her out the front, leaning against your patrol car. I think she's contemplating slashing your tyres. Are you sure you don't want me to call for backup?"

"That won't be necessary. Leave this to me."

"Can I give you a word of advice, Sarge?"

Kurt folded his arms.

"I couldn't help overhearing. Don't take the Major to the Top Pub. You don't want the whole town staring at you all evening. Besides, the steaks are better over at Brumby's Run. If you let her drive, she's less likely to kill you before you get there."

Kurt walked down the front steps of the police station.

Sigrid met him on the footpath. "You took long enough."

"You need to work on your people skills."

She laughed. "Are we going straight to dinner at the Top Pub, or do you want to change out of your uniform first?"

"My constable said the steak's better at Brumby's Run. If you don't mind the drive over there, I'll give you my keys. You can get my Hilux out of the garage while I change."

"I've borrowed Samson's Cruiser." Sigrid pointed across the street. "If it's okay with you, we'll take that."

"Does Samson know?"

"He knows that it's gone, but not who took it. Oliver made the arrangements."

Her grin told him she was enjoying this conversation. Kurt turned his back, half expecting her to follow him into his flat. When he arrived at his door unmolested, he shrugged off his disappointment. Kurt loitered in the hallway, using his phone to call the expensive restaurant the constable had suggested. The person he spoke to said he was fortunate. There had been a cancellation only moments before.

After changing, Kurt walked from the flat. The LandCruiser in his driveway had the engine running. Sigrid hit the accelerator, backing onto the road before he fastened his seatbelt. She was still wearing her uniform but had done something different to her hair. "I'm glad you've decided to spend the evening with me," she said, keeping her eyes on the road.

Kurt glanced at the speedometer. Sigrid matched the speed limit all the way to Brumby's Run, even on the corners where he would have slowed down. They arrived in record time.

Sigrid parked in the furthest corner of the restaurant car park. Kurt intended to open her door. By the time he arrived at the driver's side, she was already out. But then she opened the passenger door, perched sideways on the back seat and reached for her bootlaces. A pair of high-heeled shoes sat on the floor beside her. First one boot, and then the other sailed over her shoulder onto the seat.

Without hesitation, Sigrid began removing her heavy trousers.

Kurt took a step back, glancing around the car park. The sun had set, and they were in a shadowy corner, but the vehicle's interior light made it easy to see her actions. He averted his eyes. "What are you doing?"

Sigrid laughed. "You don't expect me to wear my camouflage gear to such a fancy restaurant. I came prepared."

He could not find a rational reply before she threw her discarded trousers at him. His automatic reaction was to look at her stocking covered legs.

He blinked. His 'date' was unbuttoning her shirt now. This time he was ready when the garment flew at him. Hurriedly, he bundled the discarded clothes together and passed them across before Sigrid rose, wearing those heels. She slammed the door and tugged at the skirt of her dress.

The flimsy straps that kept the garment from slipping too low accentuated her muscular shoulders. Kurt tore his eyes from the scar left behind by the bullet. He considered the complete outfit, searching for clues for how he should proceed. He froze. It was only half a dress. She reached for his arm, and a bolt of electricity shot through him.

Then, as they walked towards the restaurant, Sigrid flipped her hand to her head, and her red hair came loose. Now it cascaded over the scarred shoulder like a river reflecting a glorious sunset.

The waiter who met them at the door already knew him, saving Kurt the embarrassment of being unable to remember his own name. Sigrid took the lead, guiding him towards their table. People stared, and conversations stopped. She sashayed like a movie star, and he chastised himself for trailing after her like a besotted teenager.

Sigrid sat across from him, sipping beer straight from a tall bottle. "Happy Valentine's Day." She ordered for both of them – he couldn't remember what, except it was "medium-rare".

He raised his bottle, barely tasting the beverage. "Does Piper know you're here, dressed like that?"

"What's wrong with what I'm wearing?"

"In some countries, you'd be arrested—"

She laughed. "I look forward to seeing you try."

He frowned. Before he could decide how to answer, the phone on the table began to vibrate. He glanced at the screen. The message he read brought him to his feet. "I have to go. The Brumby's Run police station has called for backup, and I'm the closest."

He pulled out his wallet.

"You're not going anywhere without me." She turned to the waiter who appeared beside them. "Don't cancel our order. Move it back half an hour. We'll be back."

She was already halfway to the door before Kurt could respond. He hurried outside, catching up with her on the footpath.

"Which way?" she asked.

Curious diners watched them through the window. "You can't come with me. I'm not taking a civilian—"

Sigrid laughed. "Senior Sergeant Jensen, do you need a reminder that I outrank you?"

CHAPTER 46
(Thursday 14th February)

Triumphant
Reunion

☙ ☼ ☗

*Isaiah 35:10a CG - The redeemed of the Lord
will return with singing,
and everlasting joy will be upon their heads.*

☙ ☼ ☗

Standing outside the Brumby's Run Police Station, Sigrid tapped her toes. The fizzing excitement from being reunited with Kurt was intoxicating, but she remembered what her counsellor had said. "Let Kurt take the lead."

Hadn't she given him enough hints? His appreciation for her dress was evident on his face. So how could he have forgotten his attraction as soon as duty called? Her instinct was to charge inside the building and deal with whatever emergency was keeping him from her. Instead, she practised slow, deep breaths.

Kurt emerged from the station clipping something to his belt, and started walking up the street as if he were heading to his execution.

"Where are we going?" Sigrid asked. "The restaurant's back that way. And why do you need those handcuffs?"

"We're taking a stroll past the bank. The silent alarm has been triggered, and the nearest patrol car is twenty minutes away."

"A bank robbery?" Her mind spun through the implications. Was this the same bank where his brother had died? She needed to find a way to lighten his mood. "You certainly know how to organise an interesting date, Sergeant."

"It's probably a false alarm."

Sigrid grabbed his arm and snuggled against him. "At least we get to take a romantic walk. A pity there isn't a full moon."

He glanced sideways, tension radiating down his arm. "I should have insisted you stay at the restaurant. I have a bad feeling about this."

"Are you worried about me?" Sigrid asked. "Or is this bringing back difficult memories?"

Silence was Kurt's only answer.

"Perhaps this is your chance to put the ghosts to rest?" Sigrid murmured as they came to a halt at the corner.

The dim lights identifying the bank were half a block away. The street lamps that should have illuminated this street were dark. They crossed to the nearest lamp post, and glass crunched beneath their shoes.

"I don't like this," Kurt said, reaching for his phone.

"Not yet," Sigrid said. "If you report your suspicions, you'll be ordered to wait for an armed response team. Another shootout isn't going to help you deal with your nightmares. Besides, unless you've already turned down the screen illumination, you're going to give away our position. Let's get closer to the bank. I think I can hear a car engine idling, but it's too dark to see anything."

Keeping close to the darkened shop windows on the opposite side of the street, Sigrid led the way. After advancing another few metres, the clouds parted to reveal the quarter moon. The outline of a dark car appeared for a few seconds before the gloom concealed it again.

"We have to get closer," Sigrid whispered. "I have an idea. They won't expect a police officer to be playing Kiss Tag with his lover. I'll run across the road, and—"

"Wait." Kurt grabbed her arm. "What if I won't play?"

"Then I'll catch the bank robbers without your help."

"It's too dangerous."

"Can you think of a better way?" Sigrid started to dance down the middle of the road. "Hey, lover boy," she shouted. "Catch me if you can."

For a moment, Kurt stared and then he began to chase her. She kept out of his reach, laughing and teasing him. When they were almost to the parked car outside the bank, he managed to catch her hand. With a swift movement, Sigrid pulled him into her arms, spinning them both towards the car. Her lips pressed against his mouth, and she could taste his alarm as they crashed into the stationary object.

A whirring sound, a window opening, was followed by a harsh voice from within the parked car. "You two, get a room."

Sigrid shrieked like a silly schoolgirl and leapt away, pulling Kurt with her. That wonderful man held onto her waist, holding her close. She leaned down and gazed through the open window, praying that the angle was right for the locket camera. "Sorry," she giggled and skipped away with Kurt in pursuit. When they reached the building next to the bank, she swung around to face him, and he wrapped his arms around her to keep from knocking her down.

"What are you doing?" he asked as she leaned in for another kiss.

"Don't make me do all the work," she whispered and then wriggled out of his loose embrace. This time she almost made it to the corner before he caught her.

"You're crazy," he said, holding her close.

"How far away is your patrol car?" Sigrid asked. "We've entertained that driver long enough. He won't think twice if you take out your phone now. I'll pose, and you pretend to take the photos. Make sure you get that number plate in the frame."

Sigrid posed provocatively, laughing and smiling, as she backed away from Kurt.

The phone in his hand disrupted the night with multiple flashes. "You've done this before," Kurt said. "Message sent. Now we should find somewhere safe—"

"Too late," Sigrid hissed. "The driver's revving the engine. Your robbers are about to break cover. I'll distract them while you sneak up from the other side."

Without waiting for Kurt to reply, Sigrid strode purposefully towards the car. When she arrived, she knocked on the window. "Police!" she shouted. "Get out of the car. You're under arrest."

"I'm not afraid of a woman cop," a voice said from behind her and two figures stepped from the darkness. One of them put down the bag he was carrying and leapt towards her. Sigrid allowed him to wrench her hands behind her back, waiting for the right moment to make her move.

The driver of the car wound down his window. "Leave her, and let's get out of here."

"We can't leave behind a witness. We'll take her with us—"

"She's not alone," the driver said.

"He's right," Kurt said, appearing on the other side of the car. "You're making a big mistake. I'm a policeman, but Major Ericson's a trained killer. Surrender now, and she might not hurt you."

The man holding Sigrid laughed, and wrapped his elbow around her neck in a stranglehold. She thrust her head and shoulders forward, throwing her attacker over her head. He roared as he struggled to his feet and when he lunged at her, Sigrid knocked him to the ground with a single kick. The remaining aggressor swung his bag, and she ducked, allowing his momentum to bring him into range. He fell to the ground with a thud.

By the time she turned back towards the car, the quivering driver was kneeling at Kurt's feet, with his hands behind his head. "Don't let her near me."

"Good thing you brought those handcuffs," Sigrid said. "I can hear sirens. My two robbers aren't going anywhere, but the one you've arrested might escape."

While Kurt secured the driver to the doorframe, Sigrid checked her victims. She repositioned them to prevent them from suffocating. Then she attached their extended limbs to a convenient post that held up the veranda awning. Sigrid withdrew across the road as two police vehicles with flashing lights and sirens roared to a stop beside the getaway car.

Occasionally glancing in her direction, Kurt spoke to the officers. When everyone turned in her direction, she stepped into the middle of the road.

Kurt shook his head and hurried to rejoin her.

"All this police work has made me hungry," Sigrid said. "My dinner's waiting."

"I'm going to be in trouble for leaving the crime scene."

"I'm sure my locket camera recorded everything," Sigrid said, tracing the line of his jaw in the moonlight. "Piper can deal with any trouble. That's a benefit he provides for his minions."

"You have an answer for everything." He took hold of her hand.

She smiled, and they headed away from the bank. "We make a good team. Three bank robbers arrested, and nobody died."

When they rounded the corner, and the bank was no longer in sight, Sigrid paused to wrap her arms around his neck. "We were in the middle of a Valentine's Day game," she said. "You owe me another round."

"If I agree to play," Kurt said, encircling her waist with his arms, "do I get to name the prize?"

"What do you want, Kurt Jensen?"

"I want you to promise never to play this game with anyone else," Kurt said.

"That's a lot to ask a girl on a first date."

"I'll give you a ten-second head start."

Sigrid laughed, pulling against his embrace. Her heart skipped when he tightened his grip.

"You're not playing fair. You have to let me go before you can catch me."

"I let you go on the bridge, and I'm not repeating that mistake. Your ten seconds are up, and I've caught you."

"Your version of the game is *no* fun," Sigrid said.

"You know that I love you?" he asked, bringing his mouth closer to her lips.

Sigrid sighed, all her playful resistance seeping away.

"I'm waiting for your promise," Kurt said.

"Okay, I promise not to play this game with anyone else. Satisfied?"

"No. Now I want you to promise that I'm the only man you'll welcome in your bed."

Sigrid stiffened. "I'm no longer that promiscuous woman. If you expect an invitation, you'll have to marry me—"

"I thought you'd never ask," Kurt said, raising her off the ground to spin her around. He kissed her quickly, set her on her feet again and grabbed her hand. They hurried towards the restaurant.

"But let's skip the long engagement," he said. "Dinner first, and then we'll talk about our wedding. You've kept me waiting long enough."

Timeline

*May 26 (Book 4 ends)
May 27 (Chapters 1-5)

Introducing Sigrid to Meredith Crossing; Kurt & his police officers; Harry & Muriel (aka Mrs Mac) at Top Pub

May 28 (Chapters 6-13)

Introducing other Meredith Crossing characters; complications for Kurt and Sigrid including concerns about her secret mission

May 29 (Chapters 14-35)

Sigrid asks Kurt for help, before being challenged by her Melbourne friends; she meets his family and then faces an unexpected personal crisis; Kurt & the Melbourne friends intervene

May 30 (Chapters 35-36)

Complications for Kurt and Sigrid

*June 1 (*Book 5 ends)
June 1-5 (Chapters 38-44)

Sigrid's enemies catch up with her; a conspiracy is uncovered; Kurt is left to puzzle over the consequences

February 14 (Chapters 45-46)

Sigrid returns to resolve her relationship with Kurt

Character List

The River Wild Series Main Characters (MC):

Sigrid Ericson, *Operation Phoenix* Major (33) - **(MC This Book)**
    introduced in Book 3, works for Piper Maxwell
Kurt Jensen, Police Senior Sergeant (45) - **(MC This Book)**
    introduced in Book 4
Sebastian Romano (MC Book 1) - Evie's husband,
    Melbourne billionaire businessman, Piper's friend
Evie Romano (MC Book 1) - Romano's wife
Sofia Edwards (MC Book 2) - Evie's sister, John's wife,
    Marco's mother
John Edwards, Pastor (MC Book 2) - Sofia's husband
Freddie Kidman (MC Book 3) - Sigrid's friend,
    Alixanda' husband, Samson's half-brother
Alixanda Kidman (MC Book 3) - Sigrid's friend,
    Freddie's wife, Ruth's sister, works for Piper
Ruth Davidson aka Jezebel (MC Book 4) - married to Samson
Samson Davidson (MC Book 4) - Kurt's childhood friend,
    works for Piper Maxwell
Sara Messinger-Mariani (MC Book 5) - fugitive
Oliver Johnston (MC Book 5) - Sigrid's friend and supervisor
Piper Maxwell (MC Book 7, 2022-23) - Sigrid's boss,
    Maximum Security and *Operation Phoenix* commander
Jenny Prescott (MC Book 7, 2022-23) - Sigrid's supervisor,
    works for Piper

Kurt's family and close associates:

Abraham 'Brum' Callahan (18) - Eliza's son, Kurt's nephew
Bruce 'Diesel' Callahan - Eliza's husband
Eliza Callahan - Kurt's sister, Bruce 'Diesel' Callahan's wife,
    Brum and Hannah's mother
Hannah Callahan (12) - Eliza's daughter, Kurt's niece
Harry McHenry - Top Pub publican, Muriel's son
John Jensen (deceased) - Kurt's younger brother
Kimberley aka Kim aka Kimmy Kidman - Samson's half sister,
    Freddie's sister, Butch & Nikki's mother
KJ Jensen - Kurt (MC), Eliza &and John's father
Melissa Jensen aka Missie/Mrs J - Kurt, Eliza & John's mother
Muriel McHenry aka Mrs Mac - Harry's mother,
    related to the Kidmans and the Jensens
Old Jack Kidman - Samson's stepfather

Sigrid's Associates:
Butch Cassidy-Kidman (15) - Samson and Freddie's nephew
Macy Mancini - Sydney-based *Maximum Security* agent
Marco Fontana (14) - Sofia son
Nikki Kidman (12) - Butch's sister
Romano Twins - born April 26th

Additional Police Characters:
Ben King, Constable - Kurt's ally
Clayton Briggs, Constable
Des Wilmot, Constable
Gavin Mallory, Constable
Helena Avery, Probationary Constable
Superintendent Bellamy - Kurt's Police Area Commander
Tobias Lester-Angevin, Inspector - Task Force 9

Other Meredith Crossing characters:
Connor Portman - Top Pub patron
Drew Radcliffe - Top Pub patron
Hank Binshaw - Top Pub patron
Jeremiah Friedman aka Cowboy Joe - Top Pub patron
Lizette Friedman - Jeremiah's wife, Dr Chappell's receptionist
Rupert 'Roo' Armitage (18) - Brum's friend
Tim Chappell, Doctor - Samson and Kurt's friend

Other Characters:
Cosima - member of Sydney crime family
        Matteus & Quin's cousin, Rick's nephew
Dr Douglas Willowfield – Newcastle doctor
Matteus Barononi- member of Sydney crime family
Gina Gregorio - Piper's nemesis, Valentino's niece
Kylie Smith - Sigrid's estranged mother
Nero Mariani - Gina's cousin, Sara's estranged husband
Quin Barononi - member of Sydney crime family
Ricardo Barononi aka Rick - Sigrid's enemy,
Valentino Horatio - deceased (Book 2), Piper's cousin

Locations: (New South Wales, Australia)
Brumby's Run - fictional township in NSW
Forest Heights - Jensen property
Meredith Crossing fictional township in NSW
        remote mountain forested foothills & a wide valley
Mountain Rise - Kidman property
Top Pub aka Meredith Crossing Motel
Valley View - Cassidy property

Chrissy Garwood

River Wild Series

Book 1 (2019) White Rose of Promise
Book 2 (2019) When Promises Are Broken
Book 3 (2020) When Freedom is Promised
Book 4 (2020) Which Promise This Time?
Book 5 (2021) When Promises Are Forever
Book 6 (This one) Waiting For A Promise
Book 7 (2022-23) Who Pays The Piper?

These books can be read in any order. Each story stands alone, but some of the characters make an appearance in every story.
Available at www.chrissygarwood.com

White Rose of Promise

A prophetic dream she can't remember. A shameful past she can't forget. An impossible future she dare not cherish.

Evie hopes for reconciliation with her family. Her faith challenges wealthy businessman Sebastian Romano, turning his orderly world upside down. He thought he was done with his past, but his enemies have found her. Romano watches helplessly as her destiny unfolds...

When Promises Are Broken

A family curse, an evil plot, an unlucky coincidence. Three destinies entwined.

Sofia faces a choice that causes her to question everything she values. What price will she pay for a promise that could fulfil all her dreams?

When Freedom Is Promised

An unlucky coincidence? A fiendish plot?
Or a sacred design that promises freedom?

Bad things happen to good people. Abigail must survive to testify. Could the Melbourne hiding place be the answer?

When Freddie's troubled nephew and Abigail collide, her cover is blown. Her enemies are coming. But Freddie is in their way. Can Abigail trust this gentle stranger? Why would Freddie risk everything to set her free?

Which Promise This Time?

A random choice? A reckless plan?
Or an unmerited opportunity?

Jezebel has had many names. Her victims can't identify her. Lies and deception have been her currency for too long.

Samson Davidson has dedicated his life to serving others. Why is he in Sydney, and what is his secret mission?

As her enemies close in, she needs a new victim. This righteous man seems the perfect candidate. But too late, she realises her mistake...

When Promises Are Forever

A dream job, the perfect boss, and a surprise invitation. An unexpected chance for happiness? Or a mistake that will cost her everything?

Sara Messinger has earned her place in a prestigious Melbourne law firm, and has always been careful to guard her heart.

Oliver Johnson investigates a threat towards her wealthy employer and his powerful family. Sara is a potential suspect, but Oliver is certain that she an innocent bystander...

Until Sara's best friend decides to play matchmaker. The young lawyer is drawn into a world where extortion, violent intimidation and betrayal are the common currency.

Oliver is torn between his mission and an inexplicable urge to protect a woman who can never be his.

Fantasy River Series

Phoena's Quest: First Spark (2021)

The quest begins with a first spark.
It flares in isolation, untended and unknown.
Too late, the darkness tries to smother it...

An orphaned servant without a past, Phoena lacks magical talent and protections. The teenager is often targeted for magical experiments. After years of torment, she longs for invisibility. The other Westernbrooke Academy servants think her luck is running out.

Lord Karilion, the Academy's best magic-user, has beaten all challengers. The wealthy heir is also the champion swordsman. Viscount Baraapa, secure in second place, has no magic but his scientific mastery outweighs that disadvantage. The foreigner, Lord Oramis, threatens the balance when he refuses to be tested. What is the Ambassador's son hiding?

The quest selects its champions: a servant girl and three noblemen who think winning her loyalty is a game. And there's a dragon in the back garden...

Other titles in this series:
Phoena's Quest: Second Flame (2021)
Phoena's Quest: Third Fire (2022-23)

Acknowledgements

This book could not have been written without the support and encouragement of many people.

Firstly, I am grateful to God for inspiring me, for giving me the time and the persistence to bring this story into life.

My writing adventure has not been a solitary one. God provided me with a supportive team - determined to ask the right questions, demand the next instalment and keep me moving forward. Thanks to Gillian Perrett, Naomi McGlone, Belinda McGuire, Donna Bullen, Tim Berry, and Eva Bitterova for your help with *Waiting For A Promise*

I am thankful for you, dear reader. I am especially grateful for your gentle reminders to keep writing because you want to know what adventures are in store for your favourite characters.

A special thanks to Belinda Pollard, publishing mentor and editor, for taking me under her wing and for the professional advice that has helped make this book better than I could have imagined.

Last but not least, thanks to my patient husband Tony, for his constant encouragement, and ongoing support.

Chrissy

A Note From the Author

Greetings from Tasmania, Australia.

Thank you for reading my book. This is the sixth title in my
River Wild series. I hope you enjoyed it as much as I enjoyed
the writing process. If you are able, please leave a brief online
review, as this will help other readers find my work.

If you would like to receive updates on my progress
with other titles as they are released, please visit
www.chrissygarwood.com and complete the form.
Links to social media can
be accessed from my webpage.

Publishing a novel was a childhood ambition, one that I set
aside for decades. I added wife and mother, student,
childcare educator, visual artist and chaplain
to my list of achievements before I was ready to return
to that writing dream.

In that time, God has brought me through many challenging
experiences to help me appreciate the riches at my disposal.

But the adventures my characters endure are works of fiction
– a small grain of inspiration, a mountain of imagination,
and months of hard work to bring it all together.

When I first lost myself to the rediscovered joy of writing, my
horizons expanded. My fictional world has become populated
with characters who whisper their stories to me.
They are impatient for me to give their adventures a narrative
to activate the transformations which will lead them to a
Happy Ever After ending.

I have learned a lot about myself and my ambitions while
pursuing the writing dream. The confidence I am gaining as a
storyteller is enriched my character. I believe it is making me
a humbler disciple of Jesus Christ, a more determined
encourager, a better friend.

Chrissy